# COCKTAILS & CAULDRONS

UNLUCKY CHARMS BOOK 4

## T.M. CROMER

ISBN: 978-1-956941-04-3 (EPUB)
ISBN: 978-1-956941-15-9 (PAPERBACK)
ISBN: 978-1-956941-07-4 (HARDBACK)
ISBN: 978-1-956941-16-6 (LARGE PRINT)

Cover Design: Deranged Doctor Designs

Editor: Trusted Accomplice

# CHAPTER 1

"*N*o." Eoin gave a handsy art patron a smile filled with faux regret. Really, it was barely a twist of his lips, but he'd dealt with this particular woman for nigh on four years now, and he was irked she refused to keep her pudgy, bejeweled fingers to herself. In desperation, he blurted, "I'm gay."

Yelled it, in truth.

All heads in the gallery whipped their way, and Eoin closed his eyes against the painful tension headache forming.

"My apologies, Ms. Sullivan." Although his voice was only loud enough for her to hear this time, the other gallery visitors leaned forward as if they had a vested interest in the conversation. "Sure, and I hope you'll pardon me."

From across the room, he caught Reginald White's laughing jade-green gaze. Reggie was Eoin's closest friend and the inspiration for Eoin's desperate excuse. All he had to do was channel Reggie and his fussy mannerisms for the evening, and he might get through this nightmare. Reggie would surely call Eoin on the lie later, if only to tease him.

Eoin glanced at his watch and gritted his teeth. Only forty

minutes left of this torture. After tonight, he intended to tell his soon-to-be-ex business manager, Margo, he wouldn't be making any more appearances for the sake of his art. His reclusiveness would only add to the mystique of a temperamental artist and likely drive up the prices. He absolutely hated the idea of finding new representation, but Margo had become exceedingly demanding, both in the bedroom and office. Mixing business with pleasure had been a stupid idea, but Eoin tended to go with what felt right at the moment. And Margo's talented mouth on his cock had felt extremely right during negotiations.

"I'm sorry." The soft apology came from behind him and danced across his skin, sending a surge of blood to his dick and removing all thoughts of his manager. He suppressed a shiver.

*Brenna Sullivan.*

Her sultry voice was siren-like and could make him hard with a single word. And she just happened to be the grandniece to Odessa Sullivan, one of the top-five richest women in New York and the person he'd been forced to reject at every turn.

Had Brenna heard him declare that he was homosexual?

He shifted to face her.

*Yep.*

Her expression said she couldn't apologize enough for her aunt and that she wished she could crawl into a hole.

"No apology necessary," he said gruffly but equally as low.

The doubtful look she cast him said she didn't believe him. "Aunt Odessa is used to getting what she wants, and I'm afraid you're it."

"Not this time." His tone was hard, and he noticed her wince, slight though it was.

"No, of course not. I'm sure she didn't know you were... um... well, gay." Pink flooded Brenna's cheeks, and she compressed her lips together as she shoved her tortoiseshell glasses up her pert nose.

He wanted to tell her the cat-like style did nothing for her heart-shaped face, but it wasn't his place.

"However, you might want to introduce her to your partner, or she'll likely try to convert you to the other side." She grimaced as she said it.

He shuddered.

Mostly, his reaction was due to the idea of Odessa Sullivan attempting to convert him in any way.

One evening after a charity dinner, the wily, old fox had shown up in his hotel room. Eoin was still at a loss as to how she'd gotten in. He'd eventually concluded she bribed the cleaning crew. The remembered visual of her in a tight leather bustier and sheer lace skirt made his bollocks shrivel.

"I owe you a debt of gratitude for saving me last month, Brenna," he managed stiffly, still unable to discuss it with anything less than anger.

"No. It's the other way around. I owe you for not pressing charges or suing our hotel for trespass."

"Right." He'd forgotten Odessa had made the lion's share of her wealth through a hotel chain. "Well, after tonight, I'm sure part of your headache will go away."

"Oh?"

"I'm heading home." To deal with his pesky new magical abilities before someone got hurt. Probably him. He'd accidentally set fire to three of his easels this week alone. Much to Reggie's entertainment.

Last fall, he'd felt a tingle of something starting in his cells. Little did he know at the time, the family curse was in its reversal process. His brother Cian had fallen in love with Piper Thorne and had started the ball in motion. When his other brother, Carrick, reunited with Roisin Byrne, more power had flooded Eoin's veins. And when his sister Bridget accepted the Sword of Goibhniu from Ruairí O'Connor as a show of his love and commitment, the final barrier to their magic was removed. Both Eoin and his sister Dubheasa had felt the new infusion of power all the way across the pond.

"Oh." Brenna initially looked crestfallen, but rebounded enough to smile. "That should be nice. Ireland in the autumn months is beautiful, or so I'm told."

Eoin had been in the process of sipping his champagne when her comment hit him. Glass arrested halfway to his mouth, he stared.

"What?" She fiddled with the snap on her clutch, opening and closing it as if she had an attack of nerves.

"You've never been to *Éire*? *Ever*?"

"Is it so unusual?"

"For you? A Sullivan? Yeah." He took a casual sip of his drink and shook his head. "How is it you haven't gone yet? Sure, and we've only discussed my homeland in relation to my landscapes, but I always received the impression you loved it there, all the same."

She shrugged and gave him a sad half smile. "I'm positive I would *if* I had a chance to go. Aunt Odessa has been somewhat" —she glanced around then leaned in—"demanding."

A lightbulb went off in his brain. "She couldn't spare you, could she?" And by spare, he meant let go of the leash enough to give shy, unassuming Brenna freedom. Why should she? Odessa had the perfect little servant in her niece.

Eoin studied her objectively. She was a petite, benign creature with bland brown hair that couldn't decide whether it wanted to be blonde or brown, so it settled somewhere in the middle. If he were being kind, he'd say it was caramel, but calling her frizzy mop caramel would be romanticizing the unremarkable shade. Her clothing was as lackluster as the rest of her. And if there was one thing Eoin abhorred, it was uninspired clothing. Perhaps Reggie's lofty preferences were getting to him.

Brenna blinked, and tears flooded her eyes, making their

color an even brighter shade of blue. Those soulful aquamarine eyes of hers made him want to promise her the moon and stars. Eoin wasn't quite certain why.

"Sure, and you should come home with me," he blurted.

They both stared at each other in astonishment. She looked like he'd suggested they murder Odessa and dump her body off the Brooklyn Bridge. He, with his heart thudding rapidly, wondered what the hell had prompted such a suggestion. When Brenna's gaze dropped and lingered on his crotch, Eoin cleared his throat. Her skin darkened to a distressing shade of crimson and drastically clashed with her hair and dreadful glasses.

*Not her eyes, though.*

Those soul-destroying peepers of hers were enhanced by the contrast.

"I only meant, my family owns an inn. I'm happy to comp you a room," he offered. When she looked as if she'd object, he hurried to add, "To pay you back for rescuing me."

Why the hell was he pushing so hard? It was no skin off his back if she didn't set foot outside of New York. And yet, the sight of her poignant face triggered something inside him similar to the new influx of magic.

"You're kind, Mr. O'Malley, but I couldn't possibly impose."

Her rejection irritated him. "You wouldn't be imposing, now, would ya? I'm asking you to be my guest, Brenna."

BRENNA SUCKED IN HER BREATH AND STRUGGLED NOT TO CHOKE on her own spit. Eoin O'Malley had quickly become a living legend in the art world, and here he was, taking the time to converse with *her*. He'd just invited her to Ireland and acted as if her acceptance of his offer meant something to him.

She found herself nodding. Mainly because she'd always wanted to be in his orbit, to bask in the beauty of Eoin's stunning creations—and maybe get lost in those all-seeing emerald eyes of his, too.

Brenna wasn't a fool. She knew Eoin wasn't homosexual. He'd simply grasped the first excuse he could to dissuade Aunt Odessa from mauling him to death. Although Brenna wasn't interesting enough to attract a man like Eoin, she could at least be his friend, if he was willing.

"I do want to go," she said softly. She shot a glance to their left, where Aunt Odessa was, even now, copping a feel of an unfortunate server's bottom. Brenna frowned. "Um, excuse me, I have to—"

"No, you don't."

She whipped her head back to stare at Eoin, her mouth agape. "Pardon?"

"You don't have to run off to save Odessa from her own outrageous behavior. Sure, and let her suffer the consequences for once."

"You don't understand, Mr. O'Malley—"

"Eoin."

"Mr. O'M—"

"Eoin," he insisted again. "My name is Eoin."

Brenna almost melted into a puddle. Not only was he severe and assertive in his insistence, but he was focused solely on her, as if her compliance in calling him by his first name was of utmost importance to him.

"Eoin," she whispered lovingly.

His gaze sharpened on her, and Brenna almost swallowed her tongue.

"Say it again," he commanded in a low, urgent tone.

*Was it wrong to grow aroused when he got all growly and demanding?*

The corners of his eyes crinkled as if he guessed her thoughts and was entertained by them. He shifted closer, and his dark brows lifted in challenge. The musky scent of his woodsy cologne short-circuited her brain. "Say my name again, love."

"Eoin," she gushed.

His gaze grew hot and dropped to her mouth.

Her throat went bone dry, sending all the moisture to her candy land, and she licked her lips in an attempt to lubricate them for speech. She thought she heard him laugh softly. A laughing groan, really.

"Say you'll come home with me."

"Yeah. Okay. Sure. All right. I suppose I can do that." *Crud! What she wouldn't give for a little duct tape to slap over her mouth!*

"Excellent. I leave in three days' time. Do you have a passport?"

*Did* she have a passport? The reality of what he was asking sank in. Odessa wouldn't let her go. *"Three days?* I can't. Three days?"

"I ask again, do you have a passport, Brenna?"

She frowned as she gave his question more thought. *Did she?* Surely she'd gotten one at some point. "I don't know. I can't seem to remember. I—"

"Eoin O'Malley, you talented devil! Your *Heaven's End* piece is incredible."

Speaking of breathing, Brenna wanted to kiss the newcomer for distracting Eoin and shifting his hawk-like stare. The entire time he was focused on her, she hadn't been able to take a fortifying inhale. The arrival of the blonde bombshell was both a godsend and a curse.

"GiGi!" Eoin's wide, happy grin was a fist to Brenna's gut.

She studied the other woman a little closer. GiGi was tall, but then again, everyone was taller than Brenna's own five-feet. She also had a lion's mane of hair in varying shades of blonde, and it appeared to have a life of its own as it flowed down her back.

Brenna had serious hair envy. And as she watched, Eoin

wrapped GiGi in a bear hug and followed it with a full-mouth kiss. They made a stunning couple—him, dark and mysterious with his artistic vibe pulsing strong, and her, a goddess in an elegant, form-fitting dress that outlined every luscious curve.

"You're a sight for me sore eyes, me darlin' GiGi. Promise you're here to run away with me." Although the hint of an accent was always there, Eoin went all out with his Irish brogue to charm his lady friend.

Brenna wanted to throw up the half glass of wine she'd consumed.

"Don't worry, she has that effect on everyone," said a deep and somewhat thrilling voice next to her. "She's very much in love with her husband."

She looked up into twinkling sapphire eyes. The arrival and attention of this second sexy male was an overload of Brenna's senses. If anything, he was hotter than Eoin, and for her, that was saying something because she'd been obsessed with Eoin since the moment they'd first met four years ago. All she could do was gape at this newcomer, her brain having gone south for vacation.

The blond man tilted his head to the side to study her, and a small smirk played about his full lips.

She had the distinct impression he could see to the farthest reaches of her soul. "She's beautiful," Brenna blurted.

His smile widened.

She felt scorched by the warmth.

"My sister, GiGi? Yes, she is, indeed." He held out a hand. "Alastair Thorne."

"Brenna Sullivan." She placed her palm in his and jumped when a small current of electricity sparked between them. "Oh! I'm sorry. It must be static. I…" What could she say? And why the hell was she apologizing for something she couldn't control?

"Sullivan?" Alastair glanced over his shoulder to see Odessa bearing down on them. "A relation, I'm betting."

"My grandaunt. And I'm going to apologize in advance for whatever you're about to witness." Brenna's eyes flew wide, and she clapped a hand over her mouth. Never before had she been so open with a stranger!

Her gaze shot to Eoin.

He grinned. "I thought you might have a little fire inside you, love."

Oh, she'd give him all the fire he could handle if he'd continue to look at her like that for the remainder of her days.

# CHAPTER 2

"*A*lastair Thorne," Odessa breathed in delight. Her beady eyes narrowed, and a sick pleasure curled her garish lips.

Brenna wanted to hurl for real this time. Instead, she quickly grabbed a flute of champagne from a passing server and sidestepped so she was directly in her aunt's path, thereby protecting Alastair from a sexual mauling. "Here you are, Aunt," she said brightly.

Odessa glared down at her. "Stupid girl. You know I can't have more than one glass with my medication. Are you trying to put me in a coma?"

Mortification hit Brenna hard, and she didn't dare look at any of the guests, or she might cry. Of course she was aware it wasn't wise to mix alcohol with the pharmacy of drugs her aunt consumed each day. But Brenna was tired of Odessa throwing herself at unsuspecting men with little regard for their feelings or how predatory she was behaving, and she had simply sought to sabotage her aunt's obvious sexual advances, not kill her. That fantasy *did* exist, however, but only in the far reaches of her mind, back behind a closed door with criss-crossing DO NOT OPEN tape over the opening.

"No, Aunt. I merely—"

Odessa waved a hand in dismissal, effectively cutting Brenna off. "Oh, do shut up, girl. Your ignorance is showing. *Again.*"

A warm muscled forearm encircled Brenna's upper body and dragged her back against a rock-hard chest. She thought she might faint when she recognized the arm's owner. The myriad of bracelets—from leather to beaded to precious metal—gave her the clue. Only Eoin could wear such an eclectic range of jewelry and get away with it.

"Enough," he snapped. "You've no call to belittle Brenna, and I'll not stand for it."

One of Brenna's hands came up to grip his wrist in case she swooned at his feet, which was likely if he continued to hold and defend her.

"How dare you!" Odessa's jowls wobbled as her overly made-up face turned an alarming shade of purple.

"I dare a lot of things, Ms. Sullivan," Eoin assured her.

Only Brenna could feel the coiled tension in his frame, and she wondered why he'd bothered to stand up for her at all. Her aunt could make or break careers, and Brenna suspected Eoin knew it. It made the mystery of why he was protecting her that much more confounding.

She tried to pull away and put the brakes on this runaway train, for his sake. "Mr. O'Malley—"

"It's Eoin to you, love." His deep voice next to the shell of her ear made her tremble.

His grip tightened marginally, and he removed the champagne flute from her fingers, probably fearing she'd drop it in her surprise. Brenna could swear he rubbed his cheek against her hair. Her eyes widened, and she caught sight of Alastair's smile. Feeling as if she'd stepped into the middle of a hereto-unknown play, she shook her head and straightened her spine.

"Aunt Odessa, I—"

"You are dead to me, you foolish girl. Don't come crawling back when the Eoin O'Malleys of the world use you up and spit you out."

"She won't," Eoin assured Odessa.

Brenna almost swallowed her tongue. She glanced to the side, seeking help from the Thornes, but they looked highly amused by the entire incident. Her panicked gaze shot back to her aunt, but the woman was in high dudgeon, and Brenna had no way of talking her down this time.

Odessa hobbled away, and Brenna felt each sharp slap of her aunt's cane on the polished floor like a blow to her heart. Not that the old bat had ever treated her with courtesy or respect—Brenna was the poster child for Cinderella, minus the fairy godmother and singing mice—but Odessa was her only means of financial support.

"That went surprisingly well," GiGi said with a bright smile and laughing eyes.

Brenna pressed her fingertips to her temples and shook her head. "I guess this means I'm out of the will." She was only half joking. Or maybe she wasn't joking at all. "I get to be homeless for the foreseeable future."

"Never going to happen, child." GiGi pressed her flawlessly manicured hand to Brenna's cheek and gave a gentle pat. "We'll see you're taken care of."

"Right." Eoin gave her one more slight squeeze, as if he was reluctant to let her go, then he turned her to face him. "Besides, love, you're coming home with me, remember?"

Her heart plummeted to her big toe. Odessa was right—Brenna was a foolish girl.

"I can't, Mr. O—uh, Eoin," she corrected when he squinted a warning at her. "Aunt Odessa doesn't necessarily pay me. She always insinuated she'd compensate me, uh, later. After. Like, because I was her sole beneficiary." Her cheeks stung with heat, and she wanted to smack herself. She barely refrained. "I can't afford to go."

"It's going to be okay." Eoin's eyes softened, and a tender smile curled his lips.

*Clearly, the guy liked to stand up for the underdog in a fight.*

Those horrid emotions of hers—misery and embarrassment —warred for supremacy. Brenna dropped her gaze to her ugly sensible shoes because if she didn't, those around her were certain to see the tears forming.

She heard Eoin say, "Excuse us a moment, please." But as Brenna turned to go, he gripped her arm. "Not you, love. I was talkin' to GiGi and Alastair. *You* are the one I intend to converse with, don't ya know."

Embarrassment outdistanced misery by a mile, and Brenna was sure she was glowing a brilliant fire-engine red. Without looking up, she allowed him to lead her to a small alcove on the far side of the room. She heard the curtain rings clang against the metal rod as he closed them inside. Still, she couldn't raise her eyes from the floor.

"Brenna, love, look at me." He used the tips of his bejeweled fingers and lifted her chin. "Tell me. Do you know how much these paintings of mine sell for?"

She glanced around as if she could see through the curtain —if only to avoid meeting his eyes—and mentally calculated the price tags of all those sold tonight. He'd made a few million on this show alone. With a sharp nod, she settled her gaze on the base of his throat, where his shirt exposed his beautiful suntanned skin.

"I can afford to buy you a first-class ticket, don't you think?"

Squeezing her eyes tightly shut, she pressed her lips together.

*The humiliation just kept coming.*

Now he'd think she was pathetic and unable to care for herself or that she was one of those worthless art groupies of his, the ones who always expected him to pay for everything. All she wanted was to escape and hide in the closest closet. Unfortunately, he stood between her and the exit.

EOIN WATCHED THE PLAY OF EMOTIONS ON BRENNA'S EXPRESSIVE face, and he wanted to sigh his frustration. He'd gone and put his foot in it by mentioning his financial success while she was wondering where her next meal would come from. Yet he'd done it, not to embarrass her, but to assure her he'd help her transition from Odessa's unpaid lackey to whatever she cared to become.

"Look, Brenna, I'm not in the habit of offering charity, and I'm not offering it now. I extended an invitation for you to be a guest of my family before the altercation with your miserable aunt, and it was always my intention to pay for our trip." He stepped back to give her space. "But if you're feeling the need to pay your way, then I've a proposition for you."

Her head whipped up, and her eyes rounded behind her hideous tortoiseshell glasses.

"Jaysus! Not like *that*!"

Her expression, ever mercurial, shifted to what could only be horrified, and she dashed for the curtain.

Eoin was faster.

With an arm around her waist, he tugged her back against him, as he had during the confrontation with Odessa. He felt just as protective of her now as he had then. For the second time, he registered how perfectly snug her arse fit up against him. And, also for the second time, he felt his cock stir and take note.

"Brenna, as evidenced by the boner formin' against your

bum, I don't find you repellent in the least, but I'm not after shaggin' ya. I'm after offering you a job."

He felt her relax—and maybe press back into him—before she stiffened and turned around.

All her exposed skin was flushed beet red, and she had a difficult time deciding where to rest her gaze. Eoin's desire to laugh was overpowering, and he barely managed to choke back the sound.

"What do you say? Will you come work for me, love?"

"Wh-what will I b-be…" Her eyes locked on his semi-erection, and she audibly gulped.

The urge to tease her was strong, but he feared she'd bolt. So he decided to utilize her already formidable skills. "Manager. I need someone I can trust to make travel arrangements, settle up with gallery owners, and organize my schedule for future showings. Is it something you might want to do?"

Finally, after what felt like forever and a day, she raised those soul-stealing eyes to his. "I can do that," she said hesitantly. She followed it with a determined nod. With each second that passed, her resolve firmed and confidence took the place of her worry.

A grin curled his lips. "You'll start now?"

"You want me to make travel arrangements right now?"

"Well, no, but I would like you to stick beside me and run interference with the rest of the randy women."

She laughed with a suddenness that stole his breath, and he marveled at the melodious sound and the effect it had on his body. "I can do that."

"Grand." He gestured downward. "And pardon my humble friend, yeah? He's had to behave himself far too long while I shut myself off to work. He's feeling a might frisky at the moment. I didn't mean to frighten you."

Her startling eyes danced with mirth as more color rushed

to her cheeks. "So, not gay, despite what you told Aunt Odessa?"

"Oh, if you've ever a chance to speak with her again, you're to drive home the point and that a worldly woman such as her would make my flute hit a false note, to be sure." He grinned when she laughed. "But no, love. I'm not gay."

"And it's a bloody shame because I called dibs ages ago in case he ever decides to join my team."

The curtain was jerked aside, and Reggie propped his hands on his slim hips.

"Were ya eavesdroppin' again, you scut?" Eoin demanded with a mock scowl.

"Yes. Yes, I was." He sniffed and straightened the lapels of his shimmering-gold suit jacket. The bold material would make Elton John envious. "I had to protect your privacy from all those circling buzzards out there." He gestured over his shoulder with his thumb, and Eoin's gaze followed where Reggie had indicated. The crowd had shifted closer, eager for juicy gossip. Such was the celebrity associated with his newly successful career.

With his back still to the sea of gawkers, Reggie adopted a campy pose and batted his lashes. "You should kiss me and cement your claim, young scamp."

"Feck off," Eoin growled good-naturedly.

One elegant shrug of his shoulder later, Reggie shifted his sights to Brenna. "I had a small window to turn him, and you ruined it, you drab little thing."

"*Reg!*"

He waved a hand in dismissal of Eoin's unspoken reprimand. "Come, girl. Uncle Reggie is going to transform you and teach you all the things you need to be fabulous."

Eoin shifted to block Brenna. "Don't you dare alter one hair on her head."

"You're mighty protective of her, aren't you, scamp? It's absolutely delicious the way you defend her."

"Shut up, Reggie. Just shut the fuck up." Eoin clasped Brenna's hand but refused to look at her. He was afraid the mortification she'd be unable to hide would be the mirror of what he was currently experiencing with the entire gallery's attention on them. Of course, he was better at hiding it. "Let's go, Brenna."

Her cherry-red mouth formed a surprised O. "But I thought you wanted to stay until the end of the show."

"I've decided it's time we head on before I give in to my desire to maim someone. And I need a pint."

Reggie's smug smile and knowing eyes sorely tested Eoin's willpower to keep his fists to himself. "Cheers!"

Eoin flipped him off and tugged Brenna with him through the hastily parting crowd.

# CHAPTER 3

*B*renna studied her surroundings as Eoin waited on their drinks at the bar. He'd assured her this was as close as an Irish pub could get to any of the ones in *Éire*. She still found it difficult to believe he intended to fly her there.

*Ireland.*

She'd always dreamed of going.

Her gran had spent hours talking about growing up there as a child and sparked Brenna's love of a place she'd never seen. Doreen Sullivan had been a pistol. She'd born Brenna's mother out of wedlock, who did the same in turn. Neither cared one whit for what anyone thought. Gran's spinster sister, Odessa, had plenty to say, though. Which was ironic, since Gran and Brenna's mother had only loved once and Odessa nailed everything with a penis.

A mouthwatering muscled forearm with a rolled-up sleeve and an eclectic array of bracelets entered her sight line as Eoin set a wineglass in front of her. "What has you thinking so hard, lovely Brenna?"

"Ireland, and all the stories my grandmother told me."

"She was born there?"

"Yes." She sipped the drink and grimaced, but quickly masked her distaste.

"You don't like the wine?"

His deep chuckle made her knees tremble, and Brenna pressed them together under the table.

"It's fine," she lied.

He studied her for all of ten seconds, then pushed his Guinness across the table. "Here. Try this."

She guzzled a third of it before pushing it back to him with a laugh at his stunned expression. "Gran practically raised me on the stuff. What can I say? I prefer it to that overly dry red Odessa insists we drink."

"I'm an eejit for assuming," he muttered as he scooped up the wine. "I'll get you a proper drink."

Brenna watched as he conversed with the bartender and held up two fingers. The sexy twenty-something woman wore an inviting smile and leaned across the counter, showing the bulk of her wares in the low-cut red tank top. She touched Eoin's arm and laughed at whatever he'd told her. But Eoin surprised Brenna by withdrawing and shoving his fisted hands deep inside his jeans pockets. He gestured with a tilt of his head, and the woman's attention shifted to Brenna.

Brenna fought the urge to give her a finger wave.

With a careless shrug, the bartender left to build the beers.

"What did you say to her?" Brenna asked when Eoin returned.

"Nothing much." When she snorted her disbelief, he chuckled. "I may have said you were my girlfriend to get her to back off."

The desire to preen was strong, but she nodded instead. He'd used her as an excuse to tell another woman no. That didn't mean he wanted *her*, but at least she was good for something.

"What are you thinking, Brenna?"

Ever watchful, Eoin had picked up on her relentless self-deprecating thoughts. "Nothing much," she replied with a too-casual sip of the Guinness.

His lips curled into a delighted smile. "You've got sass. Sure, and I like it."

Because he felt like a friend, possibly the only true one she'd ever had, she gathered her courage to ask what had been bothering her since he practically abducted her from the gallery. "Was Reggie right? Am I drab?"

"No. Reggie's an arse."

Eoin appeared angry she'd brought it up, and she experienced a moment of misgiving. Would he think she was a needy pain in the butt who required constant attention?

"You're perfect the way you are, love. If others can't see your incredible light, it's on them."

No one had *ever* used the words incredible or perfect to describe her, but it seemed Eoin had a compassionate heart, if his words were anything to go by. Brenna knew not to invest in his compliments. If she did, she'd be disappointed when he rejected her, as he was bound to do.

"I'll not tell ya tall tales, Brenna. I'll always speak true." He scooted his chair closer to hers and picked up her hand. He waited until she met his steady regard, then said, "Could your hair do with a highlight or two? Meh. If you truly want them. Should you be left alone to shop for clothes? Abso-fecking-lutely not. Your tastes are questionable."

Appalled at his bluntness, her mouth dropped open.

He tapped it shut and warmed to the subject. "Those cat-eye glasses are atrocious, if I'm to be honest."

Brenna withdrew her hand and balled it in a fist, tempted to punch him in his flawless fucking face. "On that note, I suppose we should get down to business and off the topic of my appearance," she said stiffly, knowing her burning cheeks were a dead giveaway of her outrage.

Not one to be dissuaded, Eoin retrieved her hand and kissed her knuckles. She felt a wave of heat all the way down to her girl grotto.

"You're mistakin' me, Brenna." His tone was intimate and caring, his eyes admiring.

She thought she might've had a psychotic break. Maybe they were back in the gallery and she was still lusting from afar, caught up in the fantasy of Eoin noticing her. She cleared her throat as she surreptitiously pinched her thigh to make sure she wasn't dreaming.

"H-how do I m-mistake you?"

*Christ, she sounded like a dying bullfrog!*

"Because clothes and glasses are outer trappings. Hair can be cut and colored. But the things that are truly beautiful about you can't be purchased."

Her heart began to hammer, and she couldn't rip her gaze away from his for all the money in Odessa's bulging bank account.

"Your eyes. They're the color of the sea where the water kisses the sand. They reach in and trap a man's soul with one passin' glance. Your voice is pure music to the ears, a delightful symphony, and sweeter than a songbird's." Butterfly soft, he brushed his thumb across her cheekbone. "And your skin, it's enough to make a grown man weep at the silkiness of it. Sure, and it fosters dreams of what other parts of you might be that lovely."

Brenna's heart stopped in her chest. Just stopped. Right along with her lung and brain functions.

"But it's your generous spirit that entrances, love. You've a kindness not many do and a moral compass few possess. There's where your true beauty lies, to be sure."

He released her hand, sat back, and sipped his beer as if he didn't just leave her raw and aching to have him possess her in every way. More than ever, she wanted to cry. In all her twenty-six years, no one had truly *seen* her, outside of her gran. No one had ever cared to look beyond the surface to discover the woman hiding there, beneath the "outer trappings" Odessa had purchased for her. Only Eoin. And he'd thrown it out there in such a matter-of-fact way, it couldn't be denied or ignored—or acknowledged. To acknowledge it meant she'd reveal her true feelings for him and what his words meant to her.

Drawing on years of hiding her reactions, Brenna lifted her drink and wet her parched throat. "So, not drab, then," she finally managed as she blindly surveyed the bar.

She thought she heard him snort, but when she glanced over at him, his expression was bland. It was only when she peered closer that she noticed the laughter lurking in his eyes.

*Were his irises lighter in color?*

They certainly seemed to be. How it was possible, she didn't know, so she dismissed her fanciful thought.

"Not drab, then," he agreed.

Brenna couldn't help but grin.

"Brenna?"

Eoin heard the man's voice before he saw him, but he didn't fail to notice the way Brenna lit up as she looked at the person behind him.

"Brenna Sullivan! It *is* you! Here, and I'm shocked that old dragon has let you out of her sight."

"It's good to see you, Ronan," she said warmly as she was tugged to her feet and embraced in a bear hug by the newcomer.

*Ronan?*

A sick feeling rushed over Eoin, and he leapt to his feet. His worst fears were confirmed the instant he turned and recognized Ronan O'Connor, who until recently had been his family's enemy. Also one of the most gorgeous men in existence.

There wasn't a woman alive who didn't turn feeble minded when they saw him.

"Get your fucking hands off her," Eoin growled.

Both Brenna and Ronan stilled.

"Eoin?" Brenna's tentative voice made him feel like a shite, but no way was Ronan Fucking O'Connor getting within ten feet of her. His family had done enough harm to the O'Malleys, and Brenna wouldn't be caught in the crossfire of another stir-up. Eoin's previously tortured fingers still experienced phantom pains now and again.

"O'Connor, you get your fecking hands off her and back up, or I'll be cleaning the floor with your face. I'll not have you acting the maggot with her." Eoin probably just signed his death warrant because Ronan had recently acquired the formidable powers of a Guardian, *the* strongest magical being next to an Aether, who kept the balance between good and evil.

Ronan's hard silver-eyed stare summed up the situation in an instant. He no doubt recognized Eoin was deadly serious. With grudging respect, Ronan held up his hands and backed a step away. "I'm glad to see someone appreciates Brenna for who she is and not what they can get from her. Or are you after something more... *meaningful*, O'Malley?"

Rage exploded in Eoin's brain, and he lunged.

Brenna threw herself in front of him and barely avoided being mowed down. Only Eoin's quick reflexes allowed him to catch her and swing her to safety.

"Never do that again, Brenna," he scolded as he cradled her pale face between his palms.

She nodded shakily, and those wide, timid eyes caused his heart to ache. Her trembling body told the story of her fear.

He swept her into his tight embrace and rested a cheek on her silky-haired head. "Jaysus, Brenna. Don't be afraid of me. I'll not hurt ya."

Her arms crept around his middle, and Eoin released his

tension with a sigh. He hated that his back was to Ronan, and he expected a knife through the ribs at any moment—such was the O'Connor way—but the shaken woman in his arms was his priority.

"I know you won't, Eoin," she said in a low voice. "You're too nice."

Ronan possessed the hearing of a bat, and he snorted his disbelief at Brenna's comment. "The word 'nice' isn't usually associated with Eoin O'Malley, dear Brenna. If he's 'nice,' he wants something from you. Be careful your knickers don't end up around your ankles, all the same."

"I swear to feck, I'm going to kill him!"

With a fine sense of Eoin's intent, Brenna gripped his shirt and held tight. "Please don't."

Scrunching his eyes closed, he nodded and took pleasure in the small circles she'd begun to rub on his back.

Ronan's laughter followed the bastard to the bar, taunting Eoin with its mocking quality. When he had himself under control, he eased his hold on Brenna and tilted her pointy chin up. "He owes you for saving his life, love."

"Or maybe you do," she said with a slight twist of her lips. "Ronan's a big guy."

"You think I can't beat him?"

"I think I don't want to see either of you get hurt when you try."

It didn't sit well with Eoin that she thought he was a delicate flower. His oldest brother, Cian, had been a spy for the Witches' Council and had taught him to fight when Eoin was still in short pants. He might prefer a paintbrush to a weapon, but he still knew how to do damage, should he need to.

Yet he had nothing to prove at the moment, and so he let it go. "Are you ready to come home with me?"

For the second time in five minutes, she grew deathly pale. "I... uh... you... we..."

He placed a finger over her pillowy lips and registered her mouth was built for sin. How had he not noticed before that moment? He cleared his throat, mainly to focus on the subject at hand. "Not for sex, Brenna." But damn, he wouldn't mind that either. "You need a place to stay, and my apartment has an extra bedroom."

"Oh." Her face fell, and clear disappointment shone in her eyes. "Right. Not for sex. I knew that. Of *course* you don't want to have sex with me. I'm—"

Eoin shut down her babbling the best way he knew how.

He kissed her.

# CHAPTER 4

Nerves ate Brenna's insides, and the sensation was almost painful as she stood outside the entrance to Eoin's New York apartment. The urge to vomit was real. Her world had gone topsy-turvy in a matter of hours, and she had a dizzying sense that her life was never going to be the same. She only hoped it was a good thing.

With a twist of his wrist, Eoin unlocked and opened the door, then ushered her inside. The warm look he gave her melted her internal organs and doubled those pesky nerves.

"Are you all right, love?"

The quiet concern made her feel ashamed of herself, of the suspicions she'd had since he kissed her at the bar. Eoin treated their kiss as if it hadn't rocked his world, but Brenna couldn't be as blasé about it. She'd felt the scorching heat in places she didn't know could burn to such a degree, and she was certain some of her brain's wiring had melted and she was now dumber for it. Case in point, she'd blindly followed him here like a neglected puppy eager for affection. The man could be a serial killer, and she, his next victim. Still, if he kissed her before he took her out, what a way to go!

"Brenna?"

As soon as he said her name, she realized she'd taken too long to answer. "Oh, yeah. Sorry. Yeah. I'm... fine." Good gravy! Was she ever *not* going to babble in front of him? He must think she was a veritable nitwit. She released a heavy exhale and centered herself, or at least as much as she could. "I'm fine. I was wondering what I would do for clothing. Aunt Odessa isn't likely to allow me back to pack my things."

Eoin's gaze dropped to her dress, and he couldn't hide his judgmental grimace. "We'll shop in the morning."

"I..." What could she say? It wasn't as if she had a choice, and the clothing Odessa had purchased for her was atrocious anyway. "Thank you."

"I'll send Reggie to Odessa's tomorrow to recover your belongings. Make a list of your must-haves. Minus the clothing, because if it's anything like what I've seen to date, you're in need of a new wardrobe."

Irritation at his high-handed attitude bubbled up, but Brenna didn't argue. She gave him a sharp nod and proceeded to walk past him into his apartment. She stopped in the marbled foyer and turned back around, unsure which way to go.

Eoin locked the door and carelessly tossed his keys on the dark-wood table, roughly four feet in diameter, in the center of the entry. Brenna couldn't prevent the wince as the metal slid across the surface and clinked against what appeared to be an antique porcelain vase. Odessa would've given her a ten-minute lecture had she done anything so irresponsible.

"What?"

She glanced up from the keys to stare at him with wide-eyed trepidation. She didn't doubt she resembled a deer in the headlights. "N-nothing."

"Are you afraid of me, Brenna?"

Well, she wasn't that terrified before he'd asked, but what did she really know about him? "No?"

His lips twitched, and he pressed them into a tight line. A dimple appeared on his left cheek, and the sight of the asymmetrical indentation made her feel slightly better. As if perhaps he wasn't so perfect, after all.

"Why did your 'no' sound like a question, love?"

"Maybe because I don't really know you, and here I am, in your apartment, after cutting ties with the only family I have left in the world."

His eyes swept her troubled face. When his gaze focused on her mouth, a shiver ran the length of her spine. Goodness, she wanted him to kiss her again, to make her forget who and what she was—a pathetic hanger-on with no resources of her own.

"Why did you kiss me?" she croaked.

Eoin's eyes locked with hers. The slow, wicked smile that blossomed caused her already weak knees to tremble. "Because it was the most pleasurable way I could think of to shut you up."

Brenna's mind bypassed the word pleasurable and settled on *to shut you up*. She'd been shut up and shut down all her life. Now that she was out from under Odessa's iron fist, she needed to be more outspoken and stand up for herself once in a blue moon.

Drumming up the outrage, she placed her hands on her hips and glared for all she was worth.

"Sure, and the little kitten has claws." His smile widened as he strode to where she stood. "You'll need that fire in the coming days, love. Hold on to it, yeah?"

Uncertain what he meant, she nodded. She could only assume it was regarding her current predicament and not about sexual games.

Brenna wasn't quite sure what she'd intended to say in

response, but her need to reply was squashed when Dubheasa O'Malley sailed through the door and carelessly tossed her keys next to her brother's.

Again, Brenna winced.

"You'll never guess who showed up at my flat tonight—oh!" Dubheasa stopped short the second she realized company was present. "Brenna! Lovely to see you again, it is!"

Brenna couldn't help but smile. Dubheasa O'Malley, like her twin brother, was a force of nature. But unlike Eoin, she was engaging and open, with a ready laugh or quip for everyone. "And you, too."

Eoin led them into the living room and dropped onto the leather sofa, sprawling out and tucking a bent arm behind his head.

Brenna's body overheated in an instant from his unintentionally sexy pose, and her mind blanked when he caught her stare and winked.

Acting as if she wasn't standing, starstruck, he addressed his sister. "Ronan O'Connor."

"How did you guess?" Dubheasa demanded with a severe frown.

"We saw the bastard at the pub around the corner. He's an arrogant fecker, that one."

Brenna wanted to say he was the pot calling the kettle black, and because she had years of practice holding her tongue with Aunt Odessa, she managed to refrain from commenting. Whatever problems the O'Malley twins had with Ronan was their business.

"What did you intend to say, love?"

Brenna's gaze snapped to Eoin, carefully registering and cataloging his watchful expression. How had he guessed at her thoughts? And why was he concerned with her when no one other than her gran had ever been?

He lifted a brow, and a teasing light entered his eyes. "Sure, and you know you wanted to."

She wanted to do a lot of things where he was concerned. A tidal wave of heat washed over her, and she was certain her cheeks were a fiery red, clashing with her bland hair and dull gray dress. "I-I... Nothing. I wasn't going to say anything."

"Scarlet is your mam for the lies you tell." He grinned when she scowled. "Keep your secrets, Brenna Sullivan. I'm not after stealing them."

No, he was after stealing her heart, but she couldn't say that either.

EOIN DIDN'T KNOW WHY IT WAS SUDDENLY NECESSARY TO CAUSE Brenna's blush. He'd felt uncomfortable in the past whenever she turned those wide, guileless eyes his way. But after one taste of her, he found himself craving more, and amorous stirrings were beginning to take up important real estate in his mind. With a commission for a new series sitting in his account, he needed a clear head to create. Allowing himself to be consumed by her was a disaster in the making. She wasn't the type to fit in with his hedonistic, worldly friends.

Purposefully, he turned his attention and kiss-haunted thoughts away from Brenna to look at his sister. Dubheasa was in crisis mode over Ronan O'Connor, and he knew he should hear her out or she was likely to turn to murder, and then where would they be?

"What did O'Connor want?" he asked her.

"He was spoutin' malarky about Guardians and baby Aethers. Said the Oracle has decreed I'm to be his mate, as if that'll be happenin' in this bleedin' lifetime." In her rage, Dubheasa had lost her Americanized way of speaking and reverted back to their traditional speech pattern. It told him just how angry she was, because she tried hard to blend in here.

A choked noise had him turning in Brenna's direction.

"You're to be his mate?" She appeared somewhat scandalized and fascinated at the same time. "What does that even mean? Is it something the residents of your country often do, this claim-a-mate thing?"

The struggle not to laugh was real, and Eoin barely managed to choke back the sound. Dubheasa looked right horrified—as if Brenna were a small child with wet finger paint about to touch her mother's white skirt. His sister gave him an *"is she for real?"* look, to which he responded with a grin.

"She's clueless, she is." He winked in Brenna's direction, sending her into a tizzy and hopefully distracting her from the rest of Dubheasa's tangent about Ronan, Aethers, and Oracles. Eoin suspected Brenna's knowledge of such things was limited, and he wasn't up to a crash course in all things magic. He was still learning some of the basics himself.

"Clueless?" From the shrill tone of Brenna's voice, she'd taken umbrage with his comment, as he'd hoped. "I may not know about Guardians and babies... er... um, baby..." Her neck was the first to flush, quickly followed by the petal-soft skin of her face. Eoin suspected, like himself, Brenna's train of thought was derailed by their strange sexual chemistry. That she'd stalled where she did when she looked at him was telling. "Er, Aethers," she finished lamely.

"Baby Aethers," Dubheasa corrected absently as she paced, seemingly oblivious to what was happening between Brenna and him. "Like I'm to be some Sentinel of Magic tasked with watching over the Aether's daughter. Not feckin' likely! Eoin! Are ya even payin' attention to me here?"

When he was finally able to tear his gaze away from Brenna's striking face and focus on his sister, he found her glaring at him with her hands on her hips. Brenna was going to get an education in magic anyway, it seemed.

"Aye. You're right fierce in your determination to shun

Ronan O'Connor and avoid becoming a Sentinel of Magic. I heard ya the first time you caused me ears to bleed with your shrill banshee tone," he said dryly. "And ya can calm the feck down, Dubheasa. I'm not after lettin' ya make a mistake of that caliber by hookin' up with O'Connor."

When his sister turned as fiery red as Brenna had less than a minute before, he knew she'd already had sex with Ronan.

"Oh, feck. Tell me ya didn't already shag the man. You'll not get rid of him now." Eoin shook his head. "He'll be just like all the other poor bastards who you've shagged, and you'll not shake him until ya move to another country." He frowned as it occurred to him exactly what type of magic Ronan possessed as a Guardian. "But I suppose in his case, he'll find ya easy enough."

"That's the problem! Were ya not listening, Eoin? He knows where to find me, and he's found a way to haunt me dreams, he has!"

Ice seemed to freeze the blood in his veins. Dubheasa's fears were real if Ronan O'Connor was playing dirty and using magic to invade her sleep. Eoin sat up quickly, gripping the back of the couch to keep from hunting Ronan down and doing what he should've done earlier tonight and wiping the floor with the man's too-handsome-to-be-real face. "What's this, then?"

She threw up her hands in frustration. "I swear you've not been paying attention to me. I've a problem here, brother, and all ya seem to be interested in is toying with your little mouse." Storming toward the exit, she threw over her shoulder, "Never ya mind, then. I'll find a way to outsmart the fecker myself. See if I don't!"

After the front door slammed behind her, silence reigned for a full minute. Eoin was almost afraid to look at Brenna, sensing she wasn't over her pique. When he met her stormy gaze and saw how proudly she stood with her chin held high and her brows arched, he knew he deserved whatever she intended to dish up.

"I don't think I can make as spectacular an exit as your sister, but I can at least say I'm far from clueless, Mr. O'Malley."

Her voice was cooler than he'd ever heard it. His heart rate increased, thudding heavily inside his chest, and he was disconcerted by how turned on her frosty tone made him. And Brenna wasn't done giving him what for.

"If—and here I'll stress the word—*if* I decide to take the job you so carelessly offered earlier tonight, there's one thing you need to know about me. I have *always* been aware of how the world works. I may not participate in every conversation, and I've been forced to linger on the outskirts like a good little minion to Aunt Odessa, but believe me, working for her, I've received quite the education on human nature."

He rose and crossed to where she stood with her hands balled by her sides. With her eyes sparking fire and her pale skin a soft rose, she looked attractive in a way he'd not noticed before tonight. Not bothering with permission, he removed her ghastly glasses and tossed them on the sofa.

"I want to paint you," he stated, unconcerned by the husky quality in his voice. If she intended to stick around, she would soon learn he gave into his desires and denied himself nothing.

Her jaw fell open, and she blinked rapidly in her attempt to focus on him. "You can't be serious. I'm"—she swallowed hard —"not beautiful. Not l-like your r-regular models."

"Perhaps not, but you're far more interestin'. Say you'll pose for me."

Brenna remained quiet for the span of a minute, and Eoin waited. He hoped like hell she would say yes, because his hand itched to pick up a brush and capture the riot of emotions constantly flashing in her fascinating eyes.

"Is it a condition of my employment?" she finally asked.

Stuffing down the desire to say yes, he shook his head. "I hired you to do exactly as I proposed at the gallery, Brenna. Nothin' more."

As he saw the "no" forming on her lips, he held up a hand. "All I ask is that ya think about it, yeah?"

# CHAPTER 5

*B*renna had no idea how she'd ended up in first class on an airbus to Ireland, but there she was, courtesy of Eoin O'Malley. He was sprawled out next to her in his reclining seat, fast asleep, as if he didn't have a care in the world. She, on the other hand, had a million-and-one thoughts crowding her brain. And all of them centered around the future, or in her case, the lack thereof.

The last two days had been a whirlwind, and somehow he'd managed to secure her passport, buy her two suitcases full of clothes, and book their tickets for Ireland. So efficiently, in fact, she wondered why he needed to hire her. Which brought her thoughts around to working for him…

Employment with Eoin would be fine for the time being, but since she'd pined for him for what felt like forever, she knew she wouldn't be able to hang around him long term. Eventually, she'd give herself away or someone would notice her making cow eyes at him. Embarrassment would set in, and she'd have to shave her head, change her name, and move to a remote island where no one had ever heard of the newly famous artist, Eoin O'Malley.

"I can feel you thinking," Eoin said in a low, gravely voice, heavy with sleep. "Get some rest, yeah. Let tomorrow take care of itself, love."

Curious and surprised by his insight, she asked, "Don't you ever worry about anything?"

Lids at half mast, he studied her in a lazy, unhurried manner. "Rarely. But then I've always gone after what I wanted with a single-minded purpose. Sure, and maybe I'm a little arrogant here, but if I've a mind to get it, I do."

"I wish I were that brave," she said, almost to herself. Still, he heard.

"You are, or you wouldn't be sittin' here, next to me." Admiration, or something like it, was reflected back at her, and she wasn't quite sure how she'd earned it.

"I'm nothing special, Eoin."

His answering grin tied her stomach in knots. "Now there I'll have to tell you, you're wrong. I've kissed ya, remember?"

"How could I forget!" She cringed the second the words left her mouth, and when he laughed, she thought her cheeks would combust from the scorching heat. "I mean—"

"It was memorable for me, too, don't ya know." He closed his eyes, a smile still curling his talented mouth. "Get some rest, now. I've a feeling our time in Ireland will be eventful."

"Not like that, it won't," she said quickly. "I'm not... I don't... it's not that I wouldn't, uh, want to, because *look* at you, but... *oh God, I need to shut the fuck up!*"

His compelling eyes flared wide, and he was staring at her like he would a child's chalk drawing hanging in a gallery of masterpieces. Which was to say with something resembling horrified amusement.

She closed her eyes and slammed her head back against the seat, wishing there was a parachute handy so she could jump out of this damned plane. Yes, they were over the ocean, but she didn't care. A watery death was better than dying slowly by humiliation. Maybe she'd forgo the parachute and just jump. She'd have to ask the flight attendant to tell her when they reached maximum altitude, because with her stinking luck, she'd survive the fall but break every bone in her body and not be found for ten days. When they pulled her from the water, she'd be blotchy and sunburned from exposure, and the news article would show a picture of the rescue from the wrong angle. They'd capture her in an awkward pose, looking god-awful.

The subtle noise of Eoin shifting was overly loud to her oversensitive ears. She'd been tuned in to any sound of movement in case he decided to run screaming in the opposite direction.

"Brenna."

The gentle understanding in his voice made her weepy, and she scrunched her eyes tighter. His muffled laugh from directly beside her caused her lids to snap open.

"Do you always do the opposite of what people expect?"

His casual question threw her, and she didn't have an immediate response. Didn't have any thought other than she wanted him to kiss her like he had at the pub. Her gaze dropped to his mouth, and she licked her lips.

"Keep lookin' at me like that, Brenna Sullivan, and we'll be joinin' the mile-high club, we will." His Irish accent had thickened as an amorous glow lit his stunningly green eyes.

"We can't," she blurted.

"Oh, I assure you we can," he whispered into the shell of her ear.

A flutter of anticipation ran through her, and her fingers itched to trace his chiseled jaw. What she really should be doing was pushing him away. She'd never be anything more than a joke to him; she just wasn't one of *those* girls. The kind who inspired art or poetry. The kind who could suck on a lollipop and have every guy in a mile radius fantasizing about other things she could do with her mouth. The kind who understood their worth.

Except for a boyfriend in college, she hadn't had a serious relationship. The total sum of her sexual experience was losing her virginity to a nerd in a dorm room. Parker Harris had dumped her the next day, stating she just didn't "do it" for him, not like the character from his Final Fantasy PlayStation game. Brenna didn't even want to touch that with a ten-foot pole. Not Parker's obsession with video games, nor his micro penis. Through the school grapevine, she'd heard he died of an aneurysm a week after their one-night stand, and though she felt bad for his family and friends, she couldn't say she was too torn up about it. The guy had been an asshole.

"Where did you go just now, love?"

Eoin's husky voice startled her from dwelling on her crushing self-doubts. "Side trip," she said with a scrunch of her nose. "You should know, I take those journeys from time to time."

He chuckled. "You are a true delight, Brenna. Don't ever change who ya are for anyone, yeah?"

"It's doubtful I could."

Eoin laughed and clasped her hand in his. "Good. Now try to sleep."

It wasn't like she was going to be able to after *that*. She'd need to overanalyze every look, every single touch. Hell, by Shannon Airport, she'd have convinced herself he was halfway to crazy about her. But the only true cray-cray one was her, a pauper who had severed ties with her benefactor and practically jumped at the chance to work for a temperamental, hot-as-fuck artist.

EOIN RAN A THUMB OVER HER KNUCKLES IN A SIMPLE, comforting caress. In an odd, inexplicable way, he'd felt Brenna's mind working. It wasn't that he'd been able to hear her internal dialogue, but he'd certainly known every time her brain fired up and she experienced tumultuous thoughts. He wished she'd just relax and trust him to take care of her, but he understood why she couldn't.

The entire time they were on board, he'd been hyper aware of her beside him. All his nerve endings were sparking as if he'd handled a live wire, and he had no logical explanation for it. The only true energy connection he'd ever experienced was with Dubheasa, and that was more of a twin-bond thing. If she cut her hand, his stung as if he'd sliced it. Or if she was in turmoil, he sensed her unease. But that was nothing like what he felt since kissing Brenna. It was as if, by touching her, he'd created a cosmic link that tied him to her. She was always on the periphery of his mind, dancing just out of reach, waiting for Goddess knows what to make their bond stronger.

She had no magic that he knew of, but she'd bound him all the same, like the mysterious Siren.

*A Siren!*

Eoin dropped her hand, not as quickly as he would a scalding potato, but nearly as fast. He'd heard of all kinds of fae creatures, but legend stated Sirens were achingly beautiful individuals designed to drive a human mad with desire, then help them along to an untimely death after stealing their power. Was the insanity based on long-term exposure? Although he was distracted by Brenna, he wouldn't consider himself gone mad. But perhaps time with her was best in smaller increments.

He stole a sideways glance to see her worrying her lip and staring forward. No, Brenna was simply an intelligent but lost woman with few friends, who he found fascinating for all her contradictions. With a sigh, Eoin closed his eyes and tried to sleep. Yet it evaded him as visions of Brenna flitted through his mind. What would she look like draped in a sheet, with her hair a tangled mass of curls down her back as she looked over her shoulder at him, biting her lip in her uncertainty as she was now doing? Or perhaps her eyes would be sparkling and a mischievous half smile would curl her lips as he tried to find the ideal blend of paint to match the bloom on her cheeks.

Eoin shifted uncomfortably, suddenly conscious of where he was and who was wide awake next to him. He wasn't embarrassed by his wants or needs, but Brenna might be if she saw the tent forming in his trousers.

Peeking with one eye, he noted her thoughts were turned inward and she appeared to be in a different zip code. It bothered him that she was so worried about the future. She was young, bright, and from what he'd seen so far, resourceful. Like a cat, she'd land on her feet and be better for it. Whatever he had to do, he'd do it if it meant she could cut ties with that blackhearted bitch, Odessa.

What kind of woman forced their niece to live on the outskirts of society, wearing the equivalent of rags while working for free? The Odessa Sullivans of the world were takers. But Eoin intended to see Brenna get back some of her own, even if he had to bring down her aunt to do it. He hated injustice, and the way he saw it, what Brenna's aunt had done was an injustice of the worst sort.

He had a moment's pause but felt little guilt for upending her life. If someone hadn't stepped in, she'd be Odessa's unpaid attendant for life, and that, Eoin couldn't abide. Brenna would be safe enough with him until she could establish a life of her own. Or better still, he'd hand her off to Roisin and Bridget. They were both the motherly sort and would help Brenna develop the confidence she needed to make it in the world.

Eoin grinned as he thought about a confrontation between his sister Bridget and Odessa Sullivan. Those two hardheaded women clashing would be an epic battle, no doubt with Bridget winning, and their fight would go down in the O'Malley chronicles for their children's children to tell the tale.

With another glance Brenna's way, Eoin drew the light blanket over his shoulder and got comfortable for the long flight home. Yes, he could've teleported, but he didn't want to scare Brenna with the shocking knowledge that magic like his existed. As a Sullivan, she was probably aware witches were real, but the type of power the O'Malleys now possessed, since regaining their abilities, was enough to blow an average person's mind. He'd have to find a way to tell her so she wasn't surprised if he inadvertently used his magic in front of her.

As thoughts of learning to control his power crowded his mind, he was reminded of the O'Malley/O'Connor war that had lasted well over two hundred and fifty years. None but one enemy remained, and Moira Doyle was in the wind, so his return home should be relatively tame. He flexed his now-healed hand, remembering the excruciating pain of every finger Shane O'Connor had broken with his sadistic game of trying to extract information from Eoin and bring his son, Ruairí, to heel. Thank the Goddess for Alastair Thorne's and his sister GiGi's mega-powers, or Eoin would likely need to find a new method of creating his art.

Eoin also silently thanked the Goddess that Brenna wouldn't be embroiled in what was a centuries-old, ongoing war. He certainly didn't like the idea of her getting hurt because of his careless actions.

The sudden need to reassure himself that she was okay overwhelmed him, and he turned his head in her direction. A single tear, tragic in its solitude, trailed down her cheek, and she hurriedly brushed it away as she shot him a nervous look.

He gave her a tender smile. "It'll all be all right, love. I promise ya it will."

# CHAPTER 6

*B*renna wasn't sure what she'd expected when they reached Eoin's family home, but it wasn't the quaint Black Cat Inn or the rowdy Lucky O'Malley's pub right next door. They'd arrived late, and the bar was packed with locals and tourists alike. A ruggedly handsome Irishman strummed a guitar and sang in a voice so beguiling, Brenna had a difficult time tearing her eyes away.

"That's Cian. My brother," Eoin said over the crowd noise. "He's got a bit o' talent, yeah?"

"Yes." She hadn't heard music so hauntingly lovely since Gran sang to her. "Why isn't he a household name?"

"As in selling his music?" At her nod, Eoin shrugged. "He's no interest in anything but 'serving up the louts in his pub' and playin' a few songs now and again. Oh, and of course, Piper, his new bride. She's taking up all his spare time, to be sure." He winked, and Brenna felt another blush blossoming on her cheeks. The man constantly had her face flaming. Every word from his mouth sounded suggestive, and it triggered an immediate Pavlovian response in her. One sexy grin, one wink, a lowering of his voice, and her ovaries stood up to take notice.

*Stupid ovaries.*

"Come. Let's draw a few pints and head for the Black Cat." He placed a hand on her lower back and guided her through the throng of customers toward the bar as she cast one last look over her shoulder at Cian, bemused the two brothers looked nothing alike. But perhaps their similarity lay in their art choices. Cian, his music, and Eoin, his paintings. Each was a master of their trade.

As Eoin and Brenna reached their destination, a gorgeous redhead squealed and charged toward Eoin, arms outstretched. Brenna had no right feeling salty about all the beautiful women throwing themselves at him, but her heart and brain were on two separate wavelengths.

With a wide, engaging smile, he enfolded her in his embrace and kissed her temple. "Bridg."

"I didn't know you were comin' home! Why didn't ya tell me so I could have a room ready for ya?"

"Sure, and I wanted to surprise ya."

"Is Dubheasa here too, then?"

"Nah. She's back in New York, trying to find ways to murder Ronan O'Connor and dispose of the body." Eoin turned toward Brenna and held out a hand. "I've brought you another lamb to care for, and she's in need of a friend, she is."

Thoroughly embarrassed at being thought of as friendless, despite the truth of it, Brenna scowled and slapped his hand away. "I'm not a child, Mr. O'Malley," she said stiffly.

He grinned as the woman laughed.

"I like her," the redhead declared. She held out a hand. "Eoin's having a craic. And I'm Bridget O'Malley. This eejit's older sister," she said with a gesture of her thumb.

"Brenna Sullivan. This eejit's new personal manager, although he seems to like managing my schedule and not the other way around," Brenna replied with a pert look toward Eoin, who wore an unrepentant grin. "I'm sorry we showed up last minute with no warning. I assumed you prepared a room for us. If you'd like, I can find another place..." She trailed off, belatedly realizing she didn't have the funds to pay for another room anywhere else. The only reason she'd agreed to come was because Eoin had insisted and was comping her room.

But Bridget was having none of it and said as much. "You'll stay here, and I'll not hear a word otherwise. It won't be said that I couldn't find a spare bed for members of my own family."

"Oh, I didn't mean to offend!" Mortified at her blunder, Brenna put her hands over her mouth.

Eoin snorted and threw an arm over her shoulders, drawing her into a quick hug. "Bridget's not offended, love. She's just horrified by the thought of being the town gossip." He drew Brenna's hands down and lifted her chin. "But it's not like she hasn't been already, hookin' up with Ruairí O'Connor, known to be our family's sworn enemy, the rattled old tart."

"Pfft. I'll give ya a rattled old tart, ya arse." His sister gave him a little shove, then cast a loving smile over her shoulder. "And you'll be admittin' Ruairí's the only good O'Connor of the lot."

Bridget followed her admiring gaze to the shaggy blond-haired man behind the bar who returned Bridget's smile with one of his own. The heat between the two was liable to catch the building on fire, it was so hot.

"What am I missing here?" Brenna asked in an aside to Eoin.

"Our family has been at war with the O'Connor clan for over two hundred and fifty years. My sister fell in love with Ruairí as a child, and the two of them were inseparable for a time." He shrugged and gave a short nod in their direction. "But they had a seventeen-year feud of their own going on. As you can see, they've rekindled their romance, but only after Ruairí returned what was stolen by his ne'er-do-well family."

Brenna sighed when Ruairí stole a kiss from Bridget as she

returned to her spot behind the counter, lingering to steal a second and then a third. "How romantic!"

"Do you buy into all that nonsense, then?" he asked, a curious expression on his face.

"Why wouldn't I?" Did he really not believe in love or romance? If not, it was extremely sad he didn't.

He shrugged, and Brenna got the impression he'd seen too much through his worldly artist's eyes. Perhaps he'd become jaded.

"Why do ya look so worried, love? Surely, it's not on my behalf?"

She opened her mouth to respond, but couldn't find the words. How did one go about telling their new employer they felt sorry for what was lacking in their life, especially when she'd never had it for herself? If anyone was to be pitied, it was Brenna. And *that*, she refused to do! No self-pity allowed.

Snapping her mouth shut, she shrugged and turned her attention to her surroundings.

*Ireland.*

She was here, and it was completely surreal, as if she were in a dream.

"Do all these people know each other?" She gestured to a long table with its equally long benches occupied by flushed-faced individuals engaging in friendly conversations and a few heated debates.

"Most, but a lot of public houses are designed for their customers to gather, similar to that." He nodded to the particular table she'd focused on. "Not everyone came in together, but they're happy enough to sit and share a pint."

"Interesting."

He glanced down at her and smiled. "Aye."

Brenna got the impression he wasn't referring to the pub's customers, but to her reaction to his family's business. Exactly why, she couldn't say.

"You promised me a pint," she reminded him, desperate to turn his attention from her.

"That I did." He clasped her hand and led her to the beer taps, then proceeded to show her how to do a proper pour. "The secret is in the draw."

She groaned inwardly as she studied his long, tapered fingers as they expertly worked the beer tap handle. Her thoughts were in the gutter where Eoin O'Malley was concerned, and they weren't coming out anytime soon.

"Here. It's a family recipe." When he handed her the pint, she released an appreciative groan for real, following it with a grateful smile. The flight had dehydrated her and given her a headache, but the refreshing taste of the beer wet her whistle and soothed her frayed nerves. Funny how a single sip could work like that, chase away all her woes and transport her back to a time when Gran was alive to care for her. But the flavor of this particular brew woke up her taste buds, and she told him so, much to his delight and pride.

After Eoin had his drink in hand, he led her through a side door into an alleyway between the pub and the boarding house, only stopping when they reached the quiet comfort of the inn's abandoned kitchen.

"This was exactly what the doctor ordered." She closed her eyes as she took another sip, opening them to find him staring intently at her. "What?"

"I don't think I've ever seen a woman enjoy a pint as much as you."

"Hmm. Well, I'm not most women."

He snorted. "Of that, there is no question."

Inexplicably hurt by his agreement, she stared down at the foamy top of her beer.

"Why are ya upset, love? I was agreeing you weren't like... ah! You interpreted it the wrong way. Oh, Brenna." He clasped her hand in his and gave it a gentle squeeze. "Odessa did a number on ya, didn't she?"

"I suppose so. But if she did, it's only because I allowed her to." Turning her hand over, she laced her fingers with his, careful to keep her eyes lowered. She didn't want to see his pity or possible disgust at how easily she was manipulated. "Drowning in grief as I was, after Gran died, it just seemed easier to go along with whatever Aunt Odessa wanted, somehow. The next thing I knew, I was twenty-six and fully indebted to her."

"Indentured, more like," Eoin muttered before lifting her hand and dropping a kiss on her knuckles. "But you're your own person, yeah? No more of that. Here, with me, you'll speak your mind, and we'll both be happier for it."

"But you're my boss!" Her protest was met with laughter, and she drew away in her confusion. "Aren't you?"

"Not at all. I'm your employer, and I'll be payin' your salary. But you're *my* boss, love."

"I don't understand."

"Yes, you'll need to keep my schedule and tell me where to be. You'll deal with galleries and set up showings. You'll essentially run the business that is me. And when I'm at my cranky, temperamental worst, you'll need to make it known you're not putting up with my shite." He grinned. "In other words, you'll be in charge, love. I only want to paint."

She couldn't prevent her answering grin if she tried. The idea of being the one in charge was heady, and there was no doubt in her mind she would be a good manager. After all, she'd managed the majority of Aunt Odessa's businesses for years. The only thing lacking had been the final decision-making. Odessa Sullivan wouldn't give up control the way Eoin O'Malley was offering to do right now.

"I see ya like the idea of bossin' me about." He guzzled half his pint, then wiped the back of his wrist across his mouth.

There was still enough alcohol left behind to cause his lips to glisten, and Brenna's tongue itched to swipe the remaining beer from them.

"There you go with that look again, Brenna, me love. If you keep at it, I'll not be responsible for my actions."

Her face felt like it was on fire, and she took a sip of her pint to ease her suddenly parched throat. "You're my bo—uh, employer. There can be no hanky-panky between us, Mr. O'Malley."

"It's Eoin, and to be sure, we make the rules, love."

"What does *that* mean?" Clarification and boundaries needed to be set, but if he was determined to skirt the rules, she probably needed to find the willpower to object—but not too much. Truth be told, she liked the hot look in his eyes.

"If you want *hanky-panky*, I'll not be denyin' ya."

She seriously considered it as they drank in comfortable silence, and she eventually rejected the idea of sex with Eoin. He was far more experienced than she and would find her sadly lacking in the bedroom department. No, it was better she remain an efficient employee, where she knew what to do and wasn't likely to misconstrue or fantasize about things she couldn't have. Things like love.

"Ya turned sad there, Brenna. What was it I said to make you unhappy?"

His somberness shook her out of her self-pitying mood.

*You told yourself no self-pity, Brenna! Knock it off!*

"I'm tired, is all. You didn't say anything to make me unhappy, Eoin. I promise." How she managed to lie without giving herself away was a mystery, but he seemed to accept her comment at face value.

"Sure, and let's get you settled for sleep, yeah? Ya have to be knackered."

"Are you certain we should stay here? I don't want to take up a spare guest room."

"If the Black Cat were full, Bridget would've said, but we can check the reservations."

Five minutes later, Brenna was staring in shock at the reservation list. Only one room was available, which meant she either needed to find a hotel or bunk with Eoin, which he happily suggested.

"Coming here was a mistake," she said with a heavy sigh. "I should've begged Odessa's forgiveness."

*"Fuck. No."*

She looked up at Eoin's angry reply.

"You'll take the bed, and I'll not have ya fightin' me on it. My brother Carrick can provide a place to rest my head for the night. His is the house next door."

"I don't want to kick you out of your bed," she protested. Her self-pity returned with a vengeance and shifted to self-loathing. At twenty-six, she should know how to take care of herself. She should have a 401K started and a little money saved. Should have taken her college degree in fine art and done something with her life. Something like the job she'd currently accepted with Eoin. With a side glance at him, she shifted her thinking. Perhaps she *was* doing something with her life. Perhaps he was handing her a chance to finally be someone Gran could be proud of instead of a lifeless robot always at Odessa's beck and call.

"It's not my bed, love. I haven't lived here in a number of years."

"I—"

He placed a single finger over her lips, effectively silencing her. Those same lips grew tingly as the urge to nip the tip of his index finger struck her. An interested look crossed his face, one that said he found it hard to pull his attention from her mouth, but he managed to contain his standard sexy grin with a small shake of his head. But the twinkle in his eyes and his winking dimple told her all she needed to know. Charm oozed out of Eoin's pores like sweat out of a sinner in church. For him, it had to be as natural as breathing.

"I can see you're intent on arguin' with me, Brenna Sullivan. But I'll tell ya true, you won't win this one. I've a mind that you should stay here and work for me, and unless you can show me you've made other satisfactory arrangements, I'm not letting ya run back to that she-devil Odessa."

She curled her fingers around his and drew his hand away from her mouth. "Fine."

"You'll stay workin' for me?"

"Yes."

"And ya won't be fightin' me at every turn?"

"No."

"And you'll be giving me back my hand now?" he teased.

Mortification made her wish the ground would open and swallow her, and she swiftly released him. "Show me my room, please."

"Don't be hard on yourself, love. I quite like it when you hold my hand, I do."

"Oh, shut up, you damned flirt."

His eyes flew wide, and he barked a laugh. "You've graduated from kitten to a feral cat, ya have. Sure, and I like it, too."

With a roll of her eyes, she snatched the key card from his hand and charged for the stairs.

Voice thick with laughter, he said, "It's this way, love. You're on the first floor."

She'd never wanted to murder a person more, and she'd been living with Odessa for over two decades!

# CHAPTER 7

*F*ifteen minutes after Eoin settled Brenna in her room, he was trudging across the yard, back the way he'd come, when he heard someone shout his name from across the road.

"Reggie!" As he got closer, he noticed his friend had a different hair color and style. "What's with the new look, man? Are ya in hiding, then?"

As Reggie was want to do, he lifted a brow and sniffed, the picture of an English gentleman. Eoin couldn't contain his laugh.

"They're called lowlights. It wouldn't hurt you to add color now and again."

"I add color to canvas. No need to be addin' it to my head."

Reggie turned his attention to the pub, a queer look on his face. "It looks exactly the same. How did your family manage to do that and not raise questions from the locals after the explosion?"

Eoin figured he referred to the recent troubles with Loman O'Connor and how the man had blown up Lucky O'Malley's pub and half of the Black Cat inn. After Reggie's return to New

York from his business trip to England, Eoin had confided the entire story.

Turning to survey his family's businesses, Eoin cast an expert eye over them both. They'd been restored down to the last beam, thanks to the combined magic of the Aether and their friends, the Thornes. Together, with Eoin's siblings, they'd been able to rebuild and wipe the memories of that eventful day from the minds of the village residents.

He frowned as a thought occurred to him. "When have ya been here to see it?"

"I haven't. You've recreated the place on canvas, remember?" Reggie gave him a careless one-shoulder shrug. "I'm an observant person."

Taking the comment at face value, he explained what they, along with the Thornes and the Aether, had done to return their little village to normal.

"Interesting. I suppose it's good to have powerful friends." There was something surly in Reggie's tone as he handed Eoin a small suitcase. "It was all I could get from Odessa. She isn't the most charitable of women. It's a wonder your drab little mouse survived in that household as long as she did."

Forgetting the odd reaction, Eoin scowled, quick to take exception to the way his friend referred to Brenna. "Don't call her that. She's not a little mouse, and she's not drab. She's beauty in her soul. I don't understand why you and Dubheasa can't see that."

Eyebrows to his hairline, Reggie barked a cynical laugh. "What spell has she cast over you, scamp? From what I've seen, the poor child is afraid of her own shadow."

"No spell. I can see the intelligent woman under the exterior. Sure, and you should look harder if you can't," he snapped.

Giving him a considering look, his friend dropped his gaze to the case in Eoin's hand. "With a little persuading, Odessa found it in her heart to pass on a locket from her sister,

Doreen. Brenna's grandmother. Maybe now that she's free of her grandaunt's influence, your sweet little darling can learn to use her magic alongside you."

"Magic? Brenna's a witch like us?"

"She's a Sullivan. Of course she's a witch." Reggie sighed as if put out, and likely he was at Eoin's ignorance. But the history of magical families had never been of much interest to him in the past. All that mattered was taking the images from his mind and recreating them in art form.

"Let me guess. She doesn't know what she is, nor does she know what you are? Am I close?" Reggie compressed his lips into a thin line.

"We've not talked about it, but whether she is or isn't, it's all the same to me. I've hired her to do a job, and she'll be grand."

"Right. Well, best of luck to you, my darling scamp. I've a date with a handsome—"

Eoin held up his hand. "Kindly keep it to yourself. I'd need a feckin' spreadsheet to track your lovers, I would."

Reggie grinned and, with a devilish sparkle in his eyes, winked. "I'd give them all up for you, you know."

"So you've said, but we both know I'd not make you happy. Besides, you're playing for a team I'm not a part of. It's too late to be drafted."

"Pfft. It's never too late. You simply like your supermodels and starlets too much to consider switching." With a frown, Reggie said, "It's why I can't understand your preoccupation with the girl."

"She's a woman grown, and I'm not obsessed." But he sort of was, though he hated to admit it. "Go on with ya, man. I'm off to bed—to sleep, in response to your next comment."

"I like you, Eoin O'Malley. Damned if I don't."

"Sure, and why wouldn't ya? I'm feckin' awesome."

Reggie laughed and clapped him on the shoulder. "You should go give your little mou—er, friend her case. I'll call you

53

in a few days to see if you need anything." After kissing Eoin's cheek, Reggie turned to go.

"Reg?"

"Yes?"

"Do you want to get a pint first?" Eoin nodded toward Lucky's. "It's the least I can offer ya after the favor you did for Brenna."

With a soft smile but suddenly serious eyes, Reggie shook his head. "You know I'm more of a wine man, Eoin. Perhaps when you start stocking my preferred brand of chardonnay, I'll visit your quaint little pub."

As his friend turned and walked away, Eoin had the nagging sense Reggie was lonelier than he let on.

"You're a snob, Reg!" he hollered with a laugh but received no more than a wave in return.

With a shake of his head, Eoin turned toward the inn. Maybe when he delivered Brenna's suitcase, she'd take pity on him and let him pull up a section of floor to sleep. He was certain he could persuade her to allow him at least that, if not a place on the bed, but he was also certain Brenna was halfway to infatuated with him. If he *did* sleep in the bed, he'd likely have sex with her and probably destroy any chance of a working relationship they might have.

Not that he wouldn't enjoy the shagging—and he had no fear *he* could remain professional after—but Brenna didn't strike him as the type of woman to engage in sexual activity without her heart being involved. And Eoin wasn't exactly looking for commitment. With permanent relationships came family ties, and he didn't want a drain on his time and art right now. Marriage and *weens* were great for some, but not for him. Not at this juncture. Female demands were the reason he'd ditched Margo.

He stopped in the kitchen, surprised to find Brenna there, nursing a hot drink. He dropped the suitcase by the door and straddled the bench seat next to her. "What are ya doin' down here, love?"

"I couldn't sleep. Strange place, I guess."

And because his mind was still on shagging, he went where he shouldn't and said, "There's a cure for that, there is."

"I'm well aware what that cure would be, thank you," she stated primly, causing him to chuckle.

"Sure, then why aren't ya sound asleep by now?"

As was her standard, her response was a blush, but one that was adorable on her. He bit his lip to hold back a laugh when she shot him a death glare.

"That's none of your business, Eoin O'Malley. And I thank you not to discuss such things with your *employee*."

It belatedly occurred to him he'd practically shanghaied her into doing his bidding.

*Feck*.

He should've offered her more options. "If you don't want to work with me, Brenna, you don't have to. I'll help you find other employment."

With a sharp look, she asked, "You don't want me now?"

His brows shot up, and a laugh escaped him. "Jaysus, love. You ask loaded questions, to be sure. How do you want me to answer?"

"With the truth."

"The truth is, aye, I want you. In my bed. As my manager. As a *friend*. But I'm not into long-term relationships, and I suspect you are." He stole her mug and took a sip of her tea before handing it back. "What about you? What does Brenna Sullivan want?"

For the longest time, she remained quiet, staring down at the place where his lips had touched the rim of her mug. Finally, she sighed heavily. "I don't know what I want. Or if I do, it's probably not something I can have."

"And who's to say ya can't have what it is you want?" If it was within his power, he'd help her achieve it.

Her troubled eyes sought and held his, and she surprised him when she said, "Because I want you, too, Eoin. In my bed. As a boss. As a friend."

*Jaysus!* She was bolder than he'd given her credit for. His heart began to thud. "But?"

"But I don't live in your world. I don't understand the rules." She dropped her gaze and took a sip of her drink, swallowing hard. "I'm essentially a novice, and I'd probably screw things up. I don't know how to do casual, which is what you prefer."

"Sure, and nothing need be decided tonight." And it was a good thing, because she'd struck a nerve when she said he preferred casual. It didn't matter that, a minute before, he was admitting to that very thing, and in the past, he'd repeatedly told himself he didn't want entanglements. The fact she'd actually considered that type of arrangement with him was disturbing. Brenna deserved only the best in life, not to be used for sex and forgotten about a month later.

But after getting lost in her direct stare, he wondered if he could forget her. Her eyes and voice had haunted his dreams for four years, and he'd never acted on the urge to seduce her. He drew the line at innocents.

But was he so shallow, then? Is that how *everyone* saw him, as a player? True, he shunned real relationships to pursue his art, but when had his paintings come to mean more than people? And why did it matter if Brenna saw his selfishness when it hadn't been seen by anyone else in the past?

Dubheasa had tried to get him to go out with her and her friends a time or two, but he'd always had a project to complete first. And after he was finished, he wanted or needed a good fuck. But making time with Dubheasa's closest friends was a great way to rile his sister. That was all he needed, to break one of her girlfriend's hearts. Dubheasa would have his bollocks in a sling.

Shoving aside all the tumultuous thoughts, he stood. "Are ya hungry? I make a mean scone to go with your tea."

"You can make scones?"

He chuckled at her incredulous tone. "You don't believe men can bake?"

"Oh, I *do*, but I wouldn't expect it from *you*. I'm surprised you can see your way to anything but your studio."

"Ouch! That hurt, love. It truly did."

When she laughed, he barely resisted the urge to kiss her sassy mouth. "Just you watch me, Brenna Sullivan. I'll make ya the best fecking scones you ever had. You'll be wantin' to marry me for my cookin' alone." He did an internal eye-roll and mentally slapped himself the second the words left his mouth. If he didn't slow the feck down, he'd have her believing in happily-ever-after and rugrats.

Brenna adored this side of Eoin. A side she'd not seen prior to this moment. Playful, carefree, with no worries about pleasing the art crowd or navigating demanding patrons.

Needing a distraction so the heart on her sleeve wasn't so obvious, she nodded to the small suitcase by the door. "What's that?"

He glanced over his shoulder as if he'd forgotten what he brought inside. "Ah, Reggie dropped it by a short while ago. It's what he gathered of yours from Odessa. There's a locket inside from your gran."

Sadness filled her heart, and depression clouded her mind. Her entire existence fit in a small carry-on bag. She was a minimalist because she'd had to be. Aunt Odessa didn't hold with sentimental, so Brenna was surprised her aunt had included the locket. Whenever Brenna had wanted to speak of Gran or the past, Odessa would shut the conversation down, snapping at her to leave the dead buried. And because her aunt's gaze was darting about as if she were haunted by memories, Brenna had let the matter rest.

"You all right there, love?"

She glanced up to find Eoin watching her with a small frown. She should've known he'd tune in to her distress. The man was too observant by far, but perhaps that came with being an artist. He studied everything and everyone with a perceptive eye.

With a quick, false smile, she nodded.

He wiped the flour off his hands and turned more fully to face her. "Sure, and if you don't want to be talkin' to me, Brenna, I'll understand why, but I've got wide enough shoulders to help handle any burdens you're carrying."

Finding it hard to put into words what she was feeling, she shrugged. "It's not that I don't want to discuss it, but I guess I don't know how. I've been my own counsel for as long as I can remember, with no one to talk to."

"You don't have to be an island, love. You have people who care now, yeah?"

"Do I?" She didn't mean for her question to come out as sullen as it did, but she hadn't had any true friends in years. Now and again acquaintances of Aunt Odessa were kind to her, but mostly they looked at her with pity in their eyes.

Eoin never had.

Kindness and compassion, yes. But not pity, and that was exactly why she adored him.

He scowled. "Now, why would ya be sayin' it like that? Of course you do!"

A broken chuckle escaped her, and it turned into a full laugh when he looked even more put out. "Thank you for saying so, Eoin."

"Not just sayin'. *Meaning*, too."

Her heart swelled with love.

"Meaning, too," she dutifully parroted with a compressed smile.

As he returned to scone making, Brenna became fascinated with the process. Or rather, with how his hands worked the dough. Those artist's fingers expertly blended the butter with the flour, creating a breadcrumb-like consistency, and other than painting, she wondered what things he excelled at with those talented hands. She awkwardly shifted on the stool, belatedly realizing her fixation had turned her on to the point of uncomfortable. Here she'd been, daydreaming about how he'd touch her, when his full concentration was on creating the perfect scone.

She wished she had a magazine or fan to cool her hot face, and she prayed he didn't look her way, or her stupid complexion would give her away. Of course her prayers went unanswered, and he happened to glance up at that moment. He paused in rolling the dough as his sharp gaze swept her face. His easy smile turned wolfish, and he wiped his hands on his apron as he stalked around the counter to where she stood.

"I've a mind to be kissin' ya, Brenna. If you don't want me to, speak now, love, or forever hold your peace."

She lifted her face as he wove the fingers of one hand into the hair at the base of her neck and wrapped an arm around her waist to pull her against him.

"I'll take that as a yes, then, yeah?" he said on a soft growl. He lowered his mouth to hers after her jerky nod.

"If you're messing up Bridget's kitchen, she's going to be sooooo mad!" a female voice declared from behind him.

Eoin released Brenna like he'd been scalded by hot water, and spun around to face the newcomer. It provided her time to finger comb her hair, straighten her shirt, and send a silent *thank you* skyward to whoever's timely interruption had saved her from making a colossal mistake.

# CHAPTER 8

"Jaysus, Piper! You nearly gave me a fecking heart attack, ya did. What are ya doin' up at this hour?"

Piper shrugged, peered around his shoulder, and smiled at Brenna. "I couldn't sleep. This one's kicking because she's hungry." She rubbed her extended belly. "Anyway, I was on the phone with my cousin GiGi, and she said to keep an eye out for Brenna. Said she might need a friend."

"She has a friend. *Me!*" Eoin growled, beginning to get seriously irritated no one considered him friend material. Sure, he could be a bit absentminded in his pursuits, but that didn't mean he wouldn't be available should someone he cared about need him.

He felt Brenna place her hand on the small of his back and rub. It was as if she sensed his inner turmoil—just as he'd sensed hers earlier—and her touch immediately calmed him. It troubled him that she'd ever experienced even a moment of loneliness but he wasn't surprised she did. She'd not been allowed to socialize for more than a few minutes at a time, always needing to be at her aunt's disposal.

"Eoin was making me a bite to eat," Brenna said as she

stepped around him and held out a hand. "As you guessed, I'm Brenna Sullivan. And I'm not sure why your cousin would care one way or the other, to be honest."

Piper looked at the offered hand with surprise for a second before she grasped it and drew Brenna in for a hug instead. "Because GiGi has the biggest heart on the planet, and she saw in you someone she likes."

Disbelief and skepticism were heavy on Brenna's countenance, and it hurt Eoin's heart that she had so little faith in herself that she couldn't accept a ready friendship. He wanted to wrap his arms around her and protect her from the world, and because that urge was as strong as it was, it shocked him into taking a step back, resorting to teasing as was his like.

"Sure, and if GiGi likes you, she'll meddle in your life until you don't know what's up or down. Beware, Brenna, me love," he said with a flaring of his eyes. "You're about to have your world turned on its ear."

"I think it already was," Piper said dryly. With a commiserating look for Brenna, she walked farther into the kitchen and put on the kettle. "The moment you decided to throw in with the O'Malleys was the day you turned your own world on its ear, girlfriend."

"Now don't be trying to scare our darlin' Brenna, Piper. She's workin' for me, and nothing you can say will change her mind," Eoin warned, oddly fearful she *could* change Brenna's mind with a few unintended comments. It was suddenly very important that she stay.

"Who said anything about scaring her? I'm just warning her what she's in for. The O'Malleys are a lot to take in at once."

"Sure, and the Thornes aren't?" he countered with a scowl.

"Don't take umbrage, Eoin." Placing her arms over and under her belly, she gave him a twinkling smile. "Our families are one now. And when are you going to finish making those scones? I hope it's a double batch."

His ire faded, and he found himself ruefully shaking his head. Piper Thorne-O'Malley loved to tease and was the perfect foil for his brother Cian. The two were a match made by the Goddess herself. "Look, and how did you know that's what I was makin'?"

"I may have overheard most of your conversation. I decided to interrupt before it got steamy and embarrassed us all."

Brenna's sultry laughter was sunshine to his soul, and he turned his face toward the sound, ready to soak up the rays.

"Aye," he said huskily. "There was going to be enough steam to curl your hair, to be sure."

Her blush no longer seemed to detract from her looks, but instead, complimented her coloring and emphasized her star-bright eyes.

She quickly resorted to Prim and Proper Brenna from the gallery. "There will be no steam."

"Oh, I promise ya, love, there will be plenty o' steam if'n ya just let your hair down and live a little," he countered with a confident grin.

Piper fanned herself with the biscuit pan. "Wow. You two get a room, why don't you? You're messing with my pregnancy hormones."

Eoin winked at her. "And Cian will thank me for it… *later*."

"You're the biggest flirt of the lot. I didn't think anyone was worse than your brother."

He laughed and pulled her into a quick hug. "Cian's been tamed, and he's happier for it."

"Maybe you need a good woman to tame you, too," Piper said in a low voice, darting a meaningful look at Brenna. "But that girl is fragile, Eoin. You can tell it with one look. Don't hurt her, okay?"

"That's not my intent." He kept his voice equally as low. "She needed liberating from her aunt. Brenna has nothing to fear from me."

"Except getting her heart broken when she falls in love with her savior."

He didn't like Piper's assessment of the situation, but she wasn't necessarily wrong. "I'll not hurt her if I can help it, yeah?"

"That's all I ask."

Without comment, he went back to work on the scones.

BRENNA HAD HEARD PIPER AND EOIN TALKING, BUT SHE WASN'T able to make out the words. Based on the intensity of the conversation and the side glances her way, she assumed their discussion revolved around whatever Piper had witnessed when she first walked into the room. Brenna could only assume the other woman found her wanting.

Pretending indifference but needing to touch her last connection to Gran, Brenna squatted in front of her case and snapped open the locks. The cloying scent of Odessa's perfume mixed with a foreign smell invaded her sinuses, and she sneezed at the blast of offensive odor. A wave of dizziness hit, sending her the remaining distance to the floor. She plopped on her butt and shook her head.

Piper's cry brought Eoin running. He knelt next to her and cradled her head between his large palms. "Brenna! Are you okay, love?"

She opened her mouth to reply, but another wave of dizziness assailed her along with nausea. It took every ounce of willpower she possessed not to christen his lap with vomit. Managing a small shake of her head, she grabbed for the locket and clutched it to her chest. Wherever Eoin touched her, a burning pain hit her with such intensity, the breath in her lungs seized. She was certain that when he drew back, there would be handprints seared into her skin. He shifted to help her, managing to connect with more bare skin, and she released a hoarse scream.

"Brenna, love! What's wrong?"

"Don't touch me!" She scrambled away from him and pressed her palms to her cheek and neck, hissing at the continued pain. "It burns! It burns!"

"Alastair! I need you!" Piper called, clutching at a pendant around her neck. She gave Eoin a slight shove. "Get a soft cloth and a bowl of cold water stat!"

Brenna whimpered and rubbed at her skin, only to have her hands caught by Piper. "It's okay, Brenna. It's going to be okay."

"What the fuck is happenin' here?" Eoin demanded as he jumped to his feet and raced for the sink.

"I'm not sure, but she's acting as if you splashed her face with acid. I know water counteracts it and stops acid from eating the skin, so I thought maybe—"

The air around them grew heavy and crackled loudly. Following a popping sound, Alastair Thorne stepped toward her from thin air.

Brenna knew she descended from witches, but she'd assumed it was of the Wiccan variety that cast spells and held the odd ceremony for an equinox. The appearing-out-of-nowhere thing was new to her and startled her so badly that for a moment, she forgot her pain. The burning returned as Eoin reached for her—*and he hadn't even touched her again!*

For the second time in as many minutes, she screamed in agony.

"Back away, son," Alastair commanded. "To the other side of the room, and do it immediately."

Eoin complied, tension and concern etched in every line of his face.

"What do you think it is, Al?" Piper asked, wringing her hands.

"I'm not sure yet." He squatted next to Brenna. "Ms. Sullivan, if you'll allow me, I'm going to touch your face. I can feel the intensity of your pain, and I'd like to help take it away if I can, or at least ease the worst of it. Please tell me if I make it worse."

She nodded, responding more to the kindness in his eyes than to anything he'd said. When he skimmed her burning skin with his fingertips, she sucked in a sharp breath and held it, desperately trying not to cry. Although he didn't cause her more pain, the stinging had yet to recede.

The color of Alastair's eyes shifted from a bright sapphire blue to a murky shade of blue-gray, and Brenna worried her mind was playing tricks on her.

"Not acid," he murmured. "Or rather, not as you would know it in mortal terms. This seems like a personal attack, but from whom would be the question." His gaze dropped to the suitcase, but he didn't comment further about that particular *question*. "Goddess, hear my plea. Help me ease this child's suffering in this, her time of need," he murmured.

Once again, he ran his fingers over her fiery flesh, but this time, a purple light glowed from the tips, and the cooling sensation felt the way menthol did in the mouth; almost icy when air hit it. Within seconds, her skin was restored to normal, with no more searing pain.

"Thank you, Mr. Thorne," she managed to choke out her gratitude. "Thank you so much."

"It was nothing, my dear." With a gracefulness Brenna wished for, he rose and held out a hand to help her up. She placed hers in his and felt a zing similar to the one she'd felt at the gallery. A small chirp of surprise escaped her, and she jerked her hand back from the disturbing contact the instant she was standing.

"Why does that keep happening when I touch your hand?" she laughingly asked. "We create some serious static electricity between the two of us."

His dark-blond brows twitched, met, and rose, all within mere seconds, and his look of surprise was priceless because Brenna suspected not much threw him. "You think this is static, Ms. Sullivan?"

She sent a searching side glance toward Piper, who smiled at her with a type of bemusement. Finally, Brenna visually sought answers from Eoin. He still appeared troubled as he leaned against the wall, one foot propped back behind him on the smooth surface and his arms crossed. Her attention went by way of his drool-worthy forearms, and she forgot what the original question was. By the time she faced Alastair again, a lengthy silence had passed.

Mortified by her inability to concentrate when Eoin was around, she cleared her throat, desperate to remember the topic.

Alastair took pity on her. "It's not static you are experiencing, my dear, but powerful magic connecting to a matching source."

"I don't understand," she admitted. "I've never had any real magic in the truest sense of the word."

"There you're wrong. If you'll allow me, I'll show you."

Tentatively, she placed her hand in his, and when he turned her palm faceup, she shot a nervous look toward Eoin. He hadn't moved or spoken, as if afraid he'd send her into hysteria again.

Red light arched between Alastair's palm and hers, and a tickling sensation danced along her nerve endings, causing the hair on her body to rise up. Within seconds, a black smoke rose from her skin, slithering along the light, circling, as if alive. The instant Alastair registered the swirling darkness, he used his free hand to jerk theirs apart, his expression a thundercloud.

The kitchen's temperature turned freezing, and Brenna began shaking.

"What are you trying to pull, Ms. Sullivan?" His tone was colder than the room, if possible.

"N-nothing. I'm n-not pulling anything at all!" In a panic, she looked from one person to the other, seeking support from Eoin, though he didn't know her well enough to back her up. And though he straightened from the wall, he didn't approach.

Her teeth began to chatter. "I swear I d-didn't know m-magic like yours existed until n-now, M-Mr. Thorne."

Piper looked at Brenna like she'd grown a second head. "What the hell just happened, Al? Was that what I think it was?"

"Yes," he bit out.

"What? W-what w-was it?" If she had a mirror, Brenna was sure to find her lips blue from the frigid air.

"You, my dear Ms. Sullivan, are either a Siren or a Succubus. *And you tried to steal my power.*"

*"Fecking hell!"*

Eoin stalked from the room, leaving Brenna to face the wrath of a livid Alastair Thorne.

# CHAPTER 9

$\mathcal{O}$dessa Sullivan felt the instant her niece's magic tried to break free of her hold. It struggled and strained like the living beast it was. She'd done Brenna a favor when she absorbed her power for her own, although the ungrateful child wouldn't see it that way. If Brenna ever found out she was syphoning off the girl's natural born abilities, Odessa might have a serious problem on her hands.

That's precisely why she'd spelled her sister Doreen's locket when Reggie came for Brenna's things. The girl wouldn't be able to resist wearing it, and the curse Odessa put on it would repel Eoin O'Malley one way or the other. Without that hedonistic artist putting thoughts in Brenna's head, she might regain control.

"Can't let that blasted girl believe she can survive on her own," she muttered.

If Brenna did, Odessa might lose her own abilities in the process. No, she needed her niece under her thumb to supplement her life force, which had been fading faster and faster these days. And death, looming in the not-so-distant future, led her to ruminate on the past with more frequency.

"What would have happened if I hadn't given in to the darkness running through these veins?" she murmured. If she'd never slept with her first boyfriend, Redmond, gotten carried away, and sampled his soul? Never transitioned to the succubus she'd eventually become in exchange for riches and a longer life span?

Doreen had managed to curb her own impulse, but Odessa had loved a man's touch too much. She mourned the wholesome girl she'd been and hated the monster she'd turned herself into. If she could prevent Brenna from walking down her path, she'd do it. After all, the longer she survived, the longer she could save the girl from transitioning. Hers was the only way to justify what she'd done and why she'd kept the girl under her thumb all these years.

Waving a half circle in front of a faux wall, she dismissed the glamour hiding the room's opening, then she hobbled her way into her ceremony chamber and over to the scrying mirror. Once there, she called the Sullivan magic to her, pulling on all her ancestors and their ancestors before them, sucking in and holding a deep breath along with the mighty power.

*Oh, to feel that energy flow through her veins!*

It was life, and the beast within her wanted it at all costs. It stretched and growled its hunger, urging Odessa to find another warlock to take to her bed. If only Eoin O'Malley had been power mad and more career driven, she'd be feasting on his magic right now.

Her gaze dropped to the glass, and she almost swallowed her tongue when she saw Alastair Thorne dressing down Brenna and accusing her of being a Succubus. The poor girl had no idea what she was. And if Odessa had her way, she never would. All that frizzy hair in addition to the dreadful clothes and glasses had worked to hide her figure and keep men away. But that bloody artist had seen beneath all the trappings to the beauty lying underneath. He'd provided her with stylish outfits and new fashionable frames. Odessa should've known he would, and she should've kept Brenna far, far away from that boy.

*"But you have to control everything, don't you, sister?"* Doreen's voice whispered through her mind. *"Your insatiable appetites were what woke a sleeping monster, and now my Brenna is dealing with your mistakes."*

"Shut up!" Odessa hissed. "I can't think with you inside my head!"

Her sister's tinkling laughter turned hard. *"If you hadn't murdered me, perhaps I wouldn't haunt you now, you evil bitch."*

In place of the image of Brenna facing down Alastair, Doreen's hollowed-out eyes and skeletal face appeared. A shudder of revulsion chased along Odessa's spine as worms crawled through the openings. Normally, she wasn't one to be squeamish, but the image before her was of the body buried in the back garden under the towering weeping willow, grown twice its standard size.

"It was an accident, Doreen. You know that!"

Her sister's sneer shifted the already horrific countenance into a positively grotesque mask.

Turning away, Odessa released her hold on the combined Sullivan magic. Pain radiated in her left shoulder, and an area on the lower left side of her face became numb.

"No!" Terror tried to claw its way out of her chest, and she fought to regain control over her emotions. If she let go, if she allowed them dominance, then the threatening stroke would be the end of her. That, she couldn't allow to happen. She had Brenna to protect.

*"Not protect, sister,"* Doreen taunted. *"Destroy, as you have destroyed everyone who ever cared for you."*

With a barely suppressed sob, Odessa fled the room, snatching a small bottle of pills along the way. Medicine she'd compounded herself to stave off death. But recently, she'd had to up her dosage because she was beginning to look her age, and the resistance-melting beauty that had once lured all victims was long gone. Only the promise of financial reward lured the unscrupulous to her bed these days, and few of those people possessed enough magic to give her the boost she needed. Mainly, it was Brenna's magical battery keeping her alive. And she couldn't lose that, for too many reasons to count.

"I-I SWEAR"—BRENNA GULPED DOWN HER FEAR AND LIFTED HER chin—"I am n-not a Succubus. Or a Siren." Clearing her throat and firming her resolve, she continued. "I don't even know what they are, sir." The last came out in a rush, but at least she wasn't stuttering anymore. Was anything more mortifying than proving what a ninny she was? Eoin was gone, left in disgust, so at least she was spared that humiliation.

Her teeth chattered, but despite how miserable she felt, she tried to appear trustworthy.

By slow degrees, the room returned to a normal temperature, and the fierce scowl left Alastair's aristocratic face. Still, he retained a kingly air as he tugged at his shirt cuffs and gazed down his straight-as-a-pin nose at her. She forgot her terror as the disdain left his eyes, replaced by a thoughtfulness as he studied her in turn.

"Oddly, I believe you, Ms. Sullivan." His tone wasn't exactly warm, but it wasn't as frosty as it had been.

She exhaled a relieved breath.

However, Piper wasn't so trusting it seemed. "Wait just a damned minute, cousin! Who's to say she didn't cast a spell over you just now?" She glared at Brenna as she placed herself protectively in front of Alastair, much to the man's amusement if his twitching lips and dancing eyes were anything to go by.

"If you think I'm letting you close to any of the men I care about, lady, you have another think coming!"

Unsure how to respond to such blatant hostility, Brenna remained mute. Her face began to feel hot, and she was sure she would spontaneously combust from the fire raging under her skin.

"And for another thing—"

"Leave her be, Piper," Eoin commanded from behind Brenna, startling a blood-curdling scream from her.

He raised his brows, and his delightful dimple made an appearance as he suppressed a grin. "Sorry, love. Teleportin' was the fastest way to return."

Not sure she hadn't peed herself a little, Brenna placed her palm flat over her heart and nodded. Although she wanted to fling herself in his capable arms as relief coursed through her, she backed away from him as her face began to sting. "I get it."

His gaze dropped to her cheek, and he took two large steps backward. "Would ya be up for a little test, then? To prove you aren't either a Siren or Succubus, as Alastair claims?"

"Of course!" Brenna looked from one to the other in rapid succession, desperate to prove she was normal.

"It's a simple matter, yeah?" Eoin met Alastair's thoughtful gaze with a nod. "She passes the test, she's good in your book?"

"I suppose so." Alastair nodded slowly. "But how do you expect to prove anything, son? You can't get within ten feet of her."

"Well, sure, and we'll have to fix that problem first, but I have an idea."

"I'm all ears," the older man stated dryly.

With hands on hips, Piper shook her head. "I don't like it."

"You haven't heard anything yet, Piper. How is it you're not likin' it when ya don't know what *it* is?"

Despite the thick tension in the room, Brenna smothered an inappropriate giggle. Eoin had a way of pointing out the absurd and making light of it. That ability was one she had admired from afar whenever she heard him work his wiles on potential art critics and customers alike. He charmed everyone with whom he came in contact.

Glaring her displeasure, Piper waved a hand for him to continue.

He lifted a thick tome of a book. "The answers are in here. I remember reading about Sirens as a kid."

"Wait! No O'Malley has been able to open that book for years. Not since Goibhniu's curse, if what Cian and Bridget told me is true." Piper looked confused as hell, and Brenna felt sympathy, because she was right there with her.

With a shrug, Eoin gave Piper a secretive smile. "I like keeping some things for myself."

Trying to peer closer, Brenna leaned forward. "Is that called a grimoire?" She hadn't seen one before, or not that she remembered anyway.

Once again, Alastair scowled. "Why is no one teaching the newer generations the basics?"

Brenna and Eoin shared a look and a smile at the man's indignation.

"If you'll remember, all the O'Malleys were without until recently, and Brenna claims she didn't know true magic existed." Eoin shrugged. "So I imagine there was no one *to* teach us, yeah?"

"It's disgraceful," Alastair muttered, straightening his tie. Curling his fingers and gesturing for the book in Eoin's hand, he said, "Hand it over, and let's get busy with solving the proximity issue. If I didn't know better, I'd say she's allergic to you." He halted halfway to Eoin and slowly twisted to face Brenna. "That's it!"

"What is?" She wrung her hands and gnawed her lip.

"Your body is reacting in a negative way to Mr. O'Malley's. But not to mine and not to Piper's. That means Thorne blood seems to be fine, but perhaps O'Malley blood is not. Let's try something, shall we?" Turning slightly, Alastair kept his considering gaze on Brenna as he addressed Eoin. "Be kind enough to fetch your brothers, son. We have an experiment to conduct."

"I don't like the idea of experimenting on Brenna." Objection in every line of his face, Eoin took two steps forward only to immediately back up as she hissed in a breath from the burn. His resistance dissolved and turned to resignation. Without another word, he turned on his heel and left.

"What do you intend to do?" Brenna asked warily, rubbing the area of the receding pain.

"I'd like to know if you are reacting to all O'Malley men or just the one." He lifted one shoulder in a careless shrug. "If it's all, then it could mean bad blood between the Sullivans and O'Malleys and you're caught in between. If it's the one, the target is you. Perhaps a jealous lover or someone wishing to keep you apart."

"Not me. My only lover is dead," she blurted. When Piper gasped and Alastair looked nonplussed, she held up her hands and shook her head. "Not by me! I swear!"

After a full minute of sweat-soaking silence—mainly on Brenna's part, Piper sighed. "I think she doesn't know what the hell she is, Al."

"I'm inclined to agree, my dear. Why don't you both have a seat, and I'll conjure a bite to eat. I'll assume whatever was being prepared is now a loss."

"Eoin was about to make me scones," Brenna said lamely as she eyed the dough with regret. Ten minutes ago, everything was normal. But all that had changed with the arrival of Piper and the opening of Brenna's small suitcase. She caught her breath and pointed. "The odor from the case! It all went to crap when I sneezed!"

Without a by-your-leave, Alastair waved a hand and encased the travel bag in an iridescent dome.

"Holy spitballs!" To say Brenna was shocked was an understatement. All she could do was stare. Never had she known magic like his was possible, and she'd have called anyone who said it was a damned liar.

Piper snorted. "I think the term is *shit*balls."

"Gran didn't allow swearing in her house. Spitballs was as risky as it got."

"If this isn't all an elaborate act, then you are too cute for words."

Eoin entered on the last of their conversation. "'Tisn't an act, Piper. Our darlin' Brenna has been the same as long as I've known her."

"But you didn't notice me before your last show," Brenna protested, certain she hadn't been on his radar.

He shook his head as if baffled by her comment. "Of course, I noticed ya, love. From the first time we were introduced, I—" Whatever he intended to say was cut off when Cian and a black-haired man walked into the kitchen, followed by Bridget.

Piper smiled and walked into the arms of her husband. "Now you've done it, Al. All the O'Malleys in one room is pure trouble."

"Not all." Brenna shrugged when everyone looked her way. "Dubheasa's not here."

Eoin grinned, and she felt the warmth down to her toes. This time, it wasn't an evil magical reaction. Just a hormonal one. She really hoped whatever this new curse was about, it wouldn't last long. Although she wasn't the type of woman able to keep up with him, she loved lingering on the fringes of his world. If she lost the ability to orbit his sun, she'd die a little inside. Hell, who was she kidding? She'd die a *lot*.

# CHAPTER 10

*E*oin remained on the farthest side of the room from Brenna as his siblings each took turns approaching her, then placing a hand on her arm. And although their motives were harmless, meant to discover if she'd have an adverse reaction, his skin became too tight for his body. As if at any moment, he was going to lose his shite and bloody their noses for touching her.

And he hated it.

Hated the feeling of possessiveness he experienced when he was around her. The protectiveness he understood—or so he told himself. That was because she was naive to the ways of the world. But his desire to bundle her up and keep her far away from other men? Yeah, that was fecking odd.

Whenever her large, cautious eyes sought him out, Eoin felt ten feet tall and bulletproof. He also wanted to run as far and as fast as he could away from her. However, the contrary side of him kept taunting him with *what ifs*. What if he could have a relationship and it not be demanding of his time? What if Brenna worked beside him and made his life simpler instead of harder? What if she was the *one* and he was being a fecking eejit denying the existence of more? But mostly, what if he was just lonely and out of sorts since the attack at his apartment and was looking for a distraction that his work couldn't provide? Another project of sorts?

"Eoin?"

He hadn't realized he was staring with such intensity at Brenna until she tentatively said his name. With a slight shake of his head and a tight smile, he began to cross the room, only to stop halfway to her. The discomfort she experienced was evident in the tight lines around her eyes and her compressed lips.

"It's me, isn't it?" he asked softly.

She didn't have to answer. The truth was in her eyes for all to see. The welling of tears. The sadness. The apology. It was the apology that gutted him because she had nothing to be sorry for. None of this was her doing or remotely her fault as far as he could tell.

"It's all right, love." He wanted to enfold her within his embrace and stroke her wild hair back from her tragic face.

But he couldn't.

He couldn't touch her in any way, and the knowledge she was off-limits was a canker sore on his soul. It stung with every breath he inhaled and was irritating as hell.

Because he couldn't look at her without wanting to hold her, he sought answers from Alastair. "What the fuck, man? Why would this happen now?"

Alastair nodded toward the case, encircled by an iridescent force field that pulsed as it encapsulated the travel bag. "Who brought that to you?"

"Reggie. He got it directly from Odessa."

"Who's Reggie?"

"Sure, and you must've met him. He attends all my showings. We've been friends for a long while."

"Not that I recall, and I remember everyone I meet." From his forbidding tone, Alastair was suspicious as feck.

"Ships passing in the night, then." Eoin refused to believe Reggie had anything but his best interests at heart. Until now, his friend hadn't steered him wrong, so Eoin intended to give him the benefit of the doubt.

"I've met him," Brenna inserted. "He's quite opinionated but very nice, and he likes Eoin a lot."

If he could've touched her, Eoin would've kissed her for her support. From the instant she'd approached him in the gallery the other day, she'd had nothing but trouble on her doorstep, and yet, here she was, attempting to be another person's champion. A man she barely knew, and all because he was Eoin's friend.

Under Alastair's considering stare, she squirmed, but was brave enough to lift her chin and meet his eyes.

Eoin's heart melted a little.

"Odessa, then," Alastair concluded after a long pause. He rubbed his jaw, appearing deep in thought. "Why would she curse her own niece?"

"I can't imagine why she would. She believes I'm useless." A surge of blood rushed to Brenna's face, and while her chin remained high, she dropped her gaze to the floor, as if struggling to find a reason Odessa wasn't right about her.

"Far from useless," Eoin told her. "You've run the bulk of her business as she flitted about from one party to the next, preying on men."

"Succubus," Alastair said grimly. "I should've recognized what she was instantly."

"Brenna's no Succubus." Shaking his head, Eoin met her startled gaze. "I'd know."

It seemed the eyebrows of every occupant shot to their hairline at his pronouncement, and he felt his own blush rising.

"Not like that," he snapped. "We shared a kiss, and didn't I live to tell the tale? No weakness, no ill effects."

Narrowing his eyes, Alastair stepped toward Brenna until there was barely a whisper of space between them. "May I?"

*"Fuck no!"* Eoin charged forward, ready to stop Alastair from kissing Brenna at all costs. That was the absolute last image he needed in his head.

Turning enough for Eoin to see what he was doing, Alastair held up her glasses. "Calm down, son. No one is making time with your mate."

"She's not my mate!"

"I'm not his mate!"

Both Eoin and Brenna had denied Alastair's comment in stereo. She looked as if she would be ill at any second, and she refused to look at Eoin. The contrary part of him that had taunted him with *what ifs* earlier, now woke up and snorted a laugh at the denial. Both his and hers. That devilish part of him mocked and said stupid shite like, "But you want her to be. Almost as much as she wants you."

If he didn't fear being thought of as mad, Eoin would've yelled at that little voice in his head to shut the feck up as he was prone to if he was alone in his studio.

Alastair, damn him, smirked, and the shrewdness in his eyes chaffed. "Duly noted. You may want to back up a few steps, my boy. Any closer and you risk a reaction from Ms. Sullivan."

Frustrated beyond belief, Eoin backed away.

The older warlock returned his attention to Brenna. "Sing, child."

"Excuse me?" She acted as if he'd demanded she strip down and parade naked in front of the pub. Likely hers and Eoin's worst nightmare. He wouldn't want to fight every man in the place, but he would if they looked her way.

He rubbed his forehead. Feck, his obsession was getting out of hand.

"I asked you to sing, Brenna," Alastair replied, unperturbed by her reaction.

"I-I can't. I p-promised Gran I w-wouldn't."

"Your grandmother made you promise not to sing?" Alastair asked sharply.

Brenna once again focused on Eoin, as if the sight of him calmed her in situations like these.

Eoin nodded and gave her an encouraging smile. "It's all right, love."

Cian, presumably to put her at ease, began a popular Ed Sheeran ballad, and Brenna, after taking a bracing breath, joined him. Her large soulful eyes locked on Eoin, and she sang for him. Her irises brightened with each word she lovingly crooned, and every thought flew from Eoin's mind.

*Every. Single. One.*

With the exception of touching her, making her his.

Need engulfed him, and he charged across the room, determined to scoop her up and steal her away. Only when she stopped singing, grabbing for her cheeks, did the spell she'd woven break, and Eoin was left shaken and confused by his Neanderthal response.

"Siren," Alastair concluded, sounding a little shaken himself. "Our dear Ms. Sullivan is a Siren."

"Sure, and I've never heard so pure a sound." Cian's voice was filled with awe, and it was as if he found it difficult to stop staring at Brenna. *Until* Piper pinched his nipple through his jumper. "Ouch! Now why would you go and do that, ya she-devil? I was admiring Brenna's singin', to be sure."

"You were enthralled," Piper snapped. "And if I ever see you look at another woman like that again, I'll—" Horror flooded her face, and she turned to Alastair. "Why am I so vicious? That's beyond pregnancy hormones and jealousy."

"It's the enchantment of her voice. Men will find her irresistible. Women will want to harm their men for that attraction." Handing Brenna back her glasses, he gestured to the forgotten dough. "Mr. O'Malley, why don't you put on the kettle and finish your scones while I explain?"

BRENNA SAT DOWN, HARD. ALASTAIR'S PROCLAMATION RUNNING through her brain along with all her gran's warnings.

*"You can't ever sing in public, my darling girl. As difficult as it will be when the urge hits, you must resist. Do you understand?"*

*"Why, Gran?"* six-year-old Brenna had asked.

*"It will cause more chaos than you can imagine. Promise me. No singing outside these walls."*

The urgency in her grandmother's voice had stuck, and Brenna had kept her promise—for the most part. On occasion, she'd hum when a tune became too much to resist. What resulted were a few free drinks at the off-campus bar from nearby guys and surly looks from a few of the women closest to her. She never understood why the boys were attracted to her nerdy appearance.

In the great many years since Gran's death, Brenna hadn't wanted to sing. All the joy had left her life.

Until she'd met Eoin.

Now, Gran's warning and Alastair's pronouncement of her gift made perfect sense. One glimpse of Eoin's starstruck reaction and Piper's scowl was enough to cement the truth in her heart. She hadn't needed to see anyone else's response.

"Gran said I wasn't to sing in public," she said softly, dazed by what her gift could mean to those around her. "She said it will cause more chaos than I can imagine. I didn't know what she meant at the time."

Sitting down beside her, Alastair folded his hands in front of him, as if trying desperately not to reach for her. His tone was kind when he spoke. "Perhaps your grandmother was

81

trying to protect you, child. An ability like yours... she was correct. It *will* cause upheaval."

"But I don't even know what the ability is. Other than anger Piper, what did I do?"

"Your voice enchants. It's your ability to weave a spell and have men do your bidding in all ways."

"You said Aunt Odessa was a Succubus. How are we different?"

"Sirens who give into the urge to steal another's magic, usually freely offered after hearing one sing, become demon-like in their quest to obtain more and more power."

Brenna didn't understand the stealing of magic. "How does that happen? How does one steal another's power?"

"A Siren can absorb another's power during sexual intercourse. It's rumored—and here I haven't met one prior to you—that during the act, a Siren sings, and when both parties peak, the transfer of power happens."

She slouched back, shell-shocked and flustered by what she'd learned. "How do I get rid of it? This ability?"

"I don't know that you can, my dear. But you can follow your grandmother's advice to the letter."

Deep inside, she acknowledged the truth of his words. All the past conversations along with the current circumstances merged, and everything clicked into place. Not only did she need to get as far away from Eoin as she could, she needed to have her vocal cords removed so she wouldn't damn another to a magic-less existence.

"Does it hurt them? The loss of power?" The need to make up for her aunt's evil behavior began to build inside her, taking residence in her brainbox and refusing to budge. "It's what Aunt Odessa has done, isn't it?"

"I couldn't say with one-hundred-percent certainty," Alastair admitted. "And yes, the removal of magic from one's DNA is painful. But I don't know the long-term ramifications of what she's been doing, if that's what she *has* been doing, mind you."

But Brenna knew.

"Why would she have created a spell to make my skin burn the way it does?"

"It appears she wants to keep you away from Mr. O'Malley. That might be her misguided way of saving you both. Preventing you from giving in to the natural desires of a Siren."

Brenna nodded. In an odd way, it made sense. But Odessa hadn't been caring of her in the past.

"I need to leave here," she whispered. The decision to get as far away from Eoin and his family was an easy one. They'd been kind to her. The least she could do was leave and not bring her unexpected brand of trouble to their door.

"No, you *need* to find an antidote for the spell first, and you could use your young man's assistance. Otherwise, you won't know if it's directed solely at him or if it might affect anyone you come to care about in the future."

She didn't bother to deny she cared about Eoin. Alastair had read her like an open book since they first met. "I don't want him hurt in all of this. He's been nice to me."

Covering her hand with his, Alastair gave her a quick squeeze, then released her. "We'll make this right, my dear. Never fear."

Across the room, Eoin poured tea for the room's occupants, a dark frown on his face.

"Does he hate me, do you think?" she whispered.

"No, Brenna. I don't think he hates you in the least." Alastair followed her gaze. "Based on the scene at the gallery, I think he was enchanted by you long before hearing you sing."

# CHAPTER 11

*B*y the time Eoin removed the pan from the oven, he still hadn't wrapped his head around the fact Brenna was a Siren.

*A Siren!*

Jaysus! And hadn't he guessed it on the plane ride over without ever truly believing it?

But when she sang, her appearance had altered to such a degree that he could say, in all honesty, he'd never seen anything or anyone as beautiful. That vision would stay with him forever, and whether she wanted him to or not, he intended to paint her like that. If only to get the image out of his head so it would stop haunting him.

He snuck a glance her way, only to find her watching him with trepidation. After sending her a faux reassuring smile, he plated the scones, grabbed a crock of clotted cream along with the jam, and set the items in the center of the table for all to feast. He was careful to stay a safe distance from Brenna so he wouldn't cause her discomfort—nor his own. Though his was vastly different from hers, to be sure.

"It's getting late," Bridget said. "Alastair, I don't have a spare room at the moment, but I'm sure you'd prefer to go home, all the same." She wasn't kicking him out, simply letting him know morning came early at the Black Cat and, with it, her need to get up and care for her guests. Despite their problems, the business always came first with Bridget.

"Have I worn out my welcome?" Alastair asked dryly.

"You know you haven't, Al." She grinned and patted his shoulder. "But I also know Rorie, and she'll be wanting her man back before too long."

"True enough, but not before I sample some of these." He nodded toward the food. "And not before we make a plan going forward. Brenna can't continue on like this. There's no telling what the outcome of such a spell might be. And for once, I'm cautious about battling an unknown elemental like Odessa. I've never encountered a Succubus, and I don't know if the rules are different."

"I'm sorry, Mr. Thorne." With her arms wrapped around her middle, Brenna looked as if she was trying to avoid touching anyone. Her overall demeanor was small and apologetic, and Eoin's heart broke for her.

"Sure, and you've nothing to apologize for, love," he told her. "Not for whatever curse you activated when you opened the case. Not for the gifts you were born with. *Nothing*." If he was a little overly emphatic, well, it was mainly because he hated to see her suffering needlessly and torturing herself for things beyond her control.

"I agree, child." Alastair's tone was not unkind. "The emotions I'm sensing from you are concern, wariness, guilt… to name a few. One would question what you have to feel guilty about. The concern for the situation and wariness of strangers, yes. If you're not culpable in this little game of your aunt's, you shouldn't experience guilt or apologize for things beyond your control."

"I didn't intend to bring trouble to anyone." She shook her

head, and her arms tightened around her middle as she hugged herself.

For Eoin, who grew up with a family's love, it was hard to imagine a life without it. Hard to imagine a life of solitude and rejection. Hard to believe someone could feel so unworthy of love and help as Brenna did now. She didn't lack confidence in herself or her abilities; she simply lacked faith that anyone cared about her or those abilities.

"It'll be all right, love. Sure, and we'll get it sorted, sooner rather than later, yeah?"

"Eoin, I didn't mean to lay all this on your doorstep. I—"

He held up a hand. "Stop right there, Brenna Sullivan. If you're after tellin' me you intend to run back to your aunt with your tail between your legs, then I'm after tellin' you that you can forget all about it. You've committed to working for me, and I intend to hold ya to that commitment, I do." He smiled to take the sting from his words. "It'll be grand, love. You wait and see."

Why he was fighting so hard on her behalf when he didn't truly know her bothered him. Yet he knew he needed to because no one else would.

He shot a side glance at Alastair.

Well, perhaps the Thornes would. They never shied away from a battle in their lives, and they tended to get to the bottom of things. But had Brenna not entered Alastair Thorne's orbit, she'd have been left to flounder and probably been burned for it. Literally and figuratively.

"I need to be getting back. And I'm sorry I couldn't put you up, tonight, Eoin." Carrick rose to his feet and placed a hand on Eoin's shoulder. "Since Aeden's recovery, he's all about the sleepovers, and there are kids everywhere."

"Oh! I'm putting you out!" Brenna's expression was one of distress.

"I'll make other arrangements," Eoin told her. "Sure, and

there's no need for you to come undone over where I'll be restin' my head tonight."

Her dark brows clashed together, and she opened her mouth, only to quickly close it again and compress her lips together.

"And what have I said that has you upset, love?"

"Nothing. It's not my business where you sleep." Her tone implied *or with whom*, and Eoin was oddly pleased by her show of jealousy. But was it an aftereffect of her singing? Two days ago, he wouldn't have been pleased and probably would've caught the first train away from her. What had changed in such a short time?

"Besides, I have a place where I can probably go," Brenna said.

"What place?" It registered with him that *he* was the one who sounded jealous this time, but he'd believed Odessa was the only person she associated with. Perhaps he was an eejit to assume she didn't have other people to care about her.

"Ronan O'Connor's."

Eoin stood so fast his chair slammed into the wall. *"Are ya feckin' having me on?"*

"Not at all, and I'd thank you to mind your tone with me."

He saw red. "I'll not be mindin' me tone when you're ready to run off with Ronan Fucking O'Connor!"

Brenna stood, braced her hands on the table, and leaned forward, aqua eyes practically sparking flames with her irritation. "I'm not running off with him, and what I do—or don't do—with Ronan is none of your business."

"It fucking is!"

"It fucking is *not!*" She jerked back and shook her head. "Oh, my! Why are we angry?"

Her question gave Eoin pause, and he noted the stunned faces of his siblings and Alastair's thoughtful expression. Attention back on Brenna, Eoin shook his head. "I don't know. That was weird, yeah?"

"Extremely. Like for a second, I was possessed. You?"

"The same," Eoin replied grimly.

"If I had to guess, that's exactly what happened to you." Alastair set the other half of his scone on his plate with a heart-felt sigh. "There was an instant rage that washed over you both, and it felt foreign in nature."

"What do we do?" Brenna asked, an edge of anger left in her tone. Eoin could understand why. He was feeling a might salty himself. Odessa's manipulation tactics were unnerving.

"Nothing tonight. But I would suggest the two of you part company as quickly as possible. Whatever spell was cast is rapidly taking hold, and I'd be inclined *not* to give it fuel for the fire."

It went against Eoin's nature to leave Brenna to her own devices, but he intended to entrust her well-being to his siblings. Bridget, Carrick, and Cian would see her cared for. It had to be enough.

"Mr. O'Malley, I'm going to suggest Brenna come stay at my estate until we have this spell neutralized. I think it's safer for all parties involved." Alastair's comment was worded in such a way as to not be ignored. Yet Eoin wanted desperately to object to letting Brenna go. But for the primary reason that he didn't know if his feelings were his own or some adverse effect of this bleedin' spell, he nodded and abandoned the group.

---

BRENNA FOUND HERSELF BACK IN THE UNITED STATES LESS THAN twenty-four hours after her first journey to Ireland. This time, she didn't have an hours-long flight to sit and worry every detail of the trip in her mind. Teleportation was definitely the way to go, minus the odd warming sensation in her cells right before the jump from one place to the next. In less time than it took her to count to ten, she was standing in the garden outside Alastair Thorne's estate.

Although the sun was setting, she could still see the perfectly sculpted topiaries and endless beds with their tulips, roses, and herbs. Farther back, she glimpsed the beginning of a maze with its box hedges.

"This looks like an English garden," she breathed out in awe.

"My wife Aurora's doing." His smile rivaled the sun when he spoke his spouse's name, and Brenna longed for the type of love they shared. All she'd ever wanted was someone to care for her like Alastair did his wife. "She's English and is a bit of a plant snob."

"A *snob*? Really, darling, if anyone is the snob here, it's you." Aurora stepped into view, and Brenna had more than just relationship envy. The woman was stunning. Willowy and tall, with black hair shot through with sky-blue highlights that matched her brilliant eyes. Her hairstyle was a simple pixie cut and suited her classically beautiful face with high cheekbones.

"You knew she was there, didn't you?" Brenna asked him.

"Yes. I can feel her the moment she appears. It's like a pain in my left butt cheek." He winked when he said it, and Brenna smiled at his teasing.

His wife's laughter was throaty and surprising, coming from her thin frame. "The curse of an empath, I'm afraid." She wound her arm through his and leaned her head on his shoulder. "Are you another of Al's strays, dear?"

"Strays?" Brenna felt sick to think she was viewed as a charity case.

"That sounded worse than I intended." Aurora released Alastair and clasped both of Brenna's hands in hers. "Apologies. I only meant to say he tends to bring home people with magical problems needing to be solved. I wasn't implying you were anything less than lovely."

It was difficult to be annoyed with someone so gracious, so Brenna let her hurt go. "I'm afraid I'm another of his 'strays,' in that case," she said sheepishly. "I'm sorry for intruding."

"There is absolutely no intrusion, uh—I didn't catch your name, dear."

"Brenna Sullivan," Alastair supplied.

Aurora's head whipped back and forth between them. "From the gallery? Didn't you mention you met a sweet young girl?"

"I did, and this is her."

Unable not to, Brenna grinned at being called a sweet young girl. That she'd made an impression on someone as worldly and sophisticated as her host was flattering to the extreme.

"It's a pleasure to meet you, Brenna. My husband told me you saved him from your overeager aunt. For that, you have our thanks." Aurora groaned. "Oh! She's still your family, isn't she? I just put my foot in it again, didn't I? Blame my lack of tea. I was waiting for Al to come home before I ate." Frowning at him, she said, "Why do you look guilty? If you had tea without me..."

"Only half a scone," Brenna said quickly to stave off any conflict.

His wife shook her head and smiled widely. "Sorry, my dear, but I know my husband too well." To Alastair, she said, "She really is delightful, darling. I think she'll fit in well with our crowd."

"Uh, thank you?" Feeling confused, Brenna followed the couple into the house, pausing to sniff a rose here or trail her fingers over a leaf there. In less than a week, her life had been drastically altered. It was mind-boggling to think she was walking through such a lush landscape with honest-to-god witches like these two.

"Mr. Thorne?"

He'd halted by the French doors, patiently waiting for Brenna to follow. When she called out, he returned to her side. "Yes, Ms. Sullivan?"

"Please, call me Brenna." She inhaled deeply and asked the question upmost in her mind. "Do I have the ability to do what you did? To go from one place to the other so quickly?"

"As one of the oldest magical families in Ireland, the Sullivans possess great power. I don't know any of them personally, but I've always kept my pulse on the community as a whole." He gave her a lopsided grin. "I suppose what I'm trying to say is that, yes. I believe you should be capable of teleporting like I did."

"If I figure out how to unleash my potential abilities, will you teach me?" She hated to ask, but she had no one to show her such things. If she had, they'd have taught her already.

"I can. But I have a niece around your age who's knowledgeable about everything in our world. She has a photographic memory and can recount every enchantment or potion she's ever read." He tucked his hands behind his back and rocked on his heels. "I believe she would be better suited to teach you how to use your abilities. Don't you agree, Rorie, my dear?"

Aurora leaned forward and peeked around his shoulder. "What he's trying to say is that Spring isn't as stuffy as Al is. It might be more fun to learn from her."

He raised his brow and looked down at his outspoken mate. "You really are a pain in my left butt cheek."

She laughed and smacked his ass. "There. Now I've made it a fact." Blowing him a kiss, she headed for the house. "Tea is in two minutes, lovelies."

"Goddess, I love that woman," he said, admiration heavy in his voice.

"She's fantastic," Brenna replied.

"That, she is, child. That, she is."

# CHAPTER 12

Spring Thorne was even more beautiful than her mother. With chestnut hair, gleaming jade-green eyes, and curves that went on for days, she intimidated the heck out of Brenna. Then she opened her mouth to speak, and Brenna's ability to converse intelligently disappeared altogether. She mumbled a lame excuse and crossed to the bookshelves on the other side of the study, pretending an interest she didn't feel.

"She has that effect on everyone," Alastair said from beside her.

His comment eased Brenna's insecurity and tension enough for her to say, "I think that's a repeat of the very first words you spoke to me."

"I believe you are correct." He chuckled and handed her a glass of wine. "I imagine you've had a long day, my dear. If you want to take your wine and go to bed, you can, but I believe Spring might have insight on what's happening with you."

"I'll stay." She took a careful sip of the wine and sighed her relief upon tasting it.

"Not like the swill your aunt served at the gallery," he murmured right before walking away.

She snorted a laugh—as he'd probably meant for her to—and dutifully followed him across the room to where mother and daughter happily chatted away.

"Ah, I'm glad you decided to join us, Brenna. Spring was just telling me a delightful story about her sister Winnie's triplets. I fear they're running their parents ragged."

"Zane, Winnie's husband, has relented and agreed to a nanny," Spring added, gleeful laughter heavy in her voice. "Three babies broke him."

"Triplets?" Brenna blurted, horrified by the thought of taking care of three infants at once.

"Yep. All boys!" she chortled.

"You are delighting too much in your sister's trials, I'm afraid," Aurora scolded, but there was laughter heavy in her voice.

Spring grinned, unrepentant. "I know."

"Do you have any children?" Brenna asked her.

"Goddess, no! It's not that I don't want any, but I'm nowhere near ready to have any kids."

"I can respect that."

Spring's keen eyes swept over Brenna and finally settled on her face. "What are you?"

Brenna's heart skipped a beat. "Excuse me?"

"There's an aura about you that's different from any I've seen, and the coloring is slightly modified from any standard scale of auras."

Looking from daughter to mother and back again, she shrugged. "I'm afraid I don't know what color my aura is."

"Aqua. The shade of the Caribbean Sea. It's actually quite beautiful." Spring tilted her head and narrowed her eyes. "But it flickers heavily, like your power is unsteady or trying to snuff itself out."

"I don't have any magic," she confessed.

Aurora placed her arm around Brenna's shoulders. "That's what Spring is here to figure out. If there's a way to restore what was taken, she'll do it."

"Someone's stealing her abilities?" The outrage in Spring's tone was complete, as if it was a personal affront to her. And then she explained exactly why. A few years earlier, she'd been abducted and forced to wear magic-busting bracelets that suppressed her abilities and made it impossible to escape. Her fiancé, Knox, had found her and, with the help of the Goddess and a handful of others, brought her home again.

"Wow! I'm sorry you ever had to go through that." Brenna placed a hand over the area of her heart, aching for all the trauma the other woman had experienced. "I feel like my problems are insignificant compared to what happened to you."

Spring surprised Brenna when she hugged her. "No loss of magic is insignificant. It exacts a price, but we'll see yours is restored to you."

"There may be one little hitch," Alastair inserted. "It appears our dear Brenna is a Siren."

"A Siren!" Spring clung to Brenna's shoulders as she leaned back to look at her face. "Yes! That makes complete sense now. Considering her aura and everything. Awesome!"

Confused by the other woman's warm response, because Spring was the only one who had seemed remotely happy about the fact, Brenna asked, "Why are you excited rather than fearful?"

"I haven't met a Siren before, but I've read all about them. This *is* exciting. One thousand percent!" She hugged Brenna again. "I can't wait to find out more."

"I think I adore you," Brenna blurted.

Everyone laughed. Then Spring instantly sobered and cupped Brenna's jaw. "I want to help you if I can. I'm sorry this happened to you, Brenna."

Emotion clogged the back of her throat, making it impossible for her to reply. Turning away after offering a kind smile, Spring gave her the time she needed to compose herself. Still, from what Brenna had learned of Sirens, she wasn't positive she wanted to be one. The fear associated with the inability to control her potential power was great, and she wished Eoin was here to talk to. He was quickly becoming her lodestone and could ease her mind with a simple grin.

"I believe Nash might have something we could use in his lair," Spring told her mother and Alastair. "Should we go beard the dragon and take what we need?"

The atmosphere around them shifted, became heavy, constricting. The lamps flickered, and the walls stretched outward as if entities were attempting to push their way through the drywall.

*"What the devil?"* Alastair dove into action. Lifting his arms, he held his hands so his palms faced the threat. "Rorie, get Alfred and the security team in here. Spring, take Brenna to safety."

Light flashed, and a rift formed in the fabric of space next to Spring. Before Brenna could call out a warning, a well-built blond man with the face of an angel stepped into the room and wrapped his arms around the other woman. The opening sealed shut with the blond man on this side of the divide.

Without thought to what she was doing, Brenna launched herself at the guy, prepared to claw his eyes out if it meant helping her new friends.

"Brenna, wait!" Spring hollered. "This is Knox. He's here to help."

Adrenaline pumping through her veins and limbs trembling madly, Brenna nodded and backed away. "Sorry, I..." With fear in her heart, but hoping to be courageous for once, she faced the wall Alastair was attempting to hold by use of magical force and ran to see what she could do to assist him. "Can you, like, tap into my magic and use it to bolster yours or something?"

He didn't spare her a glance. "I could if yours was working properly." The color of his skin deepened, becoming a little flushed, and he frowned as he struggled against whatever intended to enter his home. "Please, Ms. Sullivan. Go stand beside Spring."

"Sorry, Uncle. She's on her own. Knox and I are going to amp up your power with ours." She touched her hand to his forearm as her fiancé protected her back and touched her shoulder. Presumably to fuel whatever spell Alastair was using to keep his enemies from entering his home.

Stunned stupid by the entire experience, Brenna watched as the air in the room picked up speed. Her heart pounded a rapid drumming *ta-dum*, *ta-dum* in her throat, and it felt too thick to swallow. The temperature plummeted to bone chilling, but even as she registered the cold, a fire flared to life in the hearth. A noise similar to screaming banshees tore through the room. The shriek was torturous to listen to, and Brenna clasped her hands over her ears in an effort to stem the sound.

In seconds, Aurora was in front of her, gripping her wrists and leaning in to speak. But Brenna was unable to make out the words as the shrill screeching became more pronounced. It felt as if her eardrums were about to burst, and she couldn't prevent her own scream at the unbearable agony in her head.

"Make it stop!" she hollered. *"Please!"*

A WAVE OF ANXIETY, THEN EXCRUCIATING PAIN, WASHED OVER Alastair an instant before Brenna screamed. Sweat beaded along his temples, and he fought the urge to bend double against the agony. But he'd endured worse. He wanted to help the girl, but if he took his attention from whatever was breaking through his previously indestructible wards, his family would be in serious jeopardy. And his loved ones came first. He didn't care to think of Brenna Sullivan as a casualty of war, but he wouldn't risk Aurora or Spring.

"Al, her nose is bleeding. I think it's a psychic attack. She appears to hear something we don't," Rorie hollered through the whipping winds. "I don't know how to help her."

"Leave her. We'll heal her after if we must." Focusing his energy and pulling more power from Spring and Knox, Alastair pushed back when the threat on the other side of the wall began to gain ground. "Where the devil is our security team, and when did the wards fail?" he shouted.

The dull thud of a body hitting the floor had him half turning. However, Rorie's cry of distress let him know it wasn't her but Brenna who had dropped. His conscience plagued him, but he shoved it aside to continue battling the unknown assailants.

Then, with disconcerting suddenness, the attack stopped.

The wind died, the temperature climbed back to normal, and the fire was snuffed out abruptly.

"Was that the work of our phantom threat?" He nodded to the soot coating the interior of the hearth and the scattering of items on the floor.

"I thought it was you, Uncle."

"Not me. I didn't have the energy to spare to wreak havoc on the room," he said grimly as he knelt beside Brenna. "How is she?"

"The bleeding has stopped, but I'm not sure what happened. She was clutching her head as if in great pain," Rorie told him, cradling Brenna's upper body in her lap and cleaning the blood from her face with a tissue.

A thin platinum streak developed from Brenna's forehead and raced to the ends of her once frizzy hair, which had smoothed to loose curls. The bland color turned a richer shade of brown, not quite dark, but enough so the new high-light complimented the overall look. The freckles on her cheeks faded, leaving a smooth porcelain appearance to her skin.

"Goddess! She's gorgeous!" Spring eased closer and stared down at the woman on the ground. "How could she transform like that?"

Displeased he may have missed a viper in their midst, Alastair scowled and said, "Perhaps she was glamouring to fool us all."

"Or perhaps someone else was doing it for her."

They all turned to stare up at Knox, who'd come up with that insightful nugget.

"Explain, son."

"Have you ever had that type of thing happen before tonight? Someone able to fool you completely?"

Alastair didn't need to think back. Other than his cousin, Delphine, who was a master in voodoo and black arts, no one ever had. She'd only fooled him because he trusted her and hadn't looked deeper. He should've done, and he hadn't made the mistake since. "No one I'd spare a moment's sleep over should they perish."

Knox shrugged. "We have to consider whatever that thing was, it was after her. Maybe the glamour was put in place by someone else to hide who and what she is."

"Odessa?" Rorie suggested.

"She doesn't seem the type, but we can't rule her out, that's for sure." As Alastair scooped Brenna up and rose to his feet, his security force burst into the room, led by a harried-looking Alfred. His butler was loaded for bear, and the determination on his face told Alastair the man needed a raise for his loyalty.

"A little late to the party, fellas, don't you think?" Spring said dryly.

Under her direct stare, the unflappable elderly Alfred stumbled. His butler had been smitten with her from the moment they met, as were most men. "I'm sorry, Miss Spring. The men and I were trapped in the armory."

"Trapped?" Knox's wary gaze surveyed the room around them, looking for enemies as if he was preparing for a second attack.

Martin, Alastair's head of security, stepped forward. "Yes. It was the oddest thing, sir. Whoever or whatever was behind this tried to come through the drywall, stretching it like silly putty. Like something out of a horror film, if I'm being honest." A slight tremor wracked his body, and Alastair had a difficult time containing his laugh. Martin feared nothing and was top-notch at his job.

"That's exactly how I would've described it." Alastair eased Brenna down on the closest sofa, then addressed his staff. "Let's get on the wards. I want to know why they failed."

"They didn't, sir. The perimeter hasn't been breached. This came from within." Martin shook his head. "I don't know how or why, but something inside the house caused this."

Aurora's shout caused him to turn back toward Brenna. The young woman's body was floating a foot or so above the sofa, and she was encased in a shimmering blue light.

"Spring, I'm going to need you to find out everything you can on Sirens. What would cause her to do what she did here, and why has she put herself into stasis."

"Is that what she's done? Have you ever heard of anyone in stasis floating?" Rorie inched closer, lifting a finger as she prepared to poke the glimmering bubble surrounding Brenna.

"Don't!" Alastair gripped her wrist and drew her back as an electrical current arched and struck where her hand had been. "That's a fierce protective force field she's got going on, my love. It'll knock us all into next week."

"Fascinating," Spring murmured. "Okay, I'm on it."

In seconds, she was gone with Knox on her heels.

# CHAPTER 13

Chapter 13 has been omitted because the author is of the superstitious variety. Feel free to take a break, feed your pet, and pet your spouse. Then return for the next part of Eoin & Brenna's story.

# CHAPTER 14

*W*hen Brenna dreamed, it was of Eoin.

*He was reclining, half-asleep, in the bed she'd occupied at the Black Cat, in nothing but a sheet, his back against the headboard, half-asleep.*

"Eoin."

*Opening his eyes, he tried to focus on her in the darkness as he frowned. "Brenna, love, what are ya doin' here? I thought you'd left with Alastair."*

"I did."

"Did he cure ya, then?"

*She shrugged, unsure if what happened tonight could be considered a cure. But she didn't need to answer, since she was in a dream state. Hell, maybe she was dead and not just dreaming. Wouldn't that be something? To be stuck in a loop with Eoin in the bed with her unable to be with him.*

*She sat on the edge of the mattress and stretched out a hand. "Should we try it?"*

*He placed his palm flat against hers, and when she didn't react, he curled his fingers over hers and tugged her closer. "What did you do different?"*

"What do you mean?"

Fingering a lock of her hair, he lifted it so she could see. "You've added highlights and smoothed your curls."

"I can't remember doing that," she murmured. When had that happened? Was she losing her damned mind?

"And your glasses are gone, too. Sure, and ya must be wearing contacts."

She wanted to touch a finger to her eye, but the idea of doing so gave her the heebie-jeebies. That squeamishness was the primary reason she still wore glasses. "No contacts. But I can see you just fine."

He drew her to kneel between his sprawled legs, and he ran his clever fingers over the planes of her face before burying them into her hair and tugging her face closer. "You were beautiful the way you were, Brenna Sullivan. I told ya you didn't need to change a thing."

"I didn't," she protested softly.

A twinkle lit his impossibly green eyes, and he gave her the devastating grin that always weakened her knees. "Aye, ya did, but I'll not argue the point anymore. Stay the night with me, love."

"Yes. I—"

"Ms. Sullivan! Brenna! We need you to wake up, my dear."

"Don't take this the wrong way, Eoin, but your Mr. Thorne is a pushy bastard."

Eoin chuckled as he rolled atop her and touched his lips to hers. "No man likes to hear another's name in his bed, yeah? How about you forget about anyone but us. You and me, here and now."

His tongue swept her mouth, and she moaned her pleasure. Every single time Eoin touched her, she felt as if she was about to go up in flames. And as scary as the prospect was, she wanted it more than she could bear.

"Sing for me, Brenna," he whispered.

She opened her mouth to do just that when Alastair disturbed her again.

"Brenna! You must wake up!"

"I don't want to," she practically whined.

*Pulling back, Eoin released a regretful sigh. "We don't need to do anything you don't want to. I don't believe in forcing myself on a woman."*

*"No! I want you. Of course I do. But can't you hear Alastair? He's telling me I have to go back, and I don't want to. I want to stay with you."*

*Eoin drew further away, all signs of play gone as he stared down into her face. "Alastair Thorne? He's calling to you now?"*

*"Yes."*

*In a move that surprised her into silence, Eoin sat up and snatched his phone from the nightstand. A few quick taps and he was making a call.*

*From a distance, Brenna could hear the ringing of a phone, and she sat up to see where the sound was generating from. On the far wall of the bedroom there appeared a solid glass door, and from her side, she saw Alastair standing a foot away from a floating body, Aurora at his side as a few men dressed in black t-shirts and cargo pants paced the room and peeked out of windows, guns at the ready.*

*"It's Eoin O'Malley," he said into his phone, right next to her. "I've Brenna with me, she—"*

*"Brenna! She's with you now? Right now?" Alastair gave his wife a concerned glance and backed further away from the floating body, allowing Brenna her first glimpse of who rested there.*

*Her hands flew to cover her mouth in her shock. It took her a long moment before she could speak.*

*"Eoin!"*

*His gaze shot to hers.*

*"Can you see the window into Alastair's house?"*

*In slow increments, he eased his head toward the wall she was pointing to. Turning back, he shook his head. "No, love. I don't see anything."*

*"Ask her to tell you what she sees, Mr. O'Malley," Alastair ordered.*

*She didn't need her to relay the question because she'd heard it directly from the man's own lips.* "I see him next to a floating body, with Aurora beside him."

*Eoin relayed word for word what she said, down to the detail of clothing and Aurora's shoe color.*

Through the glass, she saw Alastair turn in her direction, and she finally understood this was no dream she was in.

"Can she see how many fingers I'm holding up?"

"Tell him four," she whispered.

"She said four," Eoin replied, concern straining his features. "How is this possible?"

"She's put herself in stasis," Alastair said grimly, staring hard at the wall they were behind.

"*Jaysus!* Stasis?" Eoin ran an hand over his face, then froze, slowly turning to face Brenna more fully. "You put yourself in stasis, love? How? *Why?*"

"I don't know. I... I was there, and now I'm here, and I don't know how!" she cried tearfully. "What is stasis? Am I dead? How can you touch me if I'm dead?"

And why couldn't she see Gran? Weren't loved ones supposed to greet you when you crossed to the other side? But she wasn't, was she? If she were deceased, that would mean Eoin was, too.

Alastair took command, perhaps sensing her panic with his empathic ability. "Eoin, I hope you're dressed because I need you to teleport here, with Brenna if possible."

"Look, and isn't there some universal law about the same person appearin' in the same time and space as their earthly counterpart?"

"She's one in the same, and it's my fervent wish she'll merge when she returns here."

"Aye. I..." A look of dawning horror filled Eoin's face, and he scrambled off the bed, far away from her. "What if this isn't Brenna with me now? And if it is, how is it we can touch when we couldn't earlier?"

"I don't want to know why you were touching, son, but I'm almost positive it's Ms. Sullivan with you now." Alastair sounded less perturbed and a lot amused by what they'd been up to. "I'll text you a picture of my patio, and you try to teleport her here. I'll have my head of security meet you both and bring you inside."

"But this Brenna looks different. Like a feckin' beautiful goddess different."

"So does this one. The caterpillar shed her cocoon and became a stunning butterfly, my dear boy. I'm afraid you're sunk."

"Sure, and what the fuck does that mean?"

"I think you know. You have two minutes to arrive, Eoin. No more, no less. My wards can only be shut down that long without cooking you like a Christmas goose."

EOIN DIDN'T BOTHER SAYING GOODBYE AS HE DISCONNECTED AND hustled to find clothing. Brenna perked up the second he dropped his sheet, and her sharp-eyed gaze locked on his half erect shillelagh. Blushing like a girl of thirteen, his hands flew to cover himself. "Don't be appreciatin' my lad with hot eyes, Brenna. We've only got a minute more to get to Alastair's estate and no time for shaggin'."

Her laugh was spontaneous and throaty, and he finally saw the Siren she was meant to be. Alastair was right—he was sunk if she decided to seduce him. And how the hell had that happened? When did his shy Brenna become worldly?

He groaned when she licked her lips. "None of that, ya hear? You'll be saving that for a time when you aren't in stasis, yeah?" The thought of her in a coma sobered him, and any desire faded when the seriousness of the situation penetrated the sexual haze she'd woven around him. "And when did you start wearing perfume?" He took a tentative sniff, and when the unique scent of jasmine and bourbon with vanilla notes washed over him, he forgot why it was urgent to return her to Alastair.

Taking a step forward, he reached for her.

She rose up on her knees and opened her arms, ready and willing.

A pounding on the door snapped him out of the spell she was weaving, and it flew back on its hinges to reveal his sister. Hand shielding her eyes and rolling pin in hand, she looked as irritated as he'd ever seen her. "Why am I getting a call from Alastair Thorne in the middle of the night, telling me to rescue you from the clutches of Brenna? And why is he telling me you have less than one minute to get your arse to his garden?"

"Feck, Bridget! I'm not dressed!"

"Then get yourself dressed and hurry your eejit arse."

Without bothering to match his clothing, he drew on the jeans hanging over the end of his bed and a wrinkled shirt from a pile in the corner. If he smelled like week-old worn socks, it couldn't be helped. Within ten seconds, he'd clasped Brenna to him and pulled up the image on his phone.

"Hold tight, love."

"Mmm, yes," she purred.

Goddess help him, the delicious fragrance her skin was putting off was driving him mad, and he wanted nothing more than to take her somewhere they wouldn't be found. Shaking his head and trying to clear the enchantment, he visualized the stone terrace, praying with his total lack of concentration he didn't imbed them in the damned railing.

There were two armed guards waiting for him along with Alastair's wife, Aurora. Her meaningful look caused him to shift uncomfortably as she wordlessly separated them and rushed Brenna toward the house.

"Wait!" he shouted, only to have his forward progress blocked by the guards.

"Sorry, Mr. O'Malley, but you need to wait here. You can't interrupt the process."

"What bleedin' process?"

But they were gone.

"What the hell is happening here?" he demanded of the guards.

"There was an attack on the estate."

*"What?"* He charged toward the door only to have his way blocked again. "You'll be moving out of me fucking way or I'll rip your head from your shoulders, man," Eoin threatened, deadly serious.

"Can't do that, Mr. O'Malley. Mr. Thorne's orders."

"I don't give a feck about his orders. Brenna is inside, and I'll see her safe."

"She's safe. She's the one who staged the attack," the other guard said.

*"Jaysus!* You'd better be havin' a craic. But if you are, I'll be telling ya here and now, it's not funny, to be sure."

They had to be mistaken. His Brenna would never hurt a living soul. She didn't have a mean bone in her entire compact and mouthwateringly curvaceous body.

With a disgusted look at his partner, the first guard swung his gun behind him and gestured toward a padded bench. "Have a seat, sir. I'll explain what I can."

Casting the French doors one last frustrated look, Eoin crossed his arms and braced his legs. "I'll stand, thank you. And I'll be hearing that explanation, all the same."

"Name's Martin, by the way. And here's what I know…" Martin detailed the harrowing sight of facial-less features and claw-like hands attempting to push through the drywall. Of how it stretched and strained under the weight and how those in the control room were half convinced a zombie apocalypse was taking place. "Mr. Thorne suspects Brenna conjured the entire thing and put herself into stasis, perhaps to seek you out."

"But for what purpose? I intended to see her in the morning."

And here, Martin's expression turned sketchy as he squinted his eyes, crinkled his nose, and scratched behind one ear.

"Out with it, man."

With a wary side glance toward his partner, Martin said, "Possible seduction. So she could steal your powers."

"That's fuckin' absurd! She wouldn't—" But she almost did. When she'd arrived in his room, looking like a wet dream, he'd felt compelled to ask her to sing, and although she hesitated at first, she fully intended to do it. That's when Alastair rang the bell in her head, putting a stop to their shagging.

What did Eoin really know about her? Yes, he'd seen her at a few art functions over the years. Yes, she dressed in dowdy clothes and did nothing to enhance her appearance. And sure, she seemed withdrawn and unassuming with her shy smile, a genuine Mona Lisa, but could it all be an act? Was it meant to lure him in? If so, how had she known he'd take the bait? Had she gained insight into his character through his creations and the brief conversations they'd shared?

The idea that she might've was disturbing.

"I'm goin' in there, Martin. I've questions that need answers, and it's only Brenna who can provide them."

"Sir, I beg you—" He touched a finger to his earpiece, and nodded as if someone could see him. "You can go in, Mr. O'Malley."

Eoin scanned the roofline, finding multiple cameras pointed in his direction. He assumed Alastair had monitored the entire conversation. Again, to what end? To see if Eoin was loyal to Brenna or party to whatever mischief she was stirring up?

Mentally dismissing the guards, he stormed toward the entrance. There were more questions than shades on a color wheel, and he intended to have answers.

# CHAPTER 15

*B*renna woke in stages, and her body felt like she'd tied one on. Her pulse resounded inside her head like a gong, and her brain cringed with every hit of the mallet against the metal. Only once, at age fifteen, had she given into the need to find solace in alcohol, and she'd paid for it with a hangover that lasted two full days. She couldn't forget the feeling or the cotton mouth that went with it.

Oddly, Odessa hadn't scolded her and, instead, had plied her with tonics to help her through the worst of it. For the first time in the years since Gran died, Brenna had felt cared for. Of course, after two days were up and Brenna was almost fully restored to her former self, Odessa had reverted back to the cold-hearted, distant woman she always was.

Removing her glasses, Brenna rubbed the heels of her hands over her eyes. When she opened them, everything remained crystal clear, as it had in her dream. Or rather, in her visitation to Eoin. How had that happened? She sat up abruptly.

The first thing Brenna registered was roughly a dozen people crowding the room, half of which were security guards. The others were Alastair, Aurora, Spring, and Knox, and they all looked at her with varying stages of fascination, grimness, or suspicion. The last was Eoin, and his wariness struck her right at the center of her heart. But she understood it.

To give herself time to think, she carefully folded her glasses and set them on the table. Apparently, she was no longer blind as a bat without them. One good thing had come from this, she supposed. When she was sure she wouldn't break down and sob, she lifted her chin and faced the censorious gaze of Alastair Thorne. She couldn't bear to look at Eoin again.

"I-I..." She cleared her throat, inhaled deeply, and tried again. "I suppose you'd like to know what happened."

He lifted a brow.

She gulped.

"Yeah, well, I d-don't know. One second, c-creatures were coming through the walls..." She whipped her head around to assess the damage. Seeing none, she turned back. "Um, okay. Then I heard savage screams in my head, and the only thought I had was to get away from the sound."

"You ended up in Eoin's bedroom," Spring supplied kindly. "Why?"

"It was the only place I could come up with to go." Brenna finally looked at Eoin. "You make me feel safe," she said, barely above a whisper. "I couldn't think of anywhere else."

Eoin gave a single nod of acknowledgment but didn't say another word, and his severe expression, mixed with crossed arms, made her soul shrivel. She'd caused one drama too many for his liking. Because she couldn't stand the accusation in his gaze, she focused on Spring.

"I don't know how I did it. But I remember everything."

Spring leaned forward, excitement in every line of her body and sparkling from her jade eyes. "Sirens are incredibly powerful beings. Uncle Alastair suspects you created the monsters in the wall yourself."

"I didn't! I wouldn't. *Couldn't*," Brenna said. She held out a hand imploringly to Alastair. "You have to believe me, Mr. Thorne. I would *never* endanger your family."

"Not intentionally. Or so I assume," he acknowledged with a tug of his cuff links. "Regardless, endanger us, you did. What do you think might've happened had your creatures burst through those walls, Ms. Sullivan?"

Tears stung her eyes, and she shook her head, having no clue what to say and fighting like hell to suppress her desire to cry. Whatever relationships she thought she developed had turned to dust in a single night.

"They might've ripped my family to shreds to protect you. I believe you conjured them in your fear and insecurity over the situation." He gestured to the guards surrounding them. "It's why they are at the ready should your fear take over again."

Brenna felt cold to her soul. And friendless, though that wasn't new. "I see." With as much dignity as she could muster, she rose to her feet. "I'm not sure how I did what I did. And I certainly don't want to hurt anyone again. If I can borrow your phone, I can call Aunt Odessa. Explain to her I have to come home. Maybe it's better that she might be the one syphoning off my magic." She gave them a half-hearted shrug. "Maybe she did it for a reason."

Eoin swore a blue streak, dropped his arms, and began to pace.

Brenna winced with every expletive, but she refused to look at him directly or acknowledge his presence in any other way. If she did, she really *would* cry.

"Calm down, Eoin," Alastair said tiredly. "And you, please sit, Brenna. We have much to discuss."

Stopping only long enough to point at her, Eoin declared to the others, "She'll not go back to that bleedin' Succubus, and that's the final word on it."

Confused by his reaction and more than a little relieved not to return to her aunt's care, Brenna plopped back down on the sofa, wilting like a flower in the midsummer's sun with no water for days.

"Giving your power over to your aunt isn't the best option, child. You may not want to harm anyone, but I can guarantee she does if she's truly a Succubus. We need clearer heads to prevail here." Alastair sighed heavily and rubbed the spot between his brows.

The man had probably never been more confounded in his life.

"Okay, let's list what we know about Sirens. And by that, I mean Spring," Aurora said with a proud-as-punch smile for her daughter. "Your excitement leads me to believe you've learned a lot more."

Spring grinned. "Yes. Sirens have the ability to tap into their ancestors' power without going through Otherworld channels like the rest of us. As a result, they can double or triple their power for a short time with little effort." She warmed to the subject, giving Alfred a happy smile when he arrived with a straining tray laden with food, teacups, and a pot of what Brenna assumed was tea. "That ability makes you, and all your kind, notoriously hard to kill. I mean, it's not impossible, but it is difficult and takes some doing."

Heart rate like a sledgehammer and ready to come through her sweater, Brenna straightened in her seat. "Have you been studying how to kill me?" Her high-pitched tone made everyone, including herself, wince. "Sorry."

"You have power in your voice, Brenna," Eoin said, addressing her directly for the first time since she woke up. "Be careful with how you use it, yeah? And no one has been studying how to kill ya." He glared at the Thorne family members. "Have ya?"

Alastair looked distinctly amused, Aurora alarmed, and Spring apologetic. Knox was simply stoic and watchful.

113

"Oh, no!" Spring prepared a plate of food and handed it to Brenna.

Although her stomach thought her throat had been cut, so hungry was she, Brenna promptly set the offering aside, not certain if poisoning was the way they might take her out. The other woman laughed and crossed to sit next to her. Spring lifted the plate and took a bite of a petit four. Around a mouthful, she winked and said, "You're safe here. Promise."

Still, it was difficult to drum up the enthusiasm for food when Brenna felt like she was facing the gallows.

"I believe your aunt's hold on you is growing weaker, especially since you inadvertently tapped into your ancestors' power. Or could be, that was all you." Spring shrugged a shoulder and poured tea for all those present, then handed cups off to everyone with the exception of Alastair. "I'm sure you'd like your usual Glenfiddich, Uncle."

"You know me too well, child." He rose and gestured to one of the guards to abandon his place in front of a long sideboard. Alastair proceeded to pour himself a drink from a glass decanter. "Eoin, would you care for something stronger?"

"I would," Brenna said, to everyone's surprise. She cleared her throat. "It's been a long couple of days."

Alastair smiled, and for once, she felt as if she'd done or said something right. When he handed off a tumbler, she sniffed the antique gold liquid appreciatively. The smell brought to mind orange-flavored cake.

"I can see you know how to appreciate a fifty-year-old scotch. Well done, my dear."

"Gran loved Glenfiddich." She nodded toward the bottle with the stag emblem. "It was her favorite go-to when celebrating or imparting wisdom." Nostalgia washed over Brenna as she sipped her drink. The alcohol contained notes of orange with vanilla, and although there was an underlying taste of oak, it had a mild sweetness. The rich flavor filled her senses to full, and she silently saluted her gran on her excellent choice of whisky. With a sigh, she placed the glass on the coffee table in front of her and faced Spring. "Tell me why you think Aunt Odessa's hold is weaker, please."

"Your appearance, for one. You're nothing short of gorgeous, Brenna."

With a quick glance at Eoin, who confirmed what Spring had said with the smoldering heat in his gaze, Brenna nodded, barely suppressing the need to preen. Not once in her entire life had she been called gorgeous. The sensation was headier than the booze.

"And for two?"

"Your ability to conjure monsters in the walls. To *conjure* anything, really. My understanding from Uncle Al and Eoin was that you didn't know you were a full-blown witch before today."

Again, Brenna nodded her acknowledgment and to confirm what Spring had learned.

"The truth is, Odessa couldn't contain your power for long. A Siren is at her strongest when her desire to mate takes hold."

In the midst of taking another sip of her scotch, Brenna choked. Her throat and lungs were on fire, and she coughed until tears streamed down her cheeks. "Holy macaroni! That burns!"

Spring's musical laughter annoyed the blasted hell out of Brenna as the other woman thudded her back. Spring knew she'd get a rise out of her, and why she'd said it was questionable. Brenna daren't look at Eoin, or she'd accidentally conjure a hole in the floor to eat her up.

Quickly dismissing the image, lest she actually *do* it, Brenna ran a shaky hand under her eyes. "Mating and desire. Got it." She cleared the remaining heat from her throat. "Does this mean I can break free of the curse attached to Eoin and me? The allergic reaction, as Mr. Thorne called it?"

"We discussed it while you were sleeping, and we believe it's why you split off from yourself the way you did. As a work-around to the adverse reaction you have when he's close. You were able to manifest an entirely new form. None of us have ever seen it done or even heard about an astral projection like yours." Spring clutched Brenna's hand. "And if *I* haven't read about it, it's probably never been done. You could very well be the strongest Siren of your line!"

Her excitement was contagious, but at the same time, Brenna didn't dare embrace it. She couldn't forget what she'd done in Eoin's bedroom and how tempted she'd been to sing to him. Or how she'd rubbed herself against him like a cat in heat, practically purring when he held her to teleport here. Who was that woman? Certainly not her. Or not the her she had been.

But maybe she liked the new version of herself a little better than the old Brenna. The take-charge attitude was different for her, but it garnered results. Slowly, as she processed all she'd discovered about herself, she nodded. The way she saw it, she could either keep her abilities and hone them, or she could find a way to get rid of them once and for all. Because it didn't seem right to reject the gifts she'd been born with, Brenna decided learning to control herself was the better option of the two. For now. If at any time she became a threat to others, she'd find a way to rid herself of magic.

"So, is there some type of Hogwarts for people like me?"

Spring grinned. "I'd hoped you'd ask that."

"Spring wants you to move in with her while she trains you in the ways of a witch," Eoin said.

The crushing rejection Brenna experienced made it difficult to acknowledge him, but she kept her chin high and pretended it was no concern of hers, even though inside, her guts were churning. Was she back to being homeless and jobless? Techni-cally, she hadn't lost the homeless status, but if Eoin didn't want her working for him, she'd need to find gainful employment as soon as humanly possible.

"But sure, and I don't like the idea of you so far away," he added.

Brenna jerked her head up and met his fierce gaze. The admiration and concern for her seemed real, but were they a reaction to the seductive power of a Siren? She had no answer other than she didn't like the idea of being so far away from him either. But she couldn't tell him that, and she no longer intended to wear her heart on her sleeve. No one needed to tell her, but she instinctively understood the curse attached to her could, and probably would, become more severe should she ignore it to remain with him. If Aunt Odessa had created it to control her, then she'd have thought of contingencies should Brenna continue on her current path.

"I want you to meet someone before you make a decision, child." Alastair drained his glass and set it on the sideboard, where it promptly disappeared. Brenna wondered if she'd ever get used to things of that nature. This entire situation she found herself in seemed too fantastical to be real.

"Who?"

"His name is Damian Dethridge, and he's what is called an Aether."

"I don't know what that means. Well, other than Dubheasa and Eoin discussing a baby Aether."

After a long look at Eoin, Alastair said, "Damian is the balance between good and evil, darkness and light. He can give or take magic on a whim." He narrowed his eyes. "I want him to read your energy and determine if you are worthy of remaining around those I care for. I'll not have you endangering their lives, whether intentionally or not."

"Al—"

He held up a hand, interrupting his wife. "Do I make myself clear, Brenna?"

"Crystal." She clasped her hands in her lap, nearly cutting off the blood flow. She made a decision then and there. It used her remaining courage, but she was damned if she was going to be bossed around anymore. "And let me make myself clear, Mr. Thorne. I've had quite enough of domineering individuals. I believe you truly want to help me, and for that, I'm appreciative. However, I no longer intend to reside under someone else's thumb."

Expression arrested, as if she'd surprised him, Alastair paused for a heartbeat or two before barking out a harsh laugh. "You and Damian are going to get along famously, Brenna Sullivan. I guarantee it."

With those words, Alastair Thorne instilled a near-debilitating dread inside her. A clearer warning didn't exist.

# CHAPTER 16

*A*lastair left the room, followed by Aurora, Spring, Knox, and three members of the half-dozen security guards he employed. Brenna perched on the edge of one sofa as Eoin sat across and diagonal from her, at least ten feet apart, on the other. The distance seemed farther than any she'd experienced, especially with him. But maybe it was because, before now, the time she'd spent with Eoin, dreams of happily-ever-after with him were pure fantasy. This week, after the few mind-melting kisses, she'd allowed herself to indulge in what if.

Like Aunt Odessa said, she was a foolish girl!

Unable to meet Eoin's steady regard and come up with anything else to say, Brenna studied the room around her. The space screamed classy but comfy, and Alastair's stamp was on everything. Walls a cool gray, the study was tastefully done with matte-black leather club chairs positioned in front of a large hearth with a white-and-gray marble surround. Pictures of who she assumed was his family dotted the mantle, and she recognized Spring as the gap-toothed child on the right in a picture with three other girls. All adorable in their own right.

What might it have been like to grow up with sisters as Spring had done? Would Brenna be more confident and less of a doormat? Would she have had best friends to confide in when she was at her loneliest?

"Siblings can be a pain in the arse, love."

Eoin's comment surprised her enough to turn in his direction.

"How did you know I was wondering what it would be like to have siblings?"

"I'm not sure. It was more of a feeling. Your longing was so poignant, I felt it squeeze my heart."

She frowned, unable to fathom how he'd guessed her thoughts and experienced her emotions so clearly.

"I already miss touching you." His voice was pitched for her hearing alone, and it was as if he skimmed his fingers over her skin with each word. Her heart rate increased, and her pulse hammered painfully through her veins. The one constant in her brain was that she wanted to kiss him so badly.

"I want to kiss you, too, love. More, if I'm to be honest."

Again, he'd guessed her internal dialogue. Not just the gist, but the *exact* thing she was thinking.

*"Can you hear me, Eoin?"* she asked within the confines of her mind.

He frowned and shot a glance at the other men, then looked at her again and nodded. *"I can hear you,"* he replied telepathically. *"How the hell are we doing this?"*

*"I've no idea. It occurred to me we might be able to when you guessed what I was thinking—twice."*

*"But can you guess what I'm thinking?"* His wicked grin curled her toes.

*"I don't need to guess. Your look says it all."*

*"But did you hear the words? What I wanted to do to you? Where I wanted to place my mouth..."*

She shook her head, perhaps a might happy she couldn't. If

he triggered any more of her hormones, she was going to go up like a bonfire at a beach party.

"Sure, and I suppose that's a good thing," he said aloud.

"You're not mad at me? About all of this?" Swallowing down the thickness in her throat, she said, "I don't want you to hate me, Eoin."

He took his time answering, and when he did, she was no closer to feeling better about her current situation. Leaning forward, he picked up his drink and took a fortifying sip. "Look, and I don't know what you truly are, Brenna, or how I feel about ya. About what you can do." He shook his head. "A few days ago, you knew nothing about magic like ours. Tonight, you were able to split yourself into two beings, like a bleedin' amoeba." With a scowl, he broke his focus on the amber liquid in the glass. "My obsession with you is growing by the minute, and I don't know if the feelings are my own or if they've been enhanced by whatever powers you possess."

"I'm not purposely trying to lure you in." Lifting her hands, she stared at her palms. "This is all new to me, too. One minute I was attending a gallery opening, like a thousand times before, and the next, you were whisking me away to Ireland."

"Maybe your power came from getting away from your aunt," one of the men suggested kindly. Both Eoin and Brenna turned their attention to him. "I've seen a lot in my line of work and in the employ of Mr. Thorne. Bad people always attempt to steal or manipulate magic they don't have." The man smiled at her. "I don't think your intent is to hurt anyone, Ms. Sullivan. But I do think with a rapid influx of abilities as strong as yours, all sorts of strange and startling occurrences are going to take place until you learn to control what you have."

The desire to jump up and hug the man was real. No one else had quelled her fears so quickly. "Thank you, uh…"

"Martin," Eoin and Martin answered together.

"Thank you, Martin," she said with a heartfelt sigh,

conveying every ounce of gratitude she possessed. "I needed to hear that."

"My pleasure, Miss."

She sent a wary glance Eoin's way. "I'm sorry I embroiled you in all this. But I'm not sorry it happened."

His dark brows shot to his hairline. "You're not?"

"No. You helped me get away from a life I didn't want and that didn't serve me. From a woman who might be using me for more than my administrative skills." She grimaced her disgust at her own naiveté. "You've shown me that I need to learn to stand on my own two feet, Eoin. I'll be forever indebted to you."

"I don't want you to feel indebted. I want you to feel liberated, love." He drained his glass, set it on the table, and stood. A fierce light shone in his eyes as he stared down at her. "I want you to be who you were born to be, Brenna Sullivan. You owe me nothing because I've done nothing to earn your gratitude and respect, yeah? I dragged you away from the only home you've known, triggered a curse that burns the flesh from your bones, and now, I've embroiled you with Alastair Thorne and the Aether, who might view you as a serious threat."

"Alastair seems like a good man," she protested.

"Aye, and he is. But he also doesn't deal with fools, and he's no tolerance for anything that might hurt his family. That would be you and me, love, whether we want to or not."

She rose to her feet, desperate to touch him, to prove to him he had nothing to feel bad about. But she crossed her arms, not certain she wouldn't be burned alive should she do so. "How would you hurt them? You're not responsible for what I've conjured!"

He scoffed.

"You're not, Eoin," she insisted. "Whatever tried to come through those walls was from my subconscious, according to the others. You didn't cast the spell to awaken those monsters."

"But I kissed you, love. More than once, and we developed a bond that teleported your cloned self an ocean away. This"—he gestured between them—"whatever this is, has sparked your magic, and ya can't tell me it didn't."

"Martin said it could just be the lack of Aunt Odessa's influence," she said, desperate that he not shoulder the responsibility of her actions. "Not you, Eoin. Never you."

"Aye, but—"

"*Stop!*" she screeched, closing her eyes and cupping her hands over her ears. She couldn't take any more of his self-recriminations. He was too good. Too kind. And he'd only ever had her best interests at heart.

When she opened her eyes at the silence, it was to see everyone frozen in place. The only sound was the rhythmic tick from the mantle clock, echoing loudly in the room. Eoin's face was changing color, turning a purplish shade, as if he lacked air. She looked at Martin only to discover his face had an unhealthy bluish tinge.

A panicked glance at each person's chest showed *none* of them were breathing. "Holy cheese whiz! Okay, don't anyone freak. I've got this." She held up her hands, closed her eyes, and visualized them all healthy and hearty. With a deep breath of her own, she hummed a low C on the musical scale, and in a sing-song voice, she said, "Breathe, gang!"

Gasps and ragged inhales emboldened her to lift her lids. Two of the four stared at her with terror, guns clutched to their heaving chests. Martin and Eoin were a little less horror-stricken, but still wore looks of extreme wariness—no more than she herself was feeling!—as they sucked in lungsful of air. Reeling from what she could accomplish with a single word or two, she shook her head. She really needed to learn to control her power, and the sooner, the better. If not, she'd probably kill someone.

Careful to moderate her tone and distance her voice from

her feelings, she said, "I'm so sorry." She let her regretful gaze say what she couldn't verbalize. The two terrified guards looked to Martin for guidance.

"Stand down," he ordered them, chest still rising and falling like he'd run a marathon. The expression he turned on her wasn't as friendly as it had been moments before. "I'm going to ask that you zip it until Mr. Thorne returns, Ms. Sullivan. No offense, but I'd hate a repeat performance of that."

She nodded, not daring to speak.

"Brenna."

The compassionate way Eoin said her name cemented her love for him on the spot. He could've gotten angry, stormed from the room, washed his hands of her forever, but the tender look he graced her with said none of that would be happening.

Compressing her lips against the urge to profess her love, she simply nodded.

*"Thank you,"* she said, hoping their silent communication was still an open channel.

"Like Martin said, your intent wasn't to hurt anyone. And your recovery was grand, love."

She snorted a laugh and covered her mouth with her hand, cognizant of every sound she made.

He winked, and she knew she was forgiven.

IF THERE WAS ANYTHING TONIGHT HAD TAUGHT EOIN, IT WAS that Brenna was out of her element when it came to her new abilities. He understood the feeling. But what she *did* have was grace under pressure. In the last hours, her entire life had been turned on its ear, and she'd found out she was a Siren with untold power. For many, there would be an arrogance attached to that knowledge. They might not care who was hurt in their quest for learning and amassing more power.

Case in point one: Loman O'Connor.

Case in point two: Odessa Sullivan.

But Brenna had been mortified tonight when she was told about the havoc she'd conjured. And when Eoin had tried to take the blame on himself, she begged him to stop. It was obvious in her reaction that she didn't want to listen to him beat himself up for his part in all of it. All her angst had been collected in one shouted word. While her ability was at fault for stopping their body functions, the incident *had* been an accident. Eoin was sure of it. Then, realizing her mistake and with a clear head, she'd rectified the situation immediately.

Yes, he was cautious of her, as any person in their right mind would be, but the quicksilver emotions continually flashing on her face with each new event drew him in and tempted the artist to recreate what he'd witnessed on canvas.

Perhaps that's where his true fascination lay—her expressive face. That hauntingly gorgeous face. The beauty of those soul-branding eyes finally made sense. Only Eoin had seen behind the hideous tortoiseshell frames, and he now suspected it was because he was the only one she'd truly cared to look at, to watch from her safe place. So when their gazes had connected time and again across the crowded room, he somehow knew she was so much more than the person she'd portrayed.

*Fecking Odessa!*

*But* he also owed the woman a small thanks, because if Brenna had transitioned into a beautiful swan earlier, she and Eoin might not have met, and she wouldn't be infatuated with him now. He wasn't being arrogant in his assessment of her feelings. Every look, every gesture, every amorous thought she had, they all spoke to some beast within him, and that savage brute wanted to claim her in a very bad way. From the instant she stepped onto the airplane with him, he'd been able to sense her churning thoughts and wayward emotions. And since she set foot in his bedroom, they'd shared a psychic link. And damned if that didn't scare the bleedin' hell out of him, *but* it fascinated him, too. Especially when one small smile from him could overheat her about as much as her adoring eyes could set him alight.

Eoin wasn't ready to label his desire and preoccupation as anything other than what they were. He certainly didn't intend to throw the term "true love" into the mix, but he did care about her welfare, and he was invested in the outcome of this current drama.

And he discovered he hated to see her upset. The overwhelming need to put her at ease and to protect her in all ways confused him. Not that he was cruel or wouldn't look out for an underdog regardless, but for Brenna, he would move mountains and crush skulls simply to see her eyes shining, and catch a glimpse of her shy smile.

*Feck! He was a drowning man, in over his head, with no life preserver in sight.*

Her "thank you" rang inside his head, making him feel ten feet tall and bulletproof.

His wink and her snorted giggle had put them back in sync and assured him she'd never harm a living soul if not for her blossoming abilities. He only hoped Damian Dethridge had a solution to their little problem.

# CHAPTER 17

The Dethridges' English estate was picturesque, and though it didn't really look like the centuries-old house from Downton Abbey, Brenna's favorite show, she still felt as if she were traveling back in time as she climbed the stone steps to the terrace. Morning dew clung to everything it touched, and the rising sun highlighted the subtle shifting mists hovering above glorious green fields. Enormous oaks towered over benches and small outbuildings like sentinels, ever at the ready. Brenna didn't think it was possible to fall in love with a place, but if one could, this Gothic home was it. She never wanted to leave.

Then she met the owner.

He was as hauntingly beautiful as his place.

Until she set eyes on Damian Dethridge, the Aether and Mr. All-Powerful himself, she believed she'd seen some of the most handsome men in existence—Eoin, models, Eoin, the men associated with the Thorne family, Eoin, Ronan O'Connor, Eoin...

She sighed and leaned slightly forward to peer around Alastair at Eoin's proud profile. Brenna had Eoin O'Malley on the brain, and her ability to concentrate on anything else was nil. But he wasn't looking her way. All his attention was for the drool-worthy guy at the top of the stairs.

However, the Aether's focus was locked completely on Brenna.

She shivered.

The man saw too much.

A light flared bright in his eyes, and her entire being warmed in response. When she reached the landing, she inhaled his heady scent. The sublime smell of marshmallows and a crackling fire with a hint of citrus filled her nostrils, and the Siren within her sat up and took note from where she'd been pouting in her boudoir on her red velvet chaise lounger in boredom.

A trilling began in her head, and Brenna compressed her lips to keep the sound inside. If she allowed her inner seductress to gain control, all hell would break loose. That horny bitch desperately wanted the black-haired, black-eyed man in front of her, with his soul seemingly as old as time, and it wasn't only for his sex appeal. Here was a man who had experienced all life had to offer and who could make a woman beg for a mere drop of his magical nectar, and he held *power*.

She stopped short and caught herself in the act of licking her lips, appalled by the Siren's naughty thoughts on every which way she'd bang this guy. Ride him like a cowgirl all the way to Sunday—it was only Tuesday—and make him plead and scream for more.

Damian lifted a single dark brow, and his arch, knowing look sent a wave of fiery heat through her. If he couldn't read her thoughts, he could damned well guess at them.

A darting glance at Eoin showed him scowling at her for all he was worth.

*"What the fuck, Brenna?"*

The "fuck" in her head sounded like "fook." Even telepathically, his Irish accent was so strong it came through their connection. The righteous anger caused her to bite her lip against a laugh. Helpless, she shrugged. *"Sorry."*

*"If you're to be ridin' anyone like a cowgirl all the way to Sunday, it sure as feck won't be him. You'll only be shaggin' me from here on out, got it?"*

She did laugh then. His indignation came through loud and clear, as did the claim he'd just staked, although she doubted Eoin had registered it.

"Ms. Sullivan, Mr. O'Malley." The Aether's smirk practically guaranteed he'd heard their internal conversation. His following words confirmed it. "If you're done hashing out your plans for the week, I suggest you come in so we might discuss your options."

Brenna almost turned around and walked away then and there, so acute was her embarrassment over her Siren's thoughts.

The Siren inside scoffed. *Yeah, keep telling yourself it was me, girlfriend.*

*Shut up, you bitch.*

*You're the bitch—in heat. Ha!*

*Ohmygod! You are toast, you know that, right? I'm totally going to eradicate your slutty ass.*

"Brenna." Eoin's gentle prodding brought her back to reality.

Face burning as hot as the midday sun, Brenna forced herself to put one foot in front of the other and approached the Aether. In the lowest voice she could muster and still be heard by him—and only him—she said, "I'm sorry for anything inappropriate you may have been subjected to, sir."

"Think nothing of it," he said just as quietly. As he clasped her hand, raised it to his lips, and kissed her knuckles. His mouth twitched but otherwise didn't move. Yet as clear as the brilliant blue sky above them, she heard him say, *"It's quite flattering, really. You've made my day."*

His obsidian stare made her heart flutter.

"Can you help me get rid of her or at least tame her?"

"Why would you want to? She and you are one and the same."

With a rough shake of her head, Brenna jerked her hand back and tucked it with her other behind her. "We're not."

His shrewd eyes did a silent survey of her set features.

"The magic is great and all, but I worry I can't control it. Control her." She was helpless against the constant barrage of thoughts. Her Siren wanted everything and everyone. Brenna only wanted Eoin.

The Aether, quick to pick up on what she couldn't say, slowly nodded. "I can see you don't want her brand of trouble, and for that reason, I'll help you, Ms. Sullivan."

The immediate surge of tears stung, and she rapidly blinked them away as she swallowed the rising tide of emotion: fear of her other self, thankfulness to those willing to help her control it, longing to be relevant, inexplicable desire for the unimaginable power the Aether radiated, and last but not least, her unmistakable love for Eoin.

The trilling in her head grew stronger as her Siren fought for supremacy, and Brenna closed her eyes against the pounding headache forming. "I just want to be normal," she whispered.

Surprisingly, it was Alastair Thorne who offered the comfort she gravely needed. He did it by placing a gentle hand on her shoulder and squeezing. "It's going to be all right now, child."

She sniffed.

The next thing she knew, she was enclosed within his warm embrace, and she wished he was the father she hadn't had as she wrapped her arms around his middle and hugged him tightly. She had the vague sense of the others leaving as she quietly wept in the safety of Alastair's firm hold.

"I'm s-sorry, M-Mr. Thorne."

"No need to be, my dear. I'm a warlock and can remove tear stains from my suit with the snap of my fingers." His desert-dry comeback triggered her smile and was exactly what Brenna needed to recover her composure.

He held up his hand, and dangling from his fingertips was a pink and white polka-dotted handkerchief with smiling panda bears. "It's yours. I thought you could use a cheerful pick-me-up."

She laughed, cleaned up her face, and blew her nose. Then she stretched on tiptoes to kiss his unlined yet decidedly masculine cheek. "I think I love you, Mr. Thorne. But in a non-partner sort of way," she added hastily lest he believe her Siren was after him.

His wide, white smile was breathtaking. "I'm glad you clarified, or Rorie would dine on both our hearts after having them served on a silver platter, of course." With the tip of his index finger, he lifted her chin and examined her face. "I'm not convinced I'd have ever believed you could transform the way you have, my dear. But your Mr. O'Malley is going to be dancing to your tune for a great many years to come as soon as we neutralize the spell ensuring his distance."

"Am I truly so different?" It didn't sit well with her for Eoin to only be with her because of her looks.

"Only on the outside. It was always your inner beauty we all found attractive."

She smiled her pleasure at his insightful comment. "Thank you, sir."

"My friends call me Alastair, Brenna. I'll consider you a friend so long as you don't hurt a member of my family."

Woven within those words was a heavy warning. One Brenna heard and understood well. Odessa had been the queen of not-so-subtle threats. She nodded. "Thank you, Alastair," she said, thereby assuring him she'd never intentionally hurt his loved ones.

---

Eoin's stomach had been churning since Brenna's inner Siren woke, stretched, and mercilessly taunted Brenna, and *him* in the process. All this time, he'd believed Brenna desired him, was possibly half in love with him, but instead, she'd become enthralled with the Aether as soon as she saw him, thereby throwing Eoin out like yesterday's rubbish. Was there always going to be someone her Siren wanted more?

Once, long ago when he was still an art student, he'd believed himself in love with one of the class models. She'd led him on a merry chase, only to batter his wee heart by sleeping with another artist soon after agreeing to date Eoin exclusively. The hurt caused by her defection hadn't felt good, but it was nothing compared to what he was experiencing with the suspicion Brenna might prefer another man to him.

"It's a pleasure to see you again, Mr. O'Malley. May I speak with you privately?"

Eoin turned away from the terrace doors and from his standard pastime of watching Brenna to greet Damian. "Aye. What is it you wish to be speaking to me about?"

"Brenna."

Clenching his jaw, he lifted his brows to encourage the Aether to continue.

"Whatever turmoil you are currently going through, I feel as a scratch under my skin. And I'm here to tell you, I'm committed to my wife. I don't stray, Mr. O'Malley, whatever the temptation. Do you understand?"

"Are ya accusin' me of being jealous, man?" Why he was belligerent when Damian was trying to put him at ease, Eoin couldn't say.

"Yes."

"Well, I'm not, all the same."

"You are, but I've no intention of quibbling with you, *all the same*," the Aether retorted with a soft snort, as if he intended to drive home the point but wasn't trying to rile Eoin in the process. "Your Brenna has her power under control, which is pretty remarkable, considering she just came into her abilities within the last day."

Having already met the man and his wife, Eoin knew Damian lived for and would die for his lovely family. But the ugly green-eyed monster inside of Eoin liked to poke and prod. "Sure, and she's a remarkable woman. She's already realized her power is in her voice."

"As it is with all Sirens." Damian gazed out the window. "Have you researched what she is?"

"No. But I do know it's not safe to be with her in the physical sense of the word."

He nodded and looked Eoin square in the eye. "She'll have a difficult time restraining herself during intercourse. Especially in the beginning. Your magic will call to hers, and she'll be tempted to give into that call."

"Making her a Succubus, yeah?"

"Like most of the women in her line. Her mother included."

"Her mother?" The odd churning in Eoin's gut increased in intensity. "Are you sayin' her mother gave in to the call?"

"Yes. The only female from her line who refrained was Doreen Sullivan. Brenna's maternal grandmother."

"And how do you know all this, man?"

Damian smiled. "I'm the Aether. I have the ability to see the future, hear the thoughts of those nearest to me, and give or take magic as directed by the Authority. I've also spent over two hundred years on this earth and come in contact with a lot of our kind. Brenna's grandmother included."

"What was she like? Doreen Sullivan."

"Stunning. Like your Brenna." Damian's expression softened as he recalled the past. "Kind and full of life, preferring a pint over expensive liquor. Her hair was as golden as her smile, which was twice as bright as sunshine."

Eoin jerked at the realization the other man had deeply admired Doreen. "You were lovers?"

"A long time ago."

"You're not... uh..." Words failed him. How did he ask a man like Damian Dethridge if he was related to Brenna?

"No. I'm not her grandfather. But I knew him. Doreen met him one night in a pub as she waited for me to show, which I didn't."

"Because you had a vision of the other man, yeah?"

Damian smiled his approval at Eoin's guess. "I did. I knew he'd make her very happy for a time."

"A time?" Eoin swallowed hard. "Is that all Brenna and any man she chooses will have?"

"I can't tell you that, Mr. O'Malley."

"You can't or won't?"

"Both." Damian frowned as he watched Brenna and Alastair walk toward the French doors. "Even if I knew what your future held—"

"I never said I intended to be that man!"

The Aether lifted his brows as he looked at Eoin. "Who are you trying so hard to convince?" When Eoin remained silent, Damian continued. "As I was saying, even if I knew what your future held, it wouldn't be wise to share it with you. Altering the plan laid out by the Fates would have a ripple effect. I'm only allowed to step in should the Goddess or the Fates permit it. Such is the condition of my gift."

"But it's well known ya helped the Thornes whenever they showed up on your bleedin' doorstep," Eoin grumbled.

"True. But again, only because the Goddess allowed it."

"You've not gone against the gods or goddesses, then? Not once?"

"Oh, I've done it many times. However, there must be a damned fine reason. Your curiosity about your future isn't it." Damian's tone had turned hard, and the reprimand was undeniable, causing Eoin momentary discomfort, which he rightly deserved for his surliness.

Brenna wasn't the only one to control magic with her voice.

"Aye. Understood, man." Eoin placed his hand on the doorknob to admit Brenna, then remembering he couldn't be that close, stepped back and gestured to Damian. "It appears I'm not allowed even the most common of courtesies, or I'll hurt her."

The Aether opened the door with a simple wave of his hand, keeping his thoughtful expression locked on Eoin. He tilted his head as if listening to a sound too distant for the rest of them to hear. His brows clashed together, and he nodded, as if to himself.

"I'll help you remove whatever is blocking you both, Mr. O'Malley. And I'll—"

Into the salon skidded a pint-sized girl with black pigtails riding high on her head and a gamine grin. Her clothing was mussed, and she looked like a little hooligan as she turned her calculating gaze on the room. Eoin knew her to be Sabrina Dethridge, beloved daughter of the man in front of him. She, too, had the ability to predict the future and wasn't as reticent as her father about sharing what she knew when she received her visions.

"Beastie." Damian sighed heavily. "I thought I told you to stay with your mother while our guests were here."

"I want to see a real live Siren, Papa!" In her excitement, she practically shouted.

"Sorry, but you won't be this morning. Off with you," her father instructed with a stern, no-nonsense stare.

It didn't have the desired effect, and the child ignored her father to approach them, smiling up at Eoin and giving an aborted curtsy. "It's a pleasure to see you again, Mr. O'Malley."

"Sure, and you sound remarkably like your da." He smiled. It was impossible not to. The girl was capricious and fecking adorable. If Brenna had been blessed with a better family unit, might she have been secure in their affections and given over to sassy behavior like Sabrina Dethridge?

"Thank you." Her eyes twinkled, and Eoin got the distinct impression she was busting at the seams to tell him about a vision she'd received.

As if she knew he had guessed, she flared her eyes wide and compressed her mouth, purposely not looking at her da. With a minuscule tilt of her head in Damian's direction, the little beastie had signaled him to get rid of the adult Aether.

Damian did his best to hide his amusement. "So much drama." Bending, he swung her up until she was wrapped around him like a baby monkey, clinging to his back.

She smoothed her da's jumper at the shoulders then patted them. "You're good at that, Papa. So strong."

"Mmhmm. Don't try to play me, my love. I've been around lifetimes longer than you. I'm wise to the ways of wild and wicked little witches."

"I'm not wicked," she protested as she tightened her stranglehold around his neck. "And Mama says only a little wild."

"Tell Mr. O'Malley what you've seen and head off to break your fast."

"Mama told me to tell you to invite our guests to breakfast."

"Of course she did," Damian murmured with a slight shake

of his head as he untangled her from his person and set her on the ground. "Your vision, Beastie. Spill it."

"The Goddess said Loman O'Connor was back and seeking Siren magic to steal."

Eoin's heart dropped to his left knee.

# CHAPTER 18

"*L*oman O'Connor." Odessa had heard through the grapevine the man had died, bested by Alexander Castor in a fight to the death, but here he was standing on her doorstep. She sighed. One couldn't trust gossip in today's day and age. Back in her day, people fact-checked before spreading news.

"It's grand to see ya again, Odessa."

"Why the hell have you come here?" She wasn't fool enough to let him into her house or turn her back on him, but as a Succubus, she had more power than he and his family combined. Granted, hers were waning from longer periods between feeding, not to mention the major loss of Brenna's gifts. Still, Loman couldn't know that.

He scowled, but even angry, the fella was a looker. Yet on the inside, the man was ugly as sin, and that hadn't changed. Loman was the one person Odessa had no desire to seduce. The bastard would've found a way to use her own abilities against her if he could.

"Yeah, and is it not enough I've come to visit an old friend?"

"You don't have any friends, Loman. Don't think to kid a kidder."

"Two of a kind, then."

Her heart pinged. She didn't care to think of herself in his league, but she supposed, after all this time and all the evil acts she'd performed, she wasn't much better than the low-down, sneaky sonofabitch in front of her.

"Do ya not intend to invite me in?"

"No. I don't. I ask again, why the hell have you come here?"

"I've need of your magic," he told her with no more preamble. "And you'll be givin' it to me."

She laughed. "Not on your life, O'Connor."

"What about on *your* life, old woman?" a cold female voice asked from behind her as a razor-sharp blade plunged between her ribs.

As Odessa fell to her arthritic knees, she pressed her hands to the place on her back above her kidneys.

*Sneaky witch!*

She could heal herself, even from the black magic seeping into her veins, but she'd have to expose her vulnerable self for a harrowing few seconds during the transition to do it. Most people didn't know what to look for, didn't know that the area covering her heart was vulnerable to attack for roughly five beats. But if these two knew how to pierce her skin, they probably knew that, too.

"Why isn't she tryin' to save herself, Uncle?" her attacker asked as Loman joined her in the foyer, confirming what Odessa suspected.

She looked up at the attractive auburn-haired woman frowning down at her. Recognition struck. "Because I'm not as stupid as you believe me to be, Moira Doyle." Pretending to shift position, she touched the slate floor of her entry and drew in the energy of the ley line from beneath her home. Without closing her eyes, she envisioned the earth's healing resources, absorbing through her palm what she needed to encapsulate and expel the poison from Moira's knife.

"How did you know where to find me, O'Connor?" She asked to stall and give her body the boost it needed to defeat the pair of them when they least expected it.

"Ya think I can't read the society pages?" His tone was disgusted, as if she were too stupid to exist. Which maybe she was if she'd underestimated his drive to find her. After Doreen's death, Odessa had stopped running and hiding. She'd settled in one of the three family homes she owned. In her prime and full of arrogance, she'd always assumed no one would be foolish enough to tangle with a Succubus of her caliber. And they hadn't. But she could no longer claim to be unbeatable. Brenna would have that title now. Heavyweight Siren champ of the world.

Odessa smiled.

Loman and Moira exchanged an uneasy glance.

"My wards? How did you get past them?" Odessa had few people over, but one of them had betrayed her. She'd like to know who, so when she was finished with these two, she could pay their accomplice a visit.

"We've been testing them for weeks. It helped when you let my nephew Reginald in to retrieve the girl's things."

"Reggie? Eoin O'Malley's best friend is one of your clan?" She laughed, then frowned down at her chest as the sound of congestion rattled in her lungs. The earth's magic should be healing her faster than it currently was. "I must say, he fooled the lot of us."

"Sure, and that was the intent, it was." Loman's toothy grin didn't reach his dead eyes.

Odessa shivered. So many of them at cross purposes, each a threat to Doreen's beloved granddaughter in their own way. Her attention drifted to the shadowy figure across the room.

*Doreen.*

Come to watch Odessa finally get what was coming to her. She peered closer at her ghostly sister. Doreen didn't look smug, though. She looked fearful, and that was different from the norm. Odessa wanted to tell her she had nothing to worry about, but the poison in her veins was gaining ground.

Curiosity got the better of her, and somewhat distantly, she asked, "What was the toxin on the knife?"

"Witchbane, Belladonna, and Rosary Pea," Moira stated smugly. "And of course, the added ingredient to pierce Siren skin."

Odessa's painted brows shot up with her surprise. "One poison wasn't enough?"

"Not for a Succubus, it wasn't. You'd have found a way to heal yourself, as you're tryin' to do now, yeah?"

"Clever girl," she murmured. "But how clever, I wonder?"

Drawing on the power of the ley line and her ancestors, Odessa's blood boiled as she called the demon inside to wake. The poison was like acid in her veins, and her scream of pain ricocheted off the walls and slate floor, creating an earsplitting echo. The sound paralyzed Loman and Moira during the time they could've used to kill her.

*Suckers.*

The infusion of magic transformed her body, leaching her dyed hair of color and turning it to the palest white. From past experience, she knew her eyes would be glowing an unholy red and the horns that emerged from her temples to curl skyward were intimidating as hell.

The second set of arms always cracked ribs as they formed, but they were by far the most useful tool a demon could possess. Long claws sprouted where her fingers should be, and her skin developed a thick metallic veneer as her cells shifted from flesh to protective scales. Wings were next as the scapula took on a new shape and pushed through the new scaly barrier.

Resembling a bat's, they were human-sized with the ability to encase her entire body twice.

Moira, face frozen in fear, wasn't fast enough to dive for safety, but Loman, a wily fella always anticipating trouble, dove for the door just as the Succubus swiped her four-inch razor-sharp claws in his direction. Missing her target, her nails shredded a layer of the wood door, leaving a trail of inch-thick gouges. With the back of her left wing, she smacked Moira and sent her flying through the mahogany stair railing, splintering it like a toothpick.

"Did you honestly believe you could take on a Succubus and live, girl?" the demon spat. Each word was laced with venomous intent, and the sheer volume forced Moira to clamp her hands over her ears to protect her eardrums. Odessa's enraged Succubus had been known to shatter those of her victims a time or two and cause bleeding deep in the inner ear.

"Please," Moira sobbed. "Please, ya don't know how he is! What he forces us to do!"

The demon laughed uproariously.

Moira whimpered and curled into a ball, back to the wall. "I can help you," she shouted over the banshee-like echo of the Succubus's glee.

Tilting her head, Odessa paused in going for the kill. "How?"

"Sure, and if you let me live, I can lure Uncle Loman to a location of your choosin'. You can exact your revenge, ya can."

"Or I can hunt him down using the scent from your blood and pulverize him to dust for daring to believe he could best me," the demon told her conversationally. "I don't need you alive to find Loman O'Connor."

*"His son's a Guardian with unlimited power!"*

That stopped the Succubus in her tracks. A thrilling sensation similar to an orgasm shook her body as she imagined how easily and quickly a Guardian's magic could restore her to her prime. "I'm listening," she purred.

Tentatively, as if afraid of a trick, Moira lowered her arms from her face. "Ronan. He was the most powerful warlock I've ever seen, and that was before he became a guardian. He's got to be stronger than anyone—sure, and with the exception of you," she added, once again protecting her ears as the demon growled its displeasure.

"Nice save." Holding out a spare arm, Odessa curled her claws in a continual motion. She modulated her voice to an enticing tone. "The knife, Moira Doyle. The one you stabbed me with. I'll have it now."

Helpless to resist the command, Moira's face blanked and she reached beside her to withdraw the blade from its protective sheath. Then she held it out, handle first, and bowed her head in deference.

"The sheath and your clothing, too," Odessa cooed. It wouldn't do for Moira to have anything stained with her blood, or the crafty witch would extract it and enslave her.

Odessa refused to answer to anyone.

Standing on wooden legs, Moira undressed, her movements jerky like those of a marionette. When she was completely nude, Odessa grunted her satisfaction.

"Now be a good little Pinocchio. Climb to the top of the stairs and wait for me."

With her sulfuric breath and the flint of her claws, the demon created a fire in the hearth to destroy the clothing and the knife case. She licked the blade clean, savoring the rich coppery taste. She wasn't concerned with the remaining poison, not in Succubus form. The transformation had consumed her human cells and naturally destroyed the toxin in her bloodstream.

With one last look over her shoulder to where Doreen

stood, a silent specter watching the entire scene unfold, Odessa shrugged. "She had to know what she was getting into, sister."

*"She didn't. But the small part of her brain that isn't under your spell does now."*

The Succubus grinned. "Too bad you never gave in to the darkness. You'd have made a formidable demon."

*"I saw what it did to practically everyone I ever loved. Why would I feed the evil? Why should Brenna?"*

"Brenna..." Odessa frowned, then glanced up the stairs before addressing her sister again. "They'll be after her next," she said in a low voice.

Doreen glared at Moira. *"You should kill the bitch."*

"In good time. For now, I need her magic to satiate my demon. I plan to feed on her for days." With that, Odessa retracted her wings, extra appendages, and claws, then sauntered up the stairs. She ran a hand along Moira's graceful neck and gripped the young woman's throat. "So much magic," Odessa whispered with a deep inhale... seconds before she kissed her.

# CHAPTER 19

*B*renna walked through the doorway in time to hear the Aether's daughter's statement. She also heard a colorful round of swearing in her mind over the threat of Loman O'Connor, courtesy of both Damian and Eoin. Shoving aside their grim telepathy, she knelt in front of the girl.

The two of them studied one another for a long minute.

"I've never met a Siren before," the adorable sprite said. The light of curiosity shone brightly from her.

"And I've never met a young Aether before," Brenna replied with a warm smile. "It's a first for each of us. That makes today very special, indeed."

She didn't cringe when chocolate-coated fingers reached for her hair. After all, shampoo was a girl's best friend. But the child stopped and drew back.

"I forgot to wash my hands," she said in a stage whisper. "Mama's going to be so cross with me."

"Doubtful. I'm not sure how any mother could be cross with a daughter as awesome as you."

The girl beamed, and Brenna grinned right back.

"I'm Sabrina."

"I'm Brenna."

"I know."

"Of course you do. I've learned Aethers know all the things."

"I'm sorry everyone wants your magic." This time, when the girl reached for Brenna's hair, her hands were spotless.

"Neat party trick." Brenna sat still and let the girl finger her myriad of caramel- and mocha-colored curls. "And it's not your fault that people are greedy, though. And I won't let them have it if I can help it."

"I like you, Miss Brenna. You're different from the other one."

"The other one?" She glanced up at Damian, puzzled by his daughter's comment.

He shook his head and gave a slight shrug.

Looking at her father, Sabrina requested silent permission. Brenna found it disconcerting that she was subject to their thoughts as well as Eoin's.

"Who is the other one, and why can I hear the two of you communicate?" she asked, climbing to her feet and clasping Sabrina's small hand as the girl offered it.

As if unconcerned by the fact Brenna could hear her inner dialogue, Sabrina grinned and swung their hands between them. "The other one's older and different from you. Meaner. But you're stronger. Remember that, okay?"

Brenna shared a bemused look with Eoin, but nodded to Sabrina anyway.

"You'll understand when the time comes, Ms. Sullivan," Damian said. "The things Beastie predicts may seem vague, but they have a way of falling into place." He ran a palm over the top of his daughter's silky hair. "Now, young lady. You've met the Siren and given your prediction. It's time you run and do child things or help your mother make breakfast."

"We're witches, Papa. We conjure food." She put her hands

on her hips, the image of a saucy little minx. "Besides, I haven't given Mr. Eoin what he came for."

Brenna fell in love. The girl was too precious and precocious for words.

"And what did he come for?" Although Papa Aether's expression was skeptical, heavy indulgence weighted his tone.

"You're a pushover, Mr. Dethridge," Brenna said in an aside as Sabrina approached Eoin.

"You have no idea."

They shared a chuckle and tuned in to what Sabrina was saying.

"The Goddess said the Siren will always be your moose. Papa is to make you a special necklace."

"Sure, and don't ya mean muse?" Eoin asked her with a wide grin.

The girl cocked her head and frowned, deep in thought. "Maybe." With a careless shrug, she skipped away.

"I can't say I've been anyone's moose before," Brenna quipped.

"You can always be my moose, love. Day or night."

Right then, the sun appeared behind Eoin, creating a golden halo around him, and the rightness of the moment cheered her. She laughed, happier than she was when all this drama started. "I'd love to be your moose, Eoin O'Malley. Day or night."

Using their telepathic link, he said, *"I want to hold ya so badly my bones ache."*

*"Ditto."*

*"Ditto? I pour my heart out to ya, and that's all I get in return? You're an ungrateful wretch, Brenna Sullivan."* He ended his tirade with a grin, and Brenna responded in kind.

Keeping eye contact with Eoin, she shifted her head to the left to address the Aether. "About that necklace…"

Damian moved to stand next to her. "That's going to take a

little time, I'm afraid. And I'm going to need a small amount of blood from you."

"My blood..." A long-forgotten memory popped into Brenna's mind. One of Gran telling her not to give blood voluntarily. Not to family, not to strangers, not for a blood drive... *never*. "I don't think I can, Mr. Dethridge. Is there another way?"

"I'm afraid not. Or not one I'm familiar with." He faced the room and called out to Spring. "Are you familiar with any spell that might help our lovebirds?"

"We're not, uh, we..."

"Oh, Brenna, me darlin', give over," Eoin said on a laugh. "Sure, and we'd be lovers if we had the chance."

Heat infused her body and was likely reflected in her telltale complexion, but she lifted her chin, standing her ground. "We aren't lovebirds... *yet*."

"My apologies, Ms. Sullivan." With a slight incline of his head and a twinkle in his obsidian eyes, Damian turned back to Spring. "Are you familiar with any spell to help Ms. Sullivan and Mr. O'Malley get rid of their curse?"

"I've thought about it all night. They can wait it out, and perhaps the witch who conjured the enchantment will drop dead—of natural causes, of course"—and here her tone was drier than dirt—"or we can scry into the past to see if we can figure out who cast the spell to begin with, and have a conversation with them about the error of their ways."

"Or I can call my aunt and ask if she's the one responsible." Brenna was certain to her core Odessa was.

"The less contact you have with Odessa, the better, child," Alastair said as he perused the selection on the tea tray that had mysteriously appeared when Brenna's back was turned. He selected a small square sandwich and popped it into his mouth with a satisfied grunt.

"How can you eat at a time like this?" she asked him.

Aurora laughed. "Alastair doesn't miss a meal, dear, regardless of the circumstances."

"It's true." He glanced up from examining the interior of another sandwich. "Being held hostage and starved lends to a deep appreciation of food, and I accept it whenever it's offered, I'm afraid." His wry smile couldn't quite hide the haunted quality his words brought to his worldly eyes.

The Siren hummed a tune, and Brenna picked up the plaintive refrain and joined in harmony before she could stop herself. She'd never have believed she could produce both sounds at once, but the overall effect was a melodious duet.

They all went motionless, but not like when she'd locked Eoin and the Mod Squad earlier. The group around her had paused to listen to the music she produced, and there wasn't a dry eye in the house by the time she was done.

"Extraordinary!" Spring's awe was obvious from her tear-bright eyes to her voice. "How did you compose something so exquisite on the spot?"

Not at all sure where her newfound talent came from, Brenna shrugged. "It's as if I felt Alastair's—" She'd intended to say deep-rooted pain, but his uneasy look stopped her. "I, uh, felt Alastair's desire for entertainment and needed to quench it."

She didn't miss the grateful glance he shot her.

"Actually, that makes sense," Damian said, attracting everyone's attention. "Your grandmother once said something similar. She told me her Siren can detect the hidden emotions and desires of those around her with little effort."

"You knew Gran?" Heart hammering and breath laboring in her lungs, Brenna suddenly had an overwhelming urge to latch on to the one last connection to her grandmother.

"I did. A memorable woman, your gran."

His smile suggested a familiarity that went beyond friendship, but Brenna didn't pursue it. She'd already guessed he was way older than anyone she currently knew, though he looked no more than thirty-five or forty, max.

"Why didn't she tell me what we were?" she wondered aloud. "I could've been prepared for all of this."

"Perhaps she hoped you'd inherit more of your father's DNA than that of your mother's side," Aurora suggested kindly. "Maybe her wish was that you wouldn't have to face the struggles you're now presented with."

"You did say she told you not to let anyone hear you sing, love. Sure, and it seems that was her way of preparing you, don't ya think?"

Again, she longed for a hug from someone familiar. Preferably Eoin. But that wasn't happening anytime soon. It made it all the more obvious that she was attention starved. At that moment, her loneliness was at its greatest—and she was surrounded by people.

As Damian watched Brenna, hoping to get a better read on her intentions when it came to those he cared about, he felt a sort of kinship he hadn't truly experienced with anyone else before. No one had ever lived as long as he, and the isolation associated with the job of Aether was great. The young woman in front of him understood that isolation. Whether it had been forced on her or whether it was something she'd subconsciously embraced due to long-forgotten warnings from Doreen, he couldn't say.

For a great many years, Doreen had others to share her secret. Her sisters. Him for a short period of time. And eventually, the love of her life, though that relationship had been short lived. Lasting only long enough to produce twin daughters. One had run away from home at an early age, and a part of Doreen's soul was fatally wounded the day Narissa disappeared. The girl had covered her tracks so well they all believed she'd died. The other, Clarissa, had followed in her aunt's footsteps, and after the death of Brenna's father, she'd given over to the darkness and the life of a Succubus. Damian was there when Clarissa had to be relieved of her powers.

She didn't survive the process.

That day had been the last time Doreen spoke to him. She absolved him of his guilt, knowing it had to be done, but she'd ordered him to stay away from her remaining family. To see her walk away, regal head held high with a toddler in tow, hurt his heart. He'd loved her. Not as he now loved Vivian and Sabrina, but Doreen had offered true understanding with her gifts. Had helped him feel a deeper connection and fed his humanity, keeping it alive.

"If you'll come with me, I'd like to show you something, Brenna," he found himself saying, willing to share a side of himself he'd locked away ages ago.

Her wide sea-bright eyes were full of uncertainty and loneliness, and a huge part of him wanted to do this for Doreen. To provide her granddaughter whatever comfort and support she needed as a way of making up for failing Clarissa.

Brenna glanced around, her gaze seeking Eoin's like a homing pigeon looking for its roost. He nodded his encouragement and gave her a warm smile, mentally relaying that she could trust Damian. The two of them were as sweet as honey straight from a hive. Each consumed with easing the other's mind as unexpected challenges arose.

Doreen would've approved of Eoin O'Malley as a match for her granddaughter, and Damian was determined to make it happen—as long as he could assure the young man would survive the relationship and go on to live a long and happy life. That meant keeping Brenna's Siren from turning to the darkness as every member of her family had before her, with the exception of Doreen and Narissa.

"Come, Brenna. You've nothing to fear from me. I promise."

Damian held out his hand, and she tentatively took it. He chuckled when she released a small meep as their fingers connected. "Still getting used to the sensation associated with touching another witch?"

"I didn't know I was a witch like all of you until recently," she said ruefully. "I was under the impression Gran and Aunt Odessa were Wiccans who practiced under the secrecy of night."

He laughed at the idea two such powerful women practiced their craft like mortals. "It must be strange to find out differently."

"Extremely."

At the entrance to Damian's ceremony room, Brenna stopped and exclaimed her delight. Concern quickly replaced her excitement. "The power here, it may be too much for me. For *her*."

"If you resist it, she has no choice, Brenna. You control her, not the other way around. Try to remember that, won't you?"

She turned frightened eyes up at him. "I don't know that I can... resist, that is. She grows stronger with every passing minute."

He took his time answering, striving to find the proper words needed to calm her and offer the assurances she needed. "Doreen was as strong as any person, male or female, I've ever met. I see that same strength of will inside you."

"Gran was stronger and wiser than I'll ever be. Braver, too."

"You won't know what you're made of until you're tested, my dear. And I'm testing you now. I need to discover if you're worthy of Eoin O'Malley's affections." He met her fearful stare and relayed confidence in return. "Choose. You either want a future with him, or you want to remain locked in your old life. You won't be able to have both."

Grim determination tightened her mouth, and she lost her wariness. "I choose Eoin, if he'll have me."

He was able to detect her fear in the background of her churning emotions, but Damian wasn't worried about her losing control... yet. "Believe me, he will."

"But will it be for the me that was or for what I've become?" she asked in a voice a little less confident than it had been seconds before.

"It's for you, Brenna. As I've told you, the Siren and the woman are one and the same. You can control your own desires if you wish." He purposely hardened his voice for his next warning. "But if you let her have freedom, she will do what feels good, regardless of consequence. If you don't keep her contained, she'll choose the darkness every time. Do you understand what I'm telling you?"

"I do."

"You can seek your pleasure in any form you so desire. But don't give in to the temptation of stealing another's magic. *Ever.* Or you'll have me to deal with."

With a jerky nod, she blinked back the tears forming in her exquisite eyes. "If that should ever happen, the temptation part, I want you to stop me in any way you can. I couldn't bear it if I hurt Eoin."

She'd said exactly what Damian hoped she would. "Good. Now, come and let me show you what I have for you."

# CHAPTER 20

*A*s soon as Damian turned his back to Brenna, she pinched her sweater away from her chest, pumping the material to create a breeze to cool the perspiration on her skin. The man was fearsome. His entire being screamed *dangerous*, and Brenna was intelligent enough to sit up and take notice. Her Siren was, too. The two of them made a silent pact to never get on this guy's bad side if they could help it.

Lights flared to life the second Damian crossed the threshold of his private ceremony room, and as Brenna entered, she inhaled deeply. The temptation was too great not to. The magic in the air, both past and present, was a heady sensation, and she closed her eyes in ecstasy as wave after wave of power washed over her.

"What is this?" she asked in a husky, hushed voice. "It's, for lack of a better word, orgasmic."

"Isn't it?" His amused tone caused her lids to snap open.

"You brought me here to do what, exactly?"

"Experience your grandmother's magic. What you're feeling, or most of it, is from her. At any time, you can channel your ancestors without needing a room like this or a protective circle."

"That's what Spring told me earlier." Brenna stared, astounded. "I can't believe any of this is real. All this power belongs to me?"

"In a way. It's always available should you need it. And I'm going to show you how to tap into it."

Excited for the first time in forever, she pressed her hands to her chest to keep her pounding heart inside. "Are you sure I'm not dreaming? Like, should I pinch myself?"

He laughed. "Not in the least."

"You have this much magic all on your own, always, don't you?"

"I do." A shuttered look fell across his face. "But I've had over two hundred years to learn to use it, Brenna. You, on the other hand, need to learn moderation lest the Siren get the upper hand."

"You told me I could control her."

"And you can, but you can never truly let your guard down with her around this." He waved his hand to encompass the room. "Remember, she's a thief. She'll steal magic, love, and life, if she can."

"Life?" Dread made her sick to her stomach. She thought of Parker. "How can she steal life?"

He narrowed his dark eyes. "You know I can tune in to your thoughts, don't you?"

She nodded, trying desperately to keep her mind blank. But the harder she tried, the more she failed, and thoughts of her former boyfriend's death flooded her mind.

"Who was Parker Harris?" Damian's question was flat and ominous in its delivery.

"A boy I knew in college. We only went out for six weeks."

"And?"

She swallowed down her uncomfortableness and strove for honesty. "It culminated in a one-night stand."

"And he died."

She gave a single nod of confirmation, though she doubted she needed to.

"By you."

"I didn't think so at the time," she croaked. "I was told it was an aneurism."

"And how long after sex did this 'aneurism' take place?"

"A week."

The Aether's expression cleared. "Then you didn't do it."

Her shoulders sagged as she pressed a hand to her abdomen and took huge gulping breaths, relieved she'd not inadvertently murdered anyone. "How can you be sure?"

"Had your Siren drained him dry, he'd have died within twenty-four hours. And if he was left alive and was pining away for you, it would've taken him much longer. Besides, you didn't turn into a Succubus, so there was no intent."

"Wait! Back up. *Pining away for me?* What the heck does that mean? Men can pine away for a woman? That's a real thing?"

"It is for you."

Brenna scoffed. "Trust me, no man has ever pined away for me. Until tonight, I was an ugly-ass duckling with no pining prospects."

Damian's lips quirked, but he did her the courtesy of not laughing in her face. "Well, you're a stunner now, Brenna Sullivan. Have a look."

He withdrew a black velvet cloth from a wall mirror, and she nearly choked when she saw her reflection. The others had told her about her transformation, but she hadn't had time to check herself out. It had seemed odd to her that Alastair didn't have any mirrors in the main rooms of his home, but she'd just assumed he wasn't given to vanity. It occurred to her now that the Aether had none in his main rooms either.

"What is with the lack of mirrors in your home, and why do you keep this one covered?"

"Protection. To avoid letting others have a window into my inner sanctum."

"Another witch can use your mirror to see you?" And really, why was she surprised? By now, nothing should shock her.

"With the proper spell and a whole lot of power, they could. Not many are that strong, but why take the chance?"

That she could understand. The less opportunity for failure, the better. "Gran used to say, 'set yourself up for success, Brenna.'"

"Your gran was wise beyond her years," he said warmly.

"You loved her. I can feel it."

"I did. But she loved another."

Brenna scoffed. "I find *that* hard to believe. Who wouldn't pick you if they could?"

He laughed. "You're wonderful for my ego."

"Like that needs stroking. Look at *yourself* in that mirror, Mr. Dethridge."

Moving to stand beside her, he didn't look at himself, but at her. "I don't see what others see, Brenna. I see the inner soul, and mine's not clean. That's my gift and my curse."

"But you said I was a stunner."

"I did, and so you are. I should clarify." He tapped his index finger on the mirror and began to trace her outline. The image reflected back at her transformed, showing one woman superimposed on another. Both were freaking gorgeous.

"Who is the other woman?"

"You are. That's your inner self. And before you ask, not your Siren. *You.*"

"That's what you see?"

"Yes."

"But not if I was evil?"

"No. That inner self would be a lot less attractive, and

depending on the level of darkness, flat-out hideous."

She shook her head in wonder. "So all that growly talk just now, that was posturing on your part, to scare me into doing the right thing?"

He grinned, and Brenna caught her breath.

"You catch on quickly, my dear."

"Yeah, you're going to need to not do that." She gestured with a swirl of her finger toward the lower half of his face. "That packs a punch."

Again, he laughed.

"Thank you for showing me all this, Mr. Dethridge."

"Call me Damian. And I have one more gift for you." Opening an antique cabinet, he withdrew a square object covered in a black satin cloth and handed it to her. "From your grandmother."

"Gran? She gave you this to give to me?" Brenna's heart spasmed, and she felt a physical ache.

"Not personally. After she passed away, I received a package from her lawyer. There was a note inside to give this to you on your thirtieth birthday, or before if you came to seek my help first."

"She knew I'd eventually escape Aunt Odessa," she said quietly.

"I imagine she did."

When Brenna made no move to uncover her treasure, Damian reached forward and drew back the cloth for her. The box was jewel encrusted and ancient. The filigree pattern connected the myriad of gemstones and created a breathtaking tree of life.

"Wow!"

"I've seen many beautiful keepsakes in my life, but this one is by far the most incredible. It's the oldest as well. And believe me, I know old," he said dryly.

Brenna smiled as he'd intended. Fingering the clasp, she

glanced up at him. "Should I open it?"

"Here's probably the best place for it."

Nodding, she set the box on the closest surface and lifted the lid. The brilliant light nearly seared her retinas, and Brenna threw up her hands to protect her eyes. The instant the light died down to a soft glow, she peeked through her fingers. Inside, there were jewelry pieces with tags indicating who they'd belonged to and dating them from every century. A few rolled parchments were secured with ribbons, and a single key on a string tempted her to slip it around her neck, even though she didn't know what it was for. Something told her it was important if her grandmother had passed it on.

But the real treasure was Gran's journal. The sight of that journal brought burning moisture to Brenna's eyes. She remembered the many times she'd crept from bed to find her grandmother secreted away in her room, pen in hand, and gazing out over the darkened landscape. The heart-wrenching unhappiness on Gran's face had made Brenna sad. And the one time she'd questioned Doreen, she'd been shooed back to bed with a smile and a kiss, making her believe it was all imagined.

"She left me her journal," Brenna said in wonder. "I've always wondered what had happened to it. I thought I imagined her writing in it."

"It's possible there are things in there not fit for a child to read."

"I would imagine so." With reverence, she lifted the book and ran her fingertips over the top. "Do you think she wrote about you in here?"

"Perhaps. But those scrolls will tell you what you need to access your abilities. Read them carefully, Brenna."

"I want to read what Gran wrote before I make any rash future decisions, Damian. Do you think that's possible?"

"Of course. You're welcome to use my study."

She followed him from the ceremony chamber, settled into

a comfy chair by the hearth, and tucked her legs under her as he secured the door to his private room. "Will you tell the others they don't have to wait for me? They can go about their day."

He gave her a half smile and a nod, then exited.

Brenna muffled a yawn as she opened the journal. She needed answers, and now was not the time for sleep.

*My dearest Brenna...*

She pressed a hand to her mouth to hold back a startled cry. All those years, Gran had been writing this journal for *her*! Her fatigue quickly passed, and a wave of nostalgia and longing hit her with every word she read. Soon she was completely engrossed.

---

"Right this way."

Damian opened a doorway to the most magnificent studio Eoin had ever set foot in. The floor-to-ceiling windows on three full walls of the room allowed sunlight to stream and provided a view of the landscape that sang to his artist's soul.

"'Tis grand, it is. I've never seen its like."

And indeed, he hadn't. Easels and blank canvases were placed strategically at every window. Beside the easels were curved tables with clean brushes in various sizes. Paints of every shade of every color were resting in their labeled bins in a custom holder mounted to the wall.

"Have I died and gone to the Otherworld, then?"

The Aether laughed. "No, Mr. O'Malley. This is very real. I promise." He paused a moment, then continued on a more serious vein. "Vivian used to have a love of art. Before Sabrina came along, I could always find her in here, happily sketching or painting away. Her preferred medium was watercolor, but she occasionally dabbled in oils or acrylics."

There was a quality in Damian's voice that caught Eoin's notice. He gave the man a sharp glance. "She doesn't paint anymore?"

With a small shrug and a dismissive smile, Damian changed the subject. "The place is at your disposal while you wait for Brenna. I imagine she'll be a while yet."

"Sure, and can I ask ya a question?"

"You just did."

Eoin snorted. "Another, then."

"You'd like to know if Brenna will give into the lure of her Siren and possibly turn to a Succubus? I can't answer that, Eoin. Only time can. But if she's as alike Doreen as I suspect, she'll manage just fine."

"Did all the men in the Sullivan women's lives meet an early end?"

Damian strolled to the windows and peered out over his estate. "You don't miss much, do you?"

Eoin remained quiet, awaiting the answer he suspected he already knew and was dreading.

"Most did. In fact, they all did. No one truly knows why." Damian faced him, his expression curious. "Are you willing to give up what could potentially be a long life for Brenna's love?"

The Aether's question rolled about in his mind, and Eoin didn't have an answer. He cared about Brenna, desired her as he hadn't any woman before her. But love? He couldn't say he was there yet. And he certainly couldn't sentence himself to an early demise for a woman he wasn't one hundred percent committed to.

"Decide before you break her heart, Mr. O'Malley. Brenna has had enough heartache to last her two lifetimes."

After Damian left him to his own devices, Eoin picked up a piece of charcoal and began to sketch. His mind drifted to Brenna as he'd first seen her, across the gallery, desperate to fit in, but not managing to. She'd hovered on the fringes of the crowd, smiling and nodding shyly at any patrons who bothered to notice her, all the while staying attuned to Odessa, ready to answer every time the woman beckoned. Even then, Eoin was hypnotized by those wide, uncertain aquamarine eyes, the color of the Tenerife Sea where it meets the shore.

*"Are you willing to give up what could potentially be a long life for Brenna's love?"*

The Aether's pointed question haunted him. And with each line drawn, each contour shaded, the answer clarified for Eoin.

*Yes.*

Yes, he was more than willing to give up a potentially long life for Brenna's love. Because what was life without someone to share it with? He hadn't realized he was truly lonely until that exact second. Hadn't realized the life he led to that point was lacking in any way. He'd had his art, the one thing that always fed the hole in his heart that his parents had left. Bridget had tried to fill the gap, but only creating masterpieces could.

*Until Brenna.*

Oddly, other than to capture her on canvas, he hadn't once thought about his artwork or the upcoming project he'd been commissioned to do since he hired her at the gallery opening. He'd been consumed with her, with protecting her, and with the need to get her into his bed.

As the hours passed and he brought her to life with charcoal and a paintbrush, the uncertainty surrounding his feelings came into focus. He loved her. And based on the number of sketches he just finished, he'd been obsessed for a long while. Each and every one was based on a specific moment over the last four years, from the first instant he'd met her until now. With each, he could describe in detail what she'd been doing and where.

*He loved Brenna.*

# CHAPTER 21

*A*s Brenna closed the cover of Gran's journal on her final words, she gave in to the sobs she'd been holding back since she discovered the book was her grandmother's love letter directly to her. She hugged it to her chest and cried for all she'd lost: Gran, her mother, her father, who by all accounts had been a kind man, and for Eoin, who Brenna knew she had to give up.

It wasn't as if she truly had him. Desire and love were two totally different beasts. As was the Siren inside her that would kill him the first chance it got. Gran had documented how men cursed to love their kind had shorter life expectancies, confirming what Brenna had already learned. No one could say exactly why, but Gran had her suspicions, which she'd noted. It seemed the Fates always elected to give those poor souls an untimely and grizzly demise.

And Brenna couldn't sentence Eoin to such a ghastly end. If history was any judge, he'd be lucky to make it to forty, and it would kill Brenna to see so beautiful a soul snuffed out that young. For Eoin, she could be strong. For love, she would sacrifice.

With the edge of her sleeve, she scrubbed her tears from the front cover of the journal, taking the time to polish the soft red leather. Somewhere along the way, while she'd sat engrossed in reading, some thoughtful person had brought her tea and tissues without her being aware, and she used the latter now to dry her eyes and blow her nose.

"I love you, Gran," she said aloud. "I wish you were here. I miss you so flipping much."

*"I miss you, too, my darling girl."*

Fearful of losing control of her bladder, Brenna crossed her legs and inched her head around to the right to see the spirit of her gran sitting serenely in a chair by the main door.

"I've lost my fucking mind," Brenna whispered.

*"Don't swear, Brenna Marie!"* Gran scolded with a narrowed-eyed glare.

Frozen to the spot, Brenna could only stare. Only Gran could affect that look and tone. "You're really here, aren't you? How is that possible?"

A warm smile lit Gran's face, and her eyes crinkled with amusement. *"You conjured me, darling."*

"But how?"

*"You wished for me. And like Damian said and I informed you in my journal, you have the power to call your ancestors to you at any time."*

"I can always talk to you this way?"

*"Yes."*

"I suppose if I have to give up Eoin, having you again is the next best thing," Brenna said on a soft sob.

*"Why would you have to give him up, darling?"*

"Aunt Odessa cursed us, and even if she hadn't, according to you"—she held up the journal—"the men we love have extremely short lives."

*"That's not a reason to shun love, Brenna Marie. It's a reason to embrace it."*

"He deserves to have a long, happy life, Gran. To create his incredible art and fall in love and have children if he wants to. To see those children grow to adulthood."

The compassion on her grandmother's face nearly broke Brenna. *"So do you, my darling girl."*

"But I won't, will I? I could give in to the darkness, and any child of mine runs the risk of turning into a Succubus like nearly all the women in our family before her." She inhaled a shuddering breath. "Should I give my power over to the Aether, end all this here and now? I thought I might want to keep it, but I'm unsure now."

*"Only you can decide, but as you now know, your mother didn't survive the process. You will need to weigh that into your decision-making."* By her tone, Gran relayed she didn't believe it was a wise idea, and Brenna had to wonder if it was the worry of her death or that she wanted Brenna to continue as she was, magical powers intact.

"Aunt Odessa really is an evil bi—uh, witch, isn't she?"

*"In this case, I'll allow bitch. And yes, she is. Or rather, the monster inside her is."* Gran sighed and rose to her feet to cross and look out over the expanse of manicured lawn. *"I helped her maintain her youthful vitality, feeding her small bits of my magic to keep her Succubus happy. I didn't know she was trying to syphon off your power and was still taking the lives of others at the same time. A little was never going to be enough for her."*

"You wrote that you intended to confront her and that you worried she'd try to kill you so she could continue as she was. That was your last entry." Brenna swallowed hard. "She did, didn't she?"

*"Yes. I woke with a feeling that I needed to check on you, and I caught her performing an enchantment over your bed. Even as a young girl, your abilities were great, and that power called to her monster."* Gran turned and faced her. *"She was stronger than I was,*

*both physically and magically, because I'd let her bleed me almost dry that morning."*

"Oh, Gran!" Pressing her palm to her breast, Brenna shook her head and swallowed down her grief. "Why didn't she kill me, too?"

*"You are her battery, darling. To kill you would be to slowly kill herself."*

"I don't understand. Wouldn't she just continue to seduce..." A lightbulb went off in Brenna's head, and with it came understanding. "Ah, I get it now. She's aging. As a woman of her advanced years, she can't lure the same quantity of people to her bed."

*"Smart girl."*

"It's why she snuck into Eoin's hotel room, isn't it? To sing and steal while he was in a dream state."

*"Yes. A tactic she employed many times, I discovered... after our purchase of the hotel chains."*

"And the dream I had of you that night. That was really you waking me and urging me to save Eoin from her *seduction*. You knew how I felt about him."

*"Yes."*

"I have to stop her. Permanently."

Gran's face scrunched up in consternation. *"Let the Aether do it. You stay as far away from her as you can, Brenna Marie."*

"He can't be the one to clean up my messes, Gran. If I'm the more powerful of the two of us, Odessa and me, then I should be the one to end her reign of terror and death." Firm resolve hardened Brenna's heart. "It's time she paid for what she's done."

*"Brenna—"*

The click of the doorknob disengaging heralded a newcomer. Brenna felt the youthful wash of magic as the door cracked open, and she knew who was on the other side. "Hello, Sabrina."

The little girl grinned as she poked her head around the door and pressed a finger to her lips. She crept inside, acknowledged Gran by the window with a smile, then said, "Papa will be mad if—oh, hi, Papa!"

The door was pushed back the rest of the way, and Damian stood with a forbidding expression and arms crossed over his chest. "Go ahead and finish your sentence, my love. Papa will be mad if what?"

Hands tucked firmly behind her back, Sabrina conjured a bowl and spoon. The metal clanked against the porcelain rim as she lifted it and showed him. "Papa will be mad if we eat ice cream in his office."

He narrowed his eyes. "Sabrina Dethridge."

The warning tone made Brenna's stomach flip. How the little girl's unrepentant grin remained under the censure of her father's stare was a mystery.

Gran crossed the room and stood behind Sabrina, a bitter-sweet smile on her face. *"She's a pistol, Damian,"* she said softly. *"And exactly what you deserve."*

One dark brow shot up, and his lips twisted in wry humor. "A double-edged sword."

Gran laughed, and the sound was girly and sweet. Brenna caught a glimpse of the feelings they'd once shared.

*"I have to go. Take care of my Brenna, Damian. She's a good girl, like your Sabrina."*

Dark eyes burning with deep emotion, most of it sad, he nodded and watched until Gran faded away.

"Tell Brenna what you intended to tell her, Beastie, then she and I need to get to work."

"I didn't want her to be sad, Papa," Sabrina said in a solemn little voice, and for once, the mischievous sparkle was gone. "I really was bringing her ice cream, like I brought her tea and tissues."

Brenna's heart swelled at the girl's thoughtfulness. No one

other than Eoin had cared about Brenna's comfort in a very long time. "I'm okay, Sabrina. Really." She hoped she was reassuring everyone, herself included.

"But ice cream makes everyone happy."

Brenna lifted a hand to stroke Sabrina's hair, but from the corner of her eye, she saw Damian step forward. His instinctive response to protect his daughter from her stung, but Brenna understood the reason for his reaction. She dropped her arm and managed a sweet smile. "I'm sure it does, Sabrina. And thanks for thinking of me, but your dad is right, and we have a few more things to discuss."

"Okay, but don't give away your power, Miss Brenna. You'll need it."

"Can you tell me why?" Great balls of fire, she wanted some direction. If she stayed on this freaking seesaw of indecision a moment longer, she'd lose her marbles and likely throw up from the nerves eating at her stomach.

Sabrina's wise eyes, so eerily similar to her father's, were older than a child's should be. "Papa tells me not to give away the plot. He said if everyone knew what was coming, there would be no wonderful surprises in life."

Brenna stopped short of snorting as she cast Damian an exasperated look. "He did, did he?"

Humor lit his face, but he remained quiet.

"So no hints allowed?"

"For once, my daughter has felt the need to keep her visions to herself. It's a miracle in and of itself." He took the bowl from Sabrina's hands and created a hot fudge sundae with all the trimmings, then handed it back to her. "Your kindness has made me proud, my love. Thank you."

"The necklace is the only way forward, Papa," Sabrina said absently as she shoved a heaping serving of goodness into her mouth. She paused at the door and swallowed, a heavy frown pulling at her brows. "Uncle Alex's brother will want to steal it when he finds out about it, but don't let him get it, Miss Brenna."

With that, Sabrina shrugged and skipped out the door as if she didn't have another care in the world. And perhaps she didn't. As a child of the mighty Aether, she was loved and protected in a way Brenna never had been.

"We're not indestructible, Brenna," he said quietly, almost apologetically. "I live in fear every day that someone might get to her and steal what she has."

"Is it possible to steal an Aether's magic?" She didn't want to know for any other reason than curiosity, and she hoped it came across that way.

"Yes. Through death, a transference can occur."

The idea that someone might attempt to murder his beautiful daughter caused Brenna to catch her breath. True evil existed in the world; her aunt was proof of that, but that it might touch Sabrina hurt Brenna's soul. It also firmed her resolve. No one would harm any children on her watch, not if she could help it. "Then I suppose we need to defeat as many big baddies as we can so it never happens. I don't know who her Uncle Alex is, but if his brother is as dastardly as Aunt Odessa, he needs to be stopped."

"His brother is Loman O'Connor. I believe you recognize the name, if not the man. A heinous person that shouldn't still draw air." Damian rubbed the back of his neck as he contemplated her words. "You'd be willing to turn into a Succubus to stop those with wrongful intent?"

"I would prefer to find another route and forgo becoming a Succubus altogether, but if it means protecting Sabrina and those like her, then yes, I'll do what I must."

"And you know that if you do, it will be at the expense of a relationship with Mr. O'Malley?" His question sounded more like a threat.

"I suspect that relationship has been doomed from the beginning," she said with a hollow ache inside her chest.

His gaze traveled past her to someone just beyond her shoulder.

Dreading who might be there, Brenna turned to see Eoin, hands balled into fists and indignation stiffening his entire body. His furious scowl verged on frightening.

"You'd throw what we have away, Brenna? Without speaking to me first or trying to find a solution? It doesn't matter that I love ya, then?"

Her heart pinged at his declaration, but the unloved and unwanted part of her rejected that he could ever care for her.

"What do we have, Eoin?" she asked flatly. "Nothing but a newly formed work relationship, possible friendship, and a few kisses between us. You don't know me well enough to love me. And even if you did, we have the whole burning-touch situation going on."

He stalked into the room, stopping at the proper distance to ensure it wouldn't affect her. His arms came up like he wanted to embrace or strangle her, but he dropped them as quickly. "Sure, and my family's broken curses before. We can do it again."

Her heart positively ached in the face of his bravery and determination. Emotion kept the words she longed to say lodged as a solid lump in her throat.

"And I do love you, Brenna Sullivan, because I know you. Better than anyone and better than you know yourself."

With a shake of her head, she denied his claim.

"I do, love," he said achingly, barely above a whisper. "I've seen how uncomfortable you are in a crowd, but you still attend every opening so the artist showing their work feels like he or she has someone in their corner. I know that every new piece is your favorite and how you lose yourself in the wonder someone else created." His expression was raw as he gazed at her, and it was as if he'd forgotten Damian was in the room. "You have a fierce sense of right and wrong, Brenna. And despite the fact it embarrasses you so, you'll stand up for the injured party every time. Like you saved me from Odessa's monster at the hotel, and like you put yourself in her path to prevent her from latching onto Alastair."

"None of those things make me special, Eoin."

"Now there you're wrong, love, because they do. They do to *me*." He uncurled his fists and shook them out as if he'd forgotten he had clenched them. "I want to show you something. Will you come with me?"

"It won't change anything." She could never be with him without it costing his life in the end.

"I think it will."

Helplessly, she looked at Damian, silently begging him to interfere. But he stood impassive, a complete poker face, and she understood why he was the perfect judge and jury for wayward magical beings.

"Perhaps you should go, Brenna." He finally said, giving her a half smile. "You need all the facts before making up your mind."

# CHAPTER 22

*W*ith each second Brenna took to decide, Eoin died a little inside. He'd arrived at the door to hear her claim she'd do whatever it took to fight 'big baddies' to save children like Sabrina, should they require it. Sacrifice was grand and all, but she didn't need to become inhuman to do it. In fact, he suspected if she gave in to that side of her, she'd be the one Damian would annihilate to save his daughter.

Eoin lifted his gaze and met that of the Aether, and he received the confirmation he needed. Whatever it took, Eoin needed to make sure she never gave in to the call.

"Okay," she said quietly.

His relief was profound, and he wanted to grab her and kiss her. The knowledge that if he did, he'd practically fry her to a crisp kept him firmly in place.

"It's in the tower room," he said with a gesture toward the door.

A wry smile curled her lips, and she gripped a red, leather-bound book to her chest like a lifeline. "Are you sure you aren't luring me to a far-off place to lock me away?"

He said the first thing that popped into his head. "You can

be sure if I were to ever lock you away, I'd be in the room with you and we'd be throwing away the key."

The blush he loved so much tinged her smooth porcelain skin. "What is it you wish to show me?"

He turned away to hide his grin and preceded her to the stairs leading to the art studio. When they arrived at the door, he glanced back at her. "Wait ten seconds, then come into the room."

At her nod, he entered and positioned himself, perching on the edge of a window seat centered in the room, so he could watch her face when she saw his work and registered what it meant. One look at the plethora of sketches and the single painting he'd created from his favorite memory, and she'd understand what he was trying to tell her.

Her gasp was gratifying, and she pressed her hand to her throat as she moved from easel to easel. She paused in front of the painting for the longest time, but Eoin knew her process. Knew she'd take in every brushstroke, absorb every subtle coloration as it blended into another. Knew she'd come to the proper conclusion. Lifting shimmering eyes, she stared at him, lost for words.

"I see you, Brenna. I always have. You're my *moose*."

"Oh, Eoin." Her voice broke, and the tears she'd been holding back trailed one after the other down her smooth-as-silk skin.

"We can find a way to resolve this feckin' problem together. Please say you will." Uncaring of the imploring quality of his voice, he stared at her. Afraid to blink for fear she'd disappear. "Say it, love. Say you'll fight with me, for us."

"I can't." Brenna wrapped her arms around her middle the way she'd done in the past when she was forced to do something she didn't want. A self-hug, or so he tended to consider it. "I can't, Eoin. I'm sorry."

"You *can*." Straightening to his full height, he dropped his arms to his sides. "Whatever demons are at play here, whatever worries ya have, sure, and they're for another day."

"You don't understand," she cried. "Even if we were able to be together physically, you run the risk—a high risk!—of an early death. I won't be responsible for you passing before your time, Eoin. Don't ask me to. Please."

"That's a load of malarky! You don't control the lifespan of another, Brenna. That's up to the Goddess Anu and the Fates. If I'm meant to die young, that's not on you, love."

Moving her head from side to side, she looked at him as if she wanted to believe. But her doubt tore him up inside. "They all do. All the men who love a Sullivan woman."

"Give us a chance," he said, voice hoarse and as raw as his emotions. He'd never begged for anything in his life. Not since the day he'd pleaded with his father not to leave on his last business trip. Nightmares had plagued him, leading up to that fateful day, and he knew he'd never see his da again should he go, and Da hadn't returned, just like Eoin's dreams predicted.

But Eoin begged now.

For her.

*"Please."*

After what seemed a lifetime, she nodded. "If we can find a way to neutralize what's affecting us, if Damian can help protect you from my Siren, and if we can ensure you won't have an aborted lifespan, then yes."

His knees buckled, and he sat back on the sill, expelling a breath he didn't know he was holding, sagging in his relief. "Jaysus, Brenna! Ya near gave me a heart attack, ya did!"

"Those are a lot of hurdles," she reminded him.

"I'm an expert jumper."

Her response came in the form of a smile, and it lit the room to blinding. He made a mental note to recreate that on canvas, too.

"Sure, and how 'bout we go find the Aether so we can remove this fecking spell and get to shaggin'?"

"I'm down for that," she replied pertly.

A bark of laughter escaped him. Damn, he loved her saucy side.

But she made no move to leave the room, instead turning back to the portrait he'd painted.

Nerves made his fingers tingle, and he wondered what she saw. "It's not finished, but I had to show you, all the same."

"Is this truly how you saw me?"

"Yes." He studied his own work, an exact replica of what she'd looked like after the first time he kissed her in that New York pub. With her sparkling eyes full of joyous wonder and lips swollen with a hint of glistening moisture highlighting her lower lip, she looked wanton and very much in love. "And I've never seen a more beautiful sight."

"Pfft. I know the Irish enjoy their tall tales, but—"

"No, love. I'd never stretch the truth on a moment as meaningful as this."

Brenna met his serious gaze, and confusion tugged at her brow. "You really mean it. How can you when I looked like an abandoned house cat left in an alley to fend for itself?"

"You didn't. And like I told ya before, your beauty lies in your generous spirit, Brenna Sullivan."

"So if I went back to those ghastly glasses, hideous clothing, and frizzy hair, you wouldn't care?" she challenged with an arch look.

"Not one second of one day. I'm in love with *you*, not your grand new face and hot-as-feck body." He rubbed his fingers over his lips to hide his grin before saying, "But I'm not saying I wouldn't let you ride me like a cowgirl all the way to Monday, any way you wanted."

"It was Sunday."

"Aye, but today's almost over, and I want the full five days of shaggin' with ya."

Laughing, she shook her head.

*I love you, too, Eoin O'Malley.*

Her telepathy came through loud and clear, and he wanted nothing more than to storm across the room and sweep her into his arms. But there would be time enough for embracing if Damian could reverse Odessa's mischief. If indeed it *was* Brenna's aunt who had created their problem.

---

"GRAN SAID NEVER TO GIVE MY BLOOD TO ANYONE." BRENNA'S stomach was in knots. She'd been repeating that phrase like Dustin Hoffman in Rain Man for the better part of an hour. The Aether could help, but only if she offered up the one thing she shouldn't.

"It's for the amulet, and Eoin will always have it in his care," Damian explained with far more patience than she deserved at this point. "It's the only work-around I have at the moment."

"And if we show up on Odessa's feckin' door and demand she cancel her bleedin' spell? What then?" Eoin demanded, likely as frustrated as the rest of them.

Alastair had arrived with Spring after spending most of the day searching for a cure for Brenna's woes, and they were all ready to pull their hair out. Apparently, Succubus spells were close to indestructible.

"You could, and I'd gladly go with you. But Odessa is her strongest in her lair, where she can draw on her family's ancient power."

Brenna stopped pacing by the window and faced them. "But isn't her magical line and mine one and the same? Wouldn't I be able to outfight her if it came down to it?"

"You're a novice, child," Alastair said. "Even with youth and strength on your side, she's had a hundred years of craftiness on hers."

"I can't understand this level of evilness. First stealing my magic, then killing Gran—her own sister!—and now *this*? That bitch!" She pressed her head to the frosty windowpane, trying to cool down. Her temper was close to the boiling point, and she was ready to do battle with Odessa regardless of the outcome. "Okay. I'll give you what you need."

"Brenna."

She locked eyes with Eoin.

"You'll be makin' yourself vulnerable, love. Tread carefully here. No decisions need be made today, yeah?"

"I can't explain it, but I feel like our time is running out. Like if we don't do this now, we may never be able to."

He appeared troubled by her words, running his hands through his hair and causing his bracelets to click together. The sound of bead against bead against metal was loud in the stillness of the room. "Jaysus. And what if we call Ronan Fuckin' O'Connor? He's a Guardian now. Can't that scut do somethin'?"

"A Guardian isn't stronger than the Aether, son," Alastair explained. "The two can work in conjunction with their magic and, yes, easily defeat a Succubus in the process, but to break her spell, she'd need to die."

"I'm all for that," Brenna inserted heatedly. "Not that I'm bloodthirsty or anything, but she's done enough damage to last a lifetime."

Eoin grinned in the wake of her declaration. "Sure, and she's angered the wrong woman, she has."

"Damned straight!" She clenched her fists, ready to teleport to Odessa's house and end this nightmare. Well, she would if she knew how to teleport, that was.

Alastair rose to his feet and crossed to Brenna. He took his time studying her face, making her wonder what he saw. "I understand your rage, my dear. More than anyone here, I think. But trust the process. Odessa Sullivan will get hers when the time is right."

"She killed my gran," Brenna retorted, still reeling from what she'd discovered about the events of that day so long ago.

"And she'll pay. I promise you, she will."

"How can you be so sure, Alastair? If she's so hard to defeat, how can you know?"

"Because she won't be able to syphon your magic any longer once Damian finishes your amulet. It will protect you and deflect any future spells." He tugged at his cuffs and gave a small sniff, as if the thought of Odessa's treachery was odious. "Without a large infusion, she's powerless and will be unable to manipulate or steal from anyone else."

Left with the impression he would see to Odessa's demise personally, Brenna heaved a sigh of surrender. "What do we need to do to complete this amulet?"

"I already have, with the help of your grandmother's instruction. There's just one missing part." The Aether crossed to her and opened a black velvet box to display a silver disc, ringed with three concentric circles stamped with various runes. In the center rested a glass dome. Another silver circle with a thin lip sat as if waiting expectantly for her single drop of blood.

"Gran? But…" Brenna shook her head and threw her hands up. "Never mind. I can't keep up."

"She witnessed your tender scene in the studio and oversaw the construction of my fail-safe charm." Damian sounded a bit harried. "She reappeared to me to say I'm to reinforce the glass so no one can destroy it or I'd be subjected to her wrath."

"Sounds like Gran." Taking a deep breath, she lifted her chin. "Okay, how do you go about extracting what you need? Pin prick?"

He laughed.

Brenna felt the sound of his rich amusement down to her rosy recess and had to muffle a squeak. Suppressing the urge to fan her insta-flamed face, she said, "Okay, nothing so easy as that, then."

"Tell me. Do you remember ever cutting yourself? A scraped knee, perhaps?"

Frowning, she thought back. Never once had she had any type of open wound. "How is that possible?"

"Your skin is practically impenetrable."

"Practically?"

Damian tried not to smile, he truly did, but he lost what Brenna knew was a hard-fought battle. "If one were to dip a knife into a toxin after coating the tip with a female cat's vaginal excretion during a heat cycle, then yes, they could score your skin or stab you."

*"What?"* She gagged. "Of all the revolting, unsanitary ways to... Gah! Tell me you're joking. Please!"

"Afraid not."

"Which twisted deity thought of *that* shit?" After a second gag, she continued her rant. "Tell me this isn't common knowledge. Tell me I don't have a future of fighting off cat-twat-knife-wielding haters out for my blood. Because if that's the case, I'm out!"

Unrestrained laughter from behind the Aether had her pushing him aside to glare at Eoin. "What part of this do you find funny, you... you *jerk?*"

"Jerk? Sure, and after you said *shit* and *cat-twat-knife-wielding haters?*" He sucked in a breath and laughed harder until tears were rolling down his face. "Ah, Brenna... Of all the problems we have, you're worried about a cat's natural cycle takin' ya down?"

From where she stood ten feet away, she pointed at his head. "I hope you step on a Lego!"

A polypropylene bag of Legos dropped at his feet from thin air, and they both sucked in a breath.

*"Holy spitballs!"*

Again, Eoin laughed until he turned an unhealthy shade of red.

"If you are going to laugh at me every time we have an argument..." She squinted her eyes and compressed her lips.

"It may have been 'spitballs' that did it," Alastair murmured with a valiant attempt at a straight face.

"I hate you all," she muttered as she shoved open the doors and strode out to the garden.

*"Holy spitballs, love. That display of temper was hot as feck."*

*"Get out of my head, turd!"* She held up the middle finger as she marched toward the rose garden in the center of the lawn.

# CHAPTER 23

"She's had a lot of new information thrown her way," Damian said in what Eoin assumed was a way of excusing Brenna's temper.

"Yeah, and she's been suppressed for her entire life." Eoin shrugged and grinned. "She was bound to blow, and what a grand sight her explosion was."

Spring giggled. "Legos. Who'd have thought that was her worse insult?"

"Don't be forgettin' she called me a jerk and, in her mind, a turd."

Alastair stole a glance at Damian and murmured, "Cat-twat-knife-wielding haters."

The two men broke their stoic façades, laughing until their sides practically split as they held their stomachs and leaned against one another.

"Sure, and you're having the craic at me beloved Brenna," Eoin said, trying to keep a straight face and failing miserably, sending the other three occupants of the living room over the edge to hilarity.

"Holy... spitballs," Spring said between great wheezing breaths.

"Tell me you're not having a go at that poor girl's expense."

They all jerked to attention at the sound of a provocative feminine voice from the doorway. The woman bore an uncanny resemblance to Brenna. Belatedly, Eoin registered the accent was different than hers, more southern United States, based on the people he'd encountered in the art world.

Damian was the first to let his guard down, and he strode to the door, hand extended. "Narissa. I'd hoped you'd come."

"When you're summoned by the Aether, sugar, you hustle your butt to comply." Her "sugar" sounded more like "shoog-ha," and the slow honeyed way she spoke made men want to open doors for her and tip their hat.

"You summoned her? What the feck for?" Eoin demanded, shaking off any gentlemanly thoughts toward the woman. For sure, she had to be related to Brenna. He just didn't know how. But if the woman knew of Brenna's existence and knew of Odessa's penchant for stealing magic, then she lacked compassion in her heart. She should've never left Brenna with Odessa for all these years.

"And who is this indignant hunk of hotness?" Her salon-groomed brows began to meet but shot up as her eyes widened. "Oh! Eoin O'Malley, as I live and breathe. The famous artist here, in little ol' England."

Shoving aside his flattered inner peacock, he crossed his arms and glared, refusing to be charmed.

Amusement lit her blue-green eyes, and his heart flipped at how alike she appeared to Brenna when she found something funny.

"To help Brenna," Damian said, answering Eoin's initial question.

Though the woman hesitated, it was only for an instant, and she continued smoothly as if she didn't have a care in the world. "And who's Brenna, sugar? Am I supposed to guess?" She used her Siren's voice to soothe and scold as she sauntered into the room, hips swaying, a sexy pendulum that drew the eye like a bee to a pollen-packed garden.

Shaking his head to dislodge her unintentional spell, Eoin looked at Damian. How did the man remain unaffected? Was Eoin more susceptible because of her resemblance to the woman he loved?

Damian met his gaze and smiled. *"Sirens. They're unintentionally seductive, and the older they are, the more powerful they become."*

*"Feck."*

"I believe you're going to need fortification for this, Narissa." The Aether told her as he walked to the sideboard. "Still prefer Tennessee bourbon?" At her nod, he poured her a drink and handed it off. He waited until she swallowed a sip, then said, "Brenna, your niece. Clarissa's daughter. I believe you remember her, no?"

Narissa paled, and her gaze darted around like a trapped animal. She recovered remarkably well, lifting her chin and plastering on a wide smile. "Bless your heart, Damian. You must be mistaken. I'm an only child. You've known me for years."

All humor left the Aether's face.

Eoin's unease made itself known as a pounding heart and in his temples. It was never good when Damian Dethridge lost his indulgent courtesy.

"Are you seriously going to stand there and lie to me, Narissa Wells?" Damian leaned closer to her. "Or should I say Narissa *Sullivan?*"

The tumbler dropped from her hands, but the Aether had the reflexes of a jungle cat and froze the downward trajectory of the glass long enough to catch it and any liquid that escaped.

"I've always known who you are, my dear. I simply chose to

let you keep your secrets because it suited me at the time." He returned the drink to her. "But now, I need you to be a Sullivan. Odessa needs to be stopped, and your niece needs your help."

"I left my past behind for a reason," she said coldly. "I've no intention of walking back into that viper pit. Sullivans aren't a normal breed of witches."

"There's only one viper—Odessa. And she's been left free to syphon your niece's magic to fuel her Succubus. Brenna's innocent in all of this."

Narissa swallowed and fought to maintain her composure as she met Damian's dark, forbidding eyes. "Mama's... *gone?*"

"About eighteen years ago," Brenna said from the doorway, and her voice soft but thick with resentment. "You must be my mother's twin. Gran wrote that she always believed you were still alive."

In slow increments, Narissa turned to face her. One hand came up to cover her heart, and her face scrunched as she attempted to control whatever she was experiencing at the sight of her only niece standing in the opening to the terrace. "Lawdy, you look just like your mama, but I imagine you're nothing alike if you're under the protection of the Aether."

"I didn't know her. She died when I was a baby. Gran was all I had until I was about eight." Brenna made a face. "Well, Aunt Odessa, too, I suppose, but like Damian said, she's a viper."

Narissa dropped her hand, and a thoughtful expression settled on her exquisite visage. "Looks like you turned out okay, honey. Why do you need my help?"

"I didn't know you were still alive until I stepped through those doors. And it's doubtful I do need you." Walking the rest of the way into the room, Brenna shut the door and stalked to the sideboard. Without bothering to ask permission, she poured two fingers of the bourbon Damian had left out.

"What's your plan, sir?" she asked, facing the Aether after gulping half her drink.

"I didn't think you'd want to go the cat-excretion route," he deadpanned.

Spring giggled as Alastair coughed into his hand, the sound a poorly disguised bark of laughter.

Eoin had a hard time keeping his own humor in check as Brenna's lips twitched.

"If it doesn't involve cat twats, I'm in," she said with a toast of her glass.

Her trustingness of everyone rankled a bit, and Eoin put the brakes on that runaway train. "Sure, and we'll need to hold up for a minute, yeah? I'm not after putting my faith in a woman I've never met and who admittedly doesn't care for her family. Brenna can take care of herself just fine, she can."

She turned shining eyes on him, and her wide smile was nothing short of glorious. *"Thank you for believing in me."*

*"Always, love. Always."*

*"You two are like sweet tea on a hot day. Simply delicious."*

They both startled and stared at Narissa, mouths agape.

"Family," she said with a gesture of her finger between her and Brenna. "It's a Siren thing."

A thoughtful expression crossed Brenna's face, and she cocked her head. "Really? At what distance? Could we do it with Aunt Odessa?"

"We're an ocean away, honey. I'd just pick up a phone if I were you."

"It's doubtful she'd answer," Brenna said with a grimace. "We didn't separate on friendly terms."

Narissa's smile didn't reach her eyes, and her tone was droll when she said, "I like you more and more."

"Doubtful, but that's fine." Lifting her chin, Brenna said, "Gran provided me with the tools to make it. Both in advice and with my inheritance. I'll be fine without family."

Everything inside Eoin rose up in denial of her claim. *He* was her family, as were his siblings. "You have family, love. You have the O'Malleys."

"And, since the Thornes are related to the O'Malley clan by marriage, you have us, too, child."

Eoin could've kissed Alastair for his comment, especially when Brenna's luminous smile appeared.

"Thank you, both. I'm honored to have two such wonderful people in my corner."

"Eight," Spring said with an index-finger wave.

"Eight?"

"Where I go, so does Knox. Then there's my mom, Damian, Vivian, and Sabrina..." Spring shrugged. "Easily eight."

Brenna laughed, and it was pure joy. Everyone in the room smiled at the rapturous sound—even Narissa. "I really love you guys."

It occurred to Eoin that this was probably the first time she'd experienced true friendship and caring, and it near broke his fecking heart. Narissa met his gaze with a considering one of her own, and he realized she'd picked up on his thoughts. He wasn't sure how comfortable he was with anyone other than Brenna being able to hear him.

"May I speak with you in private, sugar?" she asked him.

"No."

Her dark brows shot to her hairline, and she appeared taken aback by his rudeness.

"Sure, and anything you plan to be saying, you can say in front of Brenna and the others."

Narissa rose to the challenge. "Fine. I intended to warn you away from loving a Siren. Men who care about women like us have short lives. And bless your heart, you seem to be head over heels."

"He's been warned, Narissa, and I'd appreciate if you didn't interfere with my life," Brenna snapped. The crackle of energy in the air popped like static electricity through clothes without a dryer sheet.

"You got it, honey. I've work to see to. You have a nice life, ya hear."

Narissa sashayed her way toward the hall door, but Damian's next words halted her forward movement.

"We're not done here, Ms. Sullivan. Not by a long shot."

She froze, her back to the room, and the stiffness in her shoulders told Eoin she was prepared to fight should she have to. This worldly woman had been in the trenches and lived to tell the tale. He made a quick decision that might impact them all. He changed his tune.

"Please," he said quietly as he approached her. "Don't be failing Brenna when she needs ya the most."

Her shoulders dropped, and she faced him, her arrogance dissolving in the face of his pleading. "She doesn't want my help, Mr. O'Malley. There's nothing I can do if she refuses."

"Your aunt began syphoning off her magic when she was just a wee girl. Your mam died trying to protect her, and she failed in the trying." He glanced back at Brenna, and all the love he felt for her was in his admiring stare. "Odessa treated her like a fecking unpaid servant, then cut her off without a bleedin' penny. And when Brenna finally managed to escape the woman's clutches, Odessa cursed her with a spell. Cursed *us*."

"What spell?" Narissa demanded angrily. "Why didn't y'all tell me what she did, so I can have all the facts straight off?"

"Brenna and I can't touch. Can't be within ten feet of each other without her skin damned near burnin' from her bones."

Narissa closed her eyes, and a cynical smile curled her lips as she shook her head and snorted. "Odessa, you wily fox."

"Why do I have the feelin' you know why she did it?"

"To keep you away, sugar. Seems Odessa believes without you, Brenna has no one to turn to. She forgot about me, and she severely underestimated the Aether's level of involvement, now, didn't she?"

"So you'll help her, then?"

"Brenna? Yes. But you remember what I said before you decide to commit."

"I'm already committed, all the same."

"Then you're a fool, Mr. O'Malley." She returned to Brenna's side and surprised everyone when she pulled her niece into a tight hug.

BRENNA'S EYES PRACTICALLY BULGED FROM HER HEAD, SO startled was she by Narissa's impulsive embrace. Her arms came up, and she found herself returning the hug, albeit awkwardly.

"You smell like Gran," she whispered through her surprise.

"Her shampoo recipe," Narissa said. She cleared her throat and drew back, running a thick strand of Brenna's new silky locks through her fingers before giving it a light tug. "I can teach you to make it if you'd like."

Unexpected tears burned behind Brenna's lids, and she nodded. "I would. Very much."

"You should know your mama was good once. A little on the wild side, Clarissa was, but good at heart." Releasing Brenna, Narissa smoothed her dress down her hips, and her expression returned to what Brenna assumed was the haughty face she presented to the outside world. "Clare-bear changed when she lost your daddy."

"But I thought you left home long before she met him."

"I did, but I couldn't completely cut ties with my only sister. We'd kept each others' secrets from birth. Walking away from your twin is harder than most people would imagine, honey. Be glad you never had to do it."

"It was hard enough leaving Aunt Odessa, and she was a miserable wench."

A wry smile kicked up one side of Narissa's mouth. "Maybe you do understand." She gestured to Eoin with her thumb over her shoulder. "You know you have to let him go."

"I tried. But he's a bit like a tick. He sticks."

Her aunt laughed. "I suppose you could've picked someone a lot worse than Eoin O'Malley for a beau. The man is as yummy as hot cakes with blueberry syrup."

"Your accent, is it for real?"

"Mostly. Spend close to twenty years in the Deep South and you pick up their speech patterns pretty quickly."

Brenna assumed she'd done it to blend in with the locals. There was no easier way to hide than in plain sight. With a tentative smile for Narissa, she faced Damian. "Since you summoned my aunt here so we don't need to go the cat-in-heat route, how is she supposed to help?"

"Her claws are the only other thing able to pierce another Siren's skin," he told her simply. "I need her to transform."

"Say what?" Brenna looked between them. "Transform? To what?"

"Mama would warn against giving your blood away, honey. Are you sure you want to do this?"

"According to Damian, Gran's the one who instructed him on the way the amulet should be made."

With a grim expression, Narissa walked to the center of the room. "You may want to clear some of these fancy pieces before I turn."

A single elegant wave of the Aether's hand moved the furniture to rest against the interior walls. "I'll need to bind your vocal cords first, Narissa. You're too powerful otherwise."

"You think I'd dare seduce y'all while under the Siren's charge?" Narissa's laughter was bitter. "I spent my entire life keeping my natural instincts at bay. I can promise you it's not likely I'll give in to the urge tonight."

"Nevertheless, the combined magic in this room is likely greater than any previous temptation you've experienced."

"True enough, sugar. Carry on with your bindin' spell."

He stepped in front of her and closed his hands around her neck, and for one heart-pounding second, he looked to be strangling her. Brenna started forward, only to be stopped by Spring.

"He's got this, Brenna. Damian knows what he's doing."

"Sing for me, Narissa."

Brenna opened her mouth, but closed it as quickly, realizing he meant her aunt.

The melody spilling from Narissa's lips called to Brenna's Siren, and she trilled inside her, struggling against Brenna's hold. She locked gazes with Narissa, and the subtle warning was there. Her look urged caution and told Brenna to keep her other self contained.

A strangled sound cut off Narissa's song, and she touched a hand to her throat in horrified wonder. Her mouth moved, but no words emerged.

"I promise to restore your gift. *After*." Damian backed away. "Please continue."

Lips compressed, she gave him a solemn, respectful nod and closed her eyes.

# CHAPTER 24

*N*arissa's transformation was horrifying and fantastical at the same time. Her skin shimmered before taking on an iridescent glow many women tried to achieve with makeup and glimmering highlighters. Her already long, bouncy curls came to life and swirled around her as the thick locks grew in length and encircled her body. The rich aqua color of her irises turned lighter and took on shades of lavender and green. The new, colorful swirling was barely discernible but continuous. The overall effect made it seem as if her eyes pulsed with new light. Her full lips darkened to a seductive berry red.

But it was the wings that shocked Eoin to hell and back. They tore through the back of her dress, appearing from her shoulder blades and expanding in size until they spanned a ten-foot width, and even then, they didn't appear to be fully extended. The wings themselves were a pearlized translucent, and the indigo veining running through each fold contained a faint pulsating light. As added appendages went, they were breathtaking and unreal.

Eoin looked at Brenna, but her gaze was locked on her aunt

in wide-eyed wonder. Her expression was frozen in her surprise, with her mouth slightly agape. Did she realize *she* could do this with the proper instruction? Oddly, the idea of her transformation into a different creature didn't turn him off. Contrarily, it fueled his artistic drive to see and draw her this way by candlelight. She'd be ethereal and magnificent in the nude with her wings used as burlesque fans, hinting at what lay underneath.

When Brenna finally turned her head in his direction, her relief came through their bond. She'd correctly read that he wasn't repulsed by what she had the potential to do but, instead, was intrigued by what could be.

He grinned and winked, prompting her answering smile.

They broke eye contact when Spring squealed excitedly.

A quick check of the room showed Narissa transforming yet again. Her graceful fingers became elongated, and amethyst nails took the place of the tips. The claw had to be easily four inches in length and another two in width. Those fecking things could rip out a man's throat with a flick of her wrist.

Narissa focused on Brenna and sent her a silent communication, which Eoin was also privy to.

*"This is what you can become, but it will drain you if you don't replenish your magic before shifting to your Siren a second time."*

He wanted to know how she was to accomplish the replenishing, but Brenna nodded slowly as she inched forward, one hand raised. *"May I?"*

After receiving a single nod of permission, she ran her fingertips over Narissa's face, wings, and fingers. "It's incredible, Narissa," she said aloud, awed. *"You're* incredible."

The Siren smiled, and Eoin felt an answering pulse in his groin. Disturbed by the sensation, he shot a questioning look at Damian.

"You and the others should go to the farthest corners of the room, Mr. O'Malley," the Aether told him in a strained voice. "You're about to experience some powerful urges."

Not caring for the sound of that, Eoin asked, "What the feck is happening?"

"Narissa's Siren is unrestrained. It will seduce who and what it can in this state."

"Brenna—"

"Is safe," Damian snapped. "Now go."

No more words of encouragement were needed for their small group, and they all hustled to the back corner of the room, away from the action.

The Aether didn't approach the woman, but he didn't back away, and the tension in his body could be felt in the suffocating air around them.

"He's trying to contain her allure to that area," Alastair explained, his voice low and shaken. "Her pull is undeniably strong."

"I want to touch her," Spring whispered as she folded her hands over her heart. "Just once."

Before Eoin could respond, Alastair latched onto her arm and urged her behind him.

"No, child. You need to resist the temptation and especially your curiosity. The Siren feeds on desires. Yours is to discover all you can about her. Never doubt they are dangerous creatures. Even if they haven't given in to the darkness, the instinct is there."

"Why take the chance?" Eoin asked angrily. "What the devil is this entire feckin' spectacle about, then?"

"Weren't you paying attention, son? Only another Siren can puncture Brenna's skin for the blood Dethridge needs." The irritation in the other man's voice slapped at Eoin, causing his skin to prickle uncomfortably.

"What's this? Are ya determined to take a poke at me?" he demanded. "Bring it!"

Alastair turned on a dime and lifted his hand. The air around them sizzled as he drew the molecules into his palm and created a swirling ball of energy.

"Uncle, this isn't you." Spring lightly touched his back and encircled the wrist of his raised arm. "Nor is it you, Eoin. Pull it back, fellas."

Confusion and uneasiness clouded Alastair's countenance, and he shook his hand out to dispel his magical weapon. "I apologize, Eoin. It appears I'm not myself at the moment."

Shoving aside his own pique, Eoin nodded. "We'll put it down to Narissa's unintentional seduction, yeah?"

Brenna's sharp cry had him ready to battle again in an instant, and he spun, prepared to charge to her defense. Alastair and Spring grabbed for his arms and drew him back to the safety of the corner.

"She's fine, son. Narissa merely scored Brenna's hand for Damian."

"Jaysus! Am I always going to be a feckin' eejit where the woman's concerned?" Placing his fingers to his temples, he dug in. "What is it about her that sparks my inner Neanderthal?"

Alastair surprised him with a short laugh. "That's love, son. No special magic involved."

Brenna couldn't believe how damned bad her palm stung, and it occurred to her she'd never endured the pain associated with a cut before. But as quickly as Narissa sliced her palm was as fast as the wound began to seal, and her blood sizzled off, dispersing in a puff of smoke.

"I need that droplet!" Damian leapt into action and gripped her wrist, only to be smacked across the room by Narissa's wing. He landed with a grunt, and with a rough shake of his head, he climbed to his feet and prepared to take on one angry-ass Siren.

"She's become territorial of you, Brenna." His voice was modulated and calm, and his expression neutral, but she could see the flare of concern in his dark eyes. "Tell her you're okay and that I need that blood."

Brenna turned back to her aunt in time to see Narissa had grown two feet in size and her wings were unfolded and positioned to protect them both. After a shaky inhale, she steadied her nerves. "Aunt Narissa. Please don't hurt him. I need him to help Eoin and me reverse Odessa's spell."

Narissa opened her mouth as if to trill, but the sound was garbled, causing her to scowl and arch her neck back as if in great pain.

"Talk through me," Brenna said softly, reaching up to touch Narissa's throat.

*"Takers! Men are takers, and you must be careful. Steal from them first."*

*"No. Not all men. The ones in this room are kind and trying to help us. You know that."*

*"They want your blood to enslave you!"*

*"No. They want it for the amulet Gran helped design. I'll be safe."* Although Brenna *did* have her misgivings.

"She's letting the Siren take over, Brenna. Continue to talk her down. I can't reach her with my words now," Damian said as he eased closer.

Brenna put her hand flat behind her to put the brakes on him joining them. She used her own soothing gift to address her aunt's creature. "Aunt Narissa, my wound has healed, and I need you to finish what we started. Can you help me? *Please?*" In her mind, she added, *"I love Eoin so much."*

The wild, panicked light left Narissa, and she shrunk back to her initial form, pulling her wings tight to her body to cover her now-threadbare clothing. With a hard look at the Aether, she lifted her claw and scored Brenna's palm a second time.

Hissing out a breath, Brenna held the wound open and rushed to Damian's side. "Hurry. Where's the amulet?"

He lifted his arm, and the necklace launched itself from the floor, where it had fallen, and rose straight up. Damian caught it with blinding speed, fisted her hand within his, and squeezed a drop of her precious, rapidly disappearing blood onto the glass. The lid slammed shut with a snap and a flash, sounding like nothing more than an exploding lightbulb. Then she got her first real glimpse of the color of the liquid running through her veins. She hadn't really registered the fact it wasn't mulberry colored like a normal person's, but a vivid indigo purple that hardened to an amethyst gemstone within the confines of the glass dome.

"Wow!"

The Aether's mouth kicked up in a half smile as he ran a finger around the metal's edge containing the runes. *"Aufer maledictionem et custodiat delectati. Prohibeo."*

"What does that mean?"

"Remove the curse and keep them happy. Protect."

Brenna's shoulders sagged under her profound relief. "Thank you, Damian."

Once again, he gripped her hand, but this time, it was to place the amulet within her grasp and close her fingers over it. "You'll need to create an enchantment that secures this around your young man's neck and cloaks it for all time. It's more than simply neutralizing Odessa's spell. It's meant to protect him from you, too, should the need arise. We'll work on his longevity later."

Unable to express her gratitude to the degree needed, she flung herself at him and hugged him for all she was worth. Really, she was shocked he didn't shove her from him, but instead, he embraced her back just as tightly. "It's going to be all right, Brenna," he said in a low voice. "Have faith, okay?"

She nodded, face firmly buried against his chest. "Thank

you for caring enough to help us, Damian," she managed past the lump in her throat. "I owe you everything."

He drew back but kept his hands on her shoulders. "You owe it to yourself and to Eoin to be happy. But you and me, we have a clean slate."

Brushing away her tears, he drew a symbol on the skin of her forehead, following it with a light kiss. His lips moved, but she had no way of knowing what he said.

"What was that?" she asked him.

"Further protection." With his head, he gestured toward the far corner of the room. "You should try your amulet out."

An instant later, she was running for Eoin and he for her. The second she slipped the chain over his neck, he swept her up and spun her around, laughing and gazing up at her with all the stars from the heavens in his eyes.

"I love you, Brenna Sullivan, and I don't care who knows."

She giggled and touched her forehead to his. "And I love you, Eoin O'Malley," she said right before she kissed him with all the pent-up frustration of the last day. She didn't know how long they stayed locked together, celebrating their love with passion, tenderness, and a few love nips, until a few throats were cleared and snickers released.

"Well, honey, I can see my work here is done."

Face on fire—but not from the curse—Brenna released Eoin with a happy sigh and almost dove back in for another round when Narissa's words registered.

"Oh!" She faced her long-lost aunt and savior, whose dress was restored, without a thread or seam out of place. Narissa was as pristine as when she'd arrived. "You're not leaving? I just found you!"

"Twenty minutes ago, you despised me."

Her lips twitched as she met Narissa's twinkling eyes. "A lot happened in twenty minutes."

"Damian has my number. And I have to pay a call to dear old Aunt Odessa one day in the not-so-distant future."

A chill swept Brenna's body. "Not alone. I'll go with you."

"Bless your heart for caring, but they'll be no bloodshed, honey." Narissa held up two fingers together. "Scout's honor."

"I think that's three fingers together, and I wasn't born yesterday."

A bold laugh was her aunt's response as she leaned in and kissed first one, then the other of Brenna's cheeks. "That old sow needs to be put down for all the trouble she's caused, but it won't be me who takes her on. Or not according to the Aether." She cupped Brenna's face. "I expect to hear from you soon. We can share stories about Mama."

Brenna hugged her, taking comfort in the familial connection. "Thank you for coming and for helping me, Aunt Narissa."

"I imagine it won't be the last time." She gestured to Eoin with her thumb. "This one here looks like trouble with a capital T. And a helluva lot of fun. Better hold on to him."

With a wink in his direction, Narissa sailed out the door and out of Brenna's life.

# CHAPTER 25

*D*amian glanced at the wall clock. "I imagine that concludes our business, friends. You're welcome to stay for dinner, but I imagine you'd like to get home and get some rest."

Eoin clasped Brenna's hand in his. "Sure, and it feels like we've been up for days, it has. But should we be fearin' retaliation from Odessa over the amulet?"

"I hadn't thought of that!" Brenna clenched her hand in his. "What should we do?"

"The necklace protects against your aunt, and as long as Eoin is wearing it, you will be fine. I can't predict if she'll come for you right away, but the possibility exists, based on Sabrina's earlier warning," the Aether replied. As if unconcerned either way, he repositioned his furniture. When he was done, he faced their small group. "My recommendation would be to find a small out-of-the-way place where she wouldn't think to search for you and ward the hell out of it. Just until you learn your craft."

A picture of Roisin's family cottage lodged itself in Eoin's mind, and he knew exactly where to take Brenna. "Carrick's wife has a cottage not far from the Black Cat Inn. We'd be close enough to my family if we need them, but far enough away that they won't be embroiled in any of the trouble should Odessa show up."

"I like that idea." Brenna nodded but still appeared unconvinced.

"Sure, and ya don't really."

With a snort, she nudged his shoulder. "I do, only I'm worried that Aunt Odessa might be able to find me anyway. If we, Sirens, can call our ancestors to us, then maybe we can call our living relatives, too."

"Valid point, child. Blood does call to like blood." Alastair tugged the cuffs of his dress shirt down past his suit jacket. "You'll stay at my home for the foreseeable future."

"No. I can't do that either." She gave him a sweet smile, and the austere expression left Alastair's face, leaving him looking like a kind parent. "We can't risk another horror-film reenactment with zombie-like creatures coming through the walls. I promised I wouldn't put your family in danger."

Respecting her decision and perhaps seeing the wisdom of her words, Alastair nodded. From his pinky, he pulled a tanzanite ring and handed it to Brenna. "Should you require my help, you only need to call out my name. This is charmed to create a telepathic link between the wearer and its creator —me."

After slipping the ring over her right index finger, she stretched up and kissed his smooth cheek. "Thank you for everything, Alastair. You'll let me know if I can ever return the favor, won't you?"

"I will, child." He startled everyone when he drew her in for a quick hug. "Be happy, my dear. You've worked hard enough for it."

After a round of hugs from Damian, Spring—and Sabrina, too, after the girl rushed back into the room—Eoin teleported

Brenna to his room at the inn. Other than the bed, which was freshly made, nothing had been disturbed.

"It seems weird we were here earlier today, doesn't it?"

"Aye. A lot has happened in a short time." When Brenna yawned, Eoin nudged her toward the bed. "Rest, love. I'll go give my family an update of today's events, yeah?"

"I can go with you..." She yawned a second time, suddenly more exhausted than she ever remembered being in her adult life.

He laughed and dropped a light kiss on her mouth. "I'll be back to snuggle down with ya soon enough."

The welcoming smile she gave him glowed with happiness. He was one lucky bastard. Unable to resist a second kiss, he trailed his fingers along her jawline as he tucked her in bed. "Thank you for bringing color to my world, Brenna."

"But you already had color." She frowned adorably.

"No. It was black and white with shades of gray until you. Looking back, my all of my best work happened after I met you."

"You're just saying that," she said with a snort. "You've always been a talent in the art world."

"Sure, and maybe I made passable pieces, but your shining eyes influenced my choices and your soft sultry voice was the one I heard in my dreams, telling me how much ya loved what I'd created. It made me want to make beautiful things for you to admire." Using the tips of his fingers, he traced her full lower lip. "With each commission, I didn't work for the buyer. I worked for you, love. All I ever wanted was for you to discuss my current projects with me."

Her eyes shimmered, and her mouth—Goddess, that sexy, generous mouth—widened with her happy smile. "And all I ever wanted was to be able to discuss those projects. I lived for whatever you designed or forged in your studio, Eoin. Your sculptures make my heart sing in a way I can never describe."

"Thank you, love."

"I should be the one thanking you. You rescued me from my drab world and breathed life into me."

"You didn't need rescuing. Just wakin' up, and you did that all on your own, ya did. You stepped in when Odessa intended to steal my powers for herself. You ran interference for Alastair at the gallery. And I suspect you began doing that a long time before we came along." His kiss was more than a simple sample this time. He tasted her completely, and with each touch, he burned hotter and wanted nothing more than to strip her bare to make love with her.

"I like the way you think of me, Eoin. How you believe I'm stronger and better than I am."

"You are, Brenna. I promise ya, you are."

He hated that he had to leave her, but Loman O'Connor's return was a serious threat, and not one he could put off telling the others about. "Sleep now, love. I'll be back soon."

After clicking the door closed, he withdrew his phone and texted his siblings, asking them to join him in the inn's kitchen. He'd just received their affirmative responses when his phone vibrated, indicating a call from Reggie.

"Reg!"

"We need to talk, scamp."

He tried to recall a time when he'd ever heard his friend so serious and couldn't do it. "All right. Where do you want to meet?"

"Your family's pub, but I need you to do something for me."

"Sure, and you're sounding dire. What the feck is going on, Reg? Are you all right, man?" Apprehension began to settle in Eoin's stomach. He wasn't going to like where this was going, to be sure.

"I have a confession, and I need you to listen to what I have to say. But I also need you to have Ronan with you when you do."

"Ronan O'Connor? What business do you have with that plonker?"

"I'll tell you at the pub in one hour. You'll need to meet me outside, though. Can you do that?"

"Aye."

After hanging up the call, Eoin wasted no time meeting Bridget, Cian, and Carrick in the kitchen. Joining them were Piper, Roisin, and Ruairí.

"What's so bleedin' important we had to drop everything to be here?" Carrick asked.

"Loman O'Connor."

"The man's dead." Bridget's confusion was only natural. Last they'd all heard, Alexander Castor had won a death match and sent Loman to hell after the man had bombed the O'Malley businesses.

"Not according to Sabrina Dethridge, he's not."

*"Fuck!"* Ruairí's response was natural. As a nephew to Loman, he would be on the man's revenge list as a betrayer of the O'Connors. In Loman's mind, Ruairí should've been fighting for their side in their centuries-old war and should've given *him* the sword instead of Bridget. Once Ruairí had sided with her and declared his loyalty to the O'Malleys, he'd sealed his fate with his evil-incarnate uncle. "Does Ronan or my Uncle Alex know yet?"

"I'm not certain." Eoin ran a hand along his jaw and scratched the stubbly growth as he suppressed a tired yawn. "We all know Ronan, Castor, and the Aether are friends, but I got the feelin' Damian's daughter was telling him for the first time, too."

Cian grew thoughtful, and he gazed out the window into the darkening night. "If he teams up with Moira again, we'll have a fierce threat on our hands."

"We can only assume he will," Piper said. "I'll call my dad and get the rest of my family on alert."

"Sure, and Alastair knows. He was at the Dethridge estate with us," Eoin informed her. "The man doesn't strike me as someone who lets grass grow under his feet. I'd bet my next commission he's already taking precautions and informin' the others."

Piper smiled at him. "You seem to understand Alastair well."

"I've seen the man in action, and only a feckin' eejit would pick a fight with so fierce an opponent."

Bridget placed her hand overtop of Eoin's. "Have ya told Dubheasa yet?"

"No." And he felt shame that he'd forgotten all about her and her problems. Drawing his phone from his pocket, he connected to the inn's Wi-Fi and then dialed her through the FaceTime app. When she picked up, he shifted his cell to show her there were others present. "Look, and we have a problem." He detailed what he'd learned at the Aether's home and finished with, "You need to have a care, Dubheasa. You should be strengthenin' the wards on your flat the second we are off the phone, yeah?"

There was a long pause on the other end. Her voice was troubled when she asked, "Have ya told Ronan?"

"No, not yet. He'll be the next call I make. Do you want to tell him, then?"

Again, she hesitated. "No. You'll do well to do it. I'll call GiGi and see what she can teach me by way of spells to keep this place secure."

"You can come home," Bridget said over Eoin's shoulder. "We miss ya, love."

"I'll be home on holiday for the winter solstice, and I'm planning to stay a while." Dubheasa gave them a tight smile. "Don't worry about me, yeah? But stay in touch, and tell me when Loman O'Connor is gone for good."

After they disconnected, Eoin used Ruairí's phone and placed a call to Ronan. He could swear he heard thunder boom and felt the inn shake the instant he delivered the news that Loman had returned to the land of the living.

"Where's Dubheasa?" Ronan demanded. "Look, and she needs to be with the rest of you so I can protect her... er, all of you."

Eoin almost laughed at the slip. He likely would've if the idea of Ronan and Dubheasa as a couple didn't make bile churn in his stomach. "She's off to seek the help of the Thornes."

Ronan had a few choice words for her independence, yet he had no choice but to let it go. "I'll teleport to the alley behind the inn in one minute. Prepare to lower the wards for my entry, O'Malley. And I better find you've been treatin' Brenna like a fecking princess, yeah? The girl doesn't deserve to be shagged and abandoned for her troubles."

"Feck off!" Eoin took umbrage with Ronan's arrogance.

"Sure, and I've gotten your back up, yeah? Grand. You've told me what I needed to know, then." There was amusement in Ronan's cool tone, as if he'd received the response he wanted. "One minute, O'Malley. Be ready to put your wards back up after I'm in."

The line clicked as Ronan disconnected.

"The fecking king has spoken," Eoin muttered as he handed the phone back to Ruairí. "I've a need to check on Brenna. Show that scut in, yeah?"

# CHAPTER 26

*A*fter checking and discovering Brenna sleeping, Eoin returned downstairs to find Ronan sipping tea and devouring Bridget's scones. Roisin was chatting happily away with the man and laughing at whatever he had to say, much to Carrick's irritation and Cian's amusement.

"I see you like to make yourself at home wherever ya go, O'Connor. Collect other men's women, too," Eoin said.

Ronan grinned, and Eoin could've sworn he heard the three women present sigh in response. It was a damned good thing Brenna wasn't party to this hen-fest, or his frayed temper would snap. The amusement disappeared from Ronan's eyes as he addressed the issue at hand.

"I don't know how Loman could be back. Castor and Damian were present when he was killed." He rubbed the back of his neck, expression grim. "Does the Aether have any reason for his return? Is it possible Moira performed some black-magic spell to revive him?"

"None of us went into detail while we were there." Eoin plucked a scone off the plate and added jam and clotted cream.

"Look, and we were too busy dealin' with curing Brenna of the curse plaguing her."

Straightening from his casual, half-slouched position, Ronan set down his teacup. "What curse?" The fierce anger in his voice made Eoin wonder if perhaps he hadn't been the only one to see beyond Brenna's disguise and appreciate what he saw. Or maybe Ronan O'Connor had a gentler side to him than any of them imagined.

Eoin spent the next few minutes explaining the situation and answering everyone's questions regarding what he'd learned about Sirens and their darker counterparts. "Odessa is dangerous and poses an additional threat to our family."

"Jaysus," Cian muttered. "We caught a glimpse when Brenna sang, but holy hell."

"That's not all, to be sure. My best mate, Reggie, called and wants to meet me at half past." Eoin nodded to the wall clock. "And for reasons all his own, he would like you there, O'Connor."

"Me?" Ronan frowned. "How does your friend..." A thoughtful look passed over his countenance before he carefully blanked his expression. "Reggie, you say?"

"Aye."

"Would ya be tellin' me how long you've known him? And how does he know who I am?"

"A few years now. And he's a warlock, so I've never thought to hide who I am from him." Ronan's stillness disturbed Eoin. "Would you be knowin' him, too, then?"

"I believe I do." Rising to his feet, Ronan scanned the room from top to bottom and corner to corner. "Where are we to meet him?"

"The street in front of the pub."

"Be a good lad and call him back. I've got another place in mind. Oh, and change the meeting to five minutes from now. I don't want him to have any time to change up his tactics should he be plannin' anything."

Keeping eye contact with Ronan, Eoin called Reggie and gave him the new location. "We'll be there in five minutes, Reg." After he hung up, he said, "It's done."

"I'm going, too."

They all turned to see Brenna standing in the doorway, rubbing sleep from her luminous eyes. As the others stared at her, likely unable to process the transformation from the shy, unassuming creature they'd met to the bold goddess she currently was, Eoin began to object.

She waved him off. "I'm not helpless anymore, Eoin. And I can be neutral in all this. You're liable to have hurt feelings if Reggie isn't who you believe he is, and it's clear Ronan thinks your friend is up to no good."

"Brenna, love…"

"I suppose I should've said, I'm not powerless anymore," she said with a self-deprecating smile. "I assume Eoin's told the rest of you about our little adventure today. If so, you know what I can do."

"I vote she goes," Bridget said with a toast of her mug.

"I second it." Piper grinned and gave Brenna two thumbs-up.

"And as I'm the only female left to vote, I'll be addin' mine to the mix with a hearty cheer for girl power," Roisin added with a laugh.

"Feck," Eoin muttered. Clearly, he was outvoted, and his brothers had no intention of weighing in. He looked at the O'Connor men who, for once, were content to hold their ofttimes waggin' tongues. "*Now* you intend to hold your *whisht?*"

The two cousins shared a laughing glance.

"Feck off, the lot of ya!" Eoin snarled.

Brenna clapped her hands together. "Awesome. Let's go!"

"Reg. Can't say it's good to see ya again." Ronan faced Reggie like he expected an attack.

Eoin looked between the two men, searching for what, he couldn't exactly say. The animosity was all on Ronan's side, but Reggie remained eerily calm, as if he was awaiting sentencing for past crimes.

A sense of wrongness unfurled in Eoin's chest. "I think I'm going to need a little history here, to be sure."

"Ronan is my cousin," Reggie said, and the complete lack of emotion in his voice after dropping *that* little bomb was discomfiting.

Brenna sucked in a breath. "Cousins?"

With a nod of his head, Reggie confirmed the truth.

White-hot rage boiled in Eoin's veins. Never had he felt more betrayed. His best friend, the man he looked up to and sought advice from, had fooled him from the start. Humiliation for his gullibility made Eoin's ears hot to the touch, and he tried to rub away the sensation as he frantically sought an explanation for such devious behavior. He could only come up with one.

"You're an O'Connor, and you lied to me about it, Reg? You did it to spy on me for your uncle?"

He wanted to beg Reggie to tell him it wasn't so, but the real regret in his faux friend's eyes stabbed him in the heart. Eoin swallowed hard and, oddly, fought the urge to mourn. Although perhaps it wasn't so odd to feel grief at the instant of a friendship's death.

Prepared for anything, Ronan scanned the tree line behind the park, where he'd insisted on meeting. Neutral ground, but they weren't without protection. The new Guardian job he'd acquired came with perks, and the ability to cast a circle without candles, salt, and other hoopla was one. Inside the ring, Ronan, Eoin, and Brenna were untouchable.

"That's how it started, scamp. But along the way, I found I like you. Not that it made a difference in the end. I still answer to Loman." He met Ronan's hard stare. "We all do in some form or another. And like you, we all gave a cheer when we thought his reign of terror ended. Unfortunately, we found out differently. Your father showed up on my doorstep quite recently, demanding help."

"And you gave it." It wasn't a question.

With a small nod of acknowledgment, Reggie confirmed Ronan's accurate guess. "But not against you, scamp. Against Odessa and, ultimately, Brenna."

Eoin shifted to stand in front of her, effectively blocking her from Reggie's view. "Why Brenna?"

"Her Siren's magic. She's got more power than any of you can imagine, and Loman wants it, along with that of her aunt's."

Brenna's outrage sparked in Eoin's mind like a live wire, and he reached back to clasp her hand.

"You can go back and report to him that ya failed, Reg. Brenna won't be part of your war with my family."

A cold, cruel smile curled Reggie's lips. "There you're mistaken, my dear scamp. She showed up on Loman's radar, which places her firmly on the front lines of the battlefield."

The smugness rankled, and blinded by rage, Eoin charged with no thought to his safety.

"O'Malley, no!"

Ronan's warning came too late. Eoin had crossed the line of protection. In a move that would do martial arts instructors everywhere proud, Reggie had gripped him by the throat and pressed the tip of a blade to his artery. Cian would never let Eoin live this one down. *If* he survived the night.

"I can tell by the fact you and your little mouse are able to touch again that Odessa's spell was neutralized," Reggie said, a sneer in his tone. "Shame that. I'm the one who gave her the idea."

Black rolling clouds gathered overhead, and a bolt of lightning illuminated the twilight sky, branching out in all directions.

Ronan frowned and shot a look at Brenna over his shoulder. And when Eoin met her stormy eyes, his heart dropped to his big toe. Reggie had inadvertently woken her Siren, and the creature was out for blood.

Her skin took on a luminescent glow, and her thick mane of hair came to life on the air's current. The more the wind blew, the wilder the strands fluttered, turning Medusa-like in nature. Brenna's hips rolled in a mouthwateringly seductive dance as she sauntered to the edge of the circle, growing taller and curvier as she approached. The stitching of her clothes couldn't take the pressure and gave way in random areas, providing tantalizing glimpses of what lay underneath. A creamy thigh here, a side view of her luscious full breasts there. She was splendid in her creature form, but Eoin wanted to cover her up and save her all for himself to slowly unwrap later.

"Let him go, Reggie, and I'll allow you to live."

The tip of the knife dipped to rest at the base of Eoin's Adam's apple, and he didn't dare swallow, or his blood would flow.

"Not a little mouse now, Reg," Ronan said with a spiteful laugh. "I'd say she's turned into an apex predator ready to rip your feckin' head from your shoulders, she has."

Hands clapped, catching the notice of their small group.

Loman O'Connor stepped into view. "Magnificent!"

Eoin gripped Reggie's wrist, preparing to break it and get to Brenna before the newest threat.

"Play along, scamp," Reggie murmured.

The urgency in his tone pierced Eoin's panic. "What the feck is happening, Reg?" he whispered.

"I'm trying to save your life, darling boy. Now kindly shut the fuck up."

"And what about Brenna's and Ronan's lives?" Eoin hissed, terrified in a way he had never been before. If anything happened to her, he'd be soulless and his world void of any color.

"I'm afraid they're on their own," Reggie said regretfully. "But look at the bright side, Loman's power is little in comparison to that of a combined Siren and Guardian."

Eoin's cells warmed to burning, and he released a guttural yell in protest. When he opened his eyes, he was in his New York apartment, and his amulet was dangling from Reggie's hand. As he reached for it, he noticed a shiny new bracelet on his wrist.

"What's this, then?"

"Call it a temporary leash. You'll be unable to use your magic to teleport back to Brenna until this is done."

With a roar of rage, he launched himself at Reggie, only to smack against an invisible barrier of sorts.

"Sorry, scamp. You'll thank me when the Siren's influence wears off."

"There's no '*influence,*' ya fecking eejit! I love her!"

"You only think you do. Time will tell."

"I'll be killin' ya before this night's out, Reg. You can take that to the grave with ya," Eoin promised.

---

RONAN REGISTERED HIS FATHER'S APPEARANCE AND THE corresponding disappearance of Eoin and Reggie with detachment. His first priority was making sure the young and untried Siren beside him didn't turn nuclear. Wrapping an arm around her waist, he pulled her to him and gritted his teeth. Her lure was otherworldly, and all he wanted to do was give over to her seductive power. But he had a job to do, and he'd promised little Sabrina Dethridge he'd do it.

"Sorry, darlin', but you don't get to tear my da apart at the moment. We'll save that for another day, yeah?"

With nowhere else to go, he teleported them to an abandoned cottage on the outskirts of a village seventy miles north of their location.

Brenna's Siren screeched her displeasure, and a piercing pain in Ronan's eardrums caused him to clap his hands over his ears and fall to his knees. He wanted to beg her to stop, but he didn't have the ability to speak under the intense pressure building in his head. Falling to the ground, he curled into a ball.

He was a fecking eejit!

Once again, he was trying to play the savior and protect a woman against her will. The irony of his death would keep Dubheasa O'Malley in high spirits for decades to come.

"Brenna!"

Ronan managed to crack his lids, and his heart jumped into his throat when he saw Odessa Sullivan and Moira walking toward them from the clearing. He truly was a dead man.

---

IN THE FAR REACHES OF BRENNA'S MIND, SHE REGISTERED THE fact her Siren was killing Ronan in her rage. The creature had claimed Eoin for her own and was furious her mate was gone. Now, Brenna understood how her mother had given in to the darkness when her father died. Eoin wasn't dead yet, only a captive of Reggie, and still, her Siren was inconsolable.

Odessa's shout brought her head around, and she knew unimaginable fear when she saw the two women heading their way. Instinctively, she understood they would stop her from saving Eoin.

In a flash, Damian's words returned to her.

*"The Siren and the woman are one and the same. You can control your own desires, if you wish. But if you let her have freedom, she will do what feels good regardless of consequence. If you don't keep her contained, she'll choose the darkness every time."*

She had to regain the upper hand. Even though her Siren wanted to exact revenge on Odessa, Brenna fought tooth and nail to prevent it and take back control.

Her Siren's echoing cry was cut off, and it trilled in an effort to cajole Brenna into leaving her in charge of the situation.

"You can control her, Brenna Marie," Odessa said. "You're the strongest of our kind."

She shook her head, bewildered by her aunt's unsolicited help. Her gaze dropped to Ronan, and although his pain had to be excruciating, he didn't move or make a sound. He simply stared at her, as if willing her to hear him.

"I'm sorry." Dropping to her knees, she drew his head to her breast in a protective hold. "I'm so sorry."

"Get out while you can, Brenna," he croaked. "They'll kill you for your magic."

"I don't know how to teleport, but you do. Save yourself, Ronan." She hadn't realized she was crying until a glistening tear fell onto his cheek. "Go to Damian. He can heal you."

An instant later, he was gone, and she'd returned to her normal self. But inside, her siren was kicking and screaming her rage. So loudly, in fact, she almost missed what the auburn-haired woman told her.

"'Tis a feckin' shame you let him go. We could've dined on his magic for days."

Rising to her feet, she faced Odessa and her new companion. "I'd kill him before I ever let you touch him, witch."

The woman's sly grin scrapped her nerves. "Are you certain ya didn't when you teleported him?"

"Me? I didn't..." But had she? Odessa's hard stare indicated Brenna had been the one to send him away. She felt more than a little ill.

# CHAPTER 27

*S*tanding in shredded clothes in front of her aunt and the unknown witch, Brenna experienced a sense of misgiving. She was vulnerable in a way she'd never been before. Not only because of the half-naked issue, but due to the feeling of her world being topsy-turvy.

The cottage and surrounding landscape could be England, Ireland, or a farm in Maine, for all she knew. She legit had no idea where the hell she was, but she certainly wished *someone* had taught her to teleport when they had the chance. Gran's scrolls might've contained the information, but she hadn't read them in time for this little shindig.

"What are you doing here, Aunt?" Brenna asked coldly. Her confidence might be waning, but she didn't have to appear that way. "And who is this sly cat you brought, eager to cause trouble?"

"I've come to help you, you ungrateful twit," Odessa snapped, irritation in every line of her weathered face. Except her eyes. Hidden in their depths was a warning or wariness Brenna had never witnessed.

"What if I don't want your help?"

"Would you rather Loman O'Connor murder you and steal your power?"

"How is that different from what you've been doing all these years?" Brenna demanded.

"You're living, aren't you?"

Well, there was that. "Am I supposed to be grateful for the fact you were syphoning my magic? That you murdered Gran?"

Odessa jerked as if struck, and a pained look settled on her countenance. "I've been sorry about that since the day it happened, Brenna. I loved Doreen."

"Let me guess. Your monster made you do it?" There was no forgiveness left in her. The disappearance of Eoin had been the last straw. From here on out, she was taking no prisoners.

"You have no reason to believe me, but it's the truth," Odessa told her.

Brenna sneered, full of bluster and fake confidence, hoping to buy time until her true friends came for her. "What do you hope to do to save me that I can't possibly do for myself?"

"Help you defeat Uncle Loman," the other witch inserted, a crafty smile on her face. "But you have to give over your power to Odessa completely."

Brenna didn't trust her as far as she could throw her, and with her scrawny arms, that wasn't very far. And if she didn't miss her guess, the woman was Irish, and that put her firmly in the suspicious category.

"Uncle? So you're related to Reggie and Ronan?" she asked, purposefully ignoring the suggestion she give up her magic. That was never going to happen. Not to these two.

"Aye. But they're feckin' useless, as you so recently witnessed."

Left with no choice but to bluff her way through this exchange, she checked her temper at the door and asked, "What's your plan?"

Sly satisfaction flared to life in the other woman's eyes, and

Brenna's blood turned cold. The first chance she got, the bitch would stab her in the back.

"You'll willingly submit to a transference of magic. You'll be the same uninspired girl you are, and I get the strength to defeat the others."

*Others?*

She shot a quick glance at her aunt. Odessa was either constipated or trying to put down something Brenna wasn't picking up.

*"Can you hear me, Aunt Odessa?"* she mentally asked, avoiding addressing her directly in front of the other woman.

From the corner of her eye, she saw her aunt give a single nod.

*"Can she?"*

A minuscule shake of Odessa's head.

*"Is this a trap?"*

Before Brenna received an answer, the red-headed witch growled. "What's with the bleedin' silent treatment? You either want our help or not."

"You still haven't outlined your plan, and I don't know your name, *friend*."

Respect shone from Odessa's rheumy eyes, and she nodded once again when the feisty woman's back was turned to her.

"Moira Doyle."

Brenna was sure she'd never heard the name, but the woman was related to that kidnapping bastard Reggie, and seriously eager to kill Ronan, who Brenna happened to like. She was putting Moira in the friends-she-never-wanted-to-have column.

"Can't say I've ever heard of you. What's your claim to fame?"

Rumor had it the Irish were well known for their fighting spirits and, in some cases, formidable tempers. This woman checked both boxes. Her color was high, and her irritation radiated off her in waves. "I'm the smartest and most powerful of the O'Connors," she snapped.

Scrunching her nose and squinting, Brenna pretended to consider it. "Mmm, but are you? Really? Because I've met a few of the others, and I have to say, they seem pretty clever to me. And other than an Aether and a Siren, who's more badass than a Guardian?"

*"Language, Brenna Marie."*

Gran.

Somehow, someway, she'd known Brenna needed her and came to lend her support.

And in her head, another voice chimed in. *"You should allow her a little freedom, Mama. A girl has to spread her wings, now and again. Don't ya, honey?"*

Narissa had joined the fray, and Brenna couldn't help her triumphant smile as her mother's twin stopped beside her, shoulder to shoulder. With the specter of Gran on one side and the very solid form of Narissa on the other, Brenna felt unstoppable.

With a snap of her fingers, Narissa restored Brenna's clothes to new, with not a speck of dirt or thread out of place. "Remind me to show you how to do that after we take out the trash, honey."

Moira grew concerned. "Where… how… who…?"

"I can answer that, Ms. Doyle." From seemingly nowhere, the Aether appeared behind Moira.

The woman's complexion turned positively green, and she whirled to face the newest and most serious threat that ever existed.

"Hello, Moira. I've been looking forward to this moment for a very long time." Damian's grin was pure menace, and the light of retribution was in his hard, frigid stare.

The wind around them began to howl, and the trees swayed to the point of snapping branches.

The Aether was one pissed-off dude.

"It was Seamus who tried to—" she ended on a gurgle. As she clawed at the invisible hand around her neck, she wildly flailed one arm and reached for Odessa.

"The plan was *yours*, and you tried to murder my child. *My* child." Damian strolled forward as if he were taking a walk in the park and had all day. But with each step, the overhead clouds darkened until he stopped only a foot away from his target. A bolt of lightning shattered a nearby tree, and the resounding crack and boom instilled fear in all of their hearts. "And for that, Moira Doyle, you've forfeited your life."

His icy words froze Brenna's breath in her lungs. Unwilling and unable to take her attention from the unfolding scene, she blindly sought and clasped Narissa's hand. For the second time, she reminded herself to never get on Damian Dethridge's bad side.

*"You got that right, honey."* Narissa's fingers tightened over hers, and she leaned into her, seeking unity.

The Aether placed his palm flat on Moira's chest, and from the marginal gap, a chartreuse light tried to escape, sending blinding beams in all directions. The woman's head dropped back, and black smoke poured out of her lurid red and grotesquely gaping mouth. It drifted up and hovered above Damian as if unsure where it should go. Without bothering to remove his focus from Moira, he lifted a hand to the sky and absorbed the dark mist into the flat of his palm.

The scent of brimstone filled the air, and fire flared to life at her feet, then licked up her legs. The flame stopped at her waist as if awaiting instruction, and it danced in its eagerness.

The tortured expression on Moira's countenance was hard to witness, and Brenna jerked free of her aunt's hold to approach the righteous Aether.

"Damian, please. Show mercy!"

"No."

"Brenna," Ronan quietly spoke her name from behind her. "Stay out of it."

She should've expected he'd get reinforcements and return, but she hadn't thought that far ahead.

"He's killing her," she hissed. And as he attempted to pull her away, Brenna tugged her arm, but was unable to break his hold.

"Let him."

The unperturbed tone bothered her. With a last look for poor Moira, Brenna called out to Damian again. "Damian, please. Please don't kill her."

Not removing his dispassionate stare from Moira, he addressed Brenna's concern. "She'd kill any and all of us where we stand, Brenna. Remember what I told you about what I see when I look at someone? She's flat-out hideous."

"Can't she be redeemed?" she cried. "Surely reform is possible?"

"Tell me this, my dear. Would you let a serial killer of young children walk away to strike again?"

Brenna remained mute. He knew she wouldn't. Couldn't.

"And not one minute ago, she intended to enslave you to do her bidding as she's managed to enslave Odessa." He spared her aunt a glance. "Tell her."

"I believed I was in control when she showed up at my home." Odessa lifted her chin, but it wobbled tellingly. "She stabbed me in the back, and when I transitioned to take her magic, she turned the tables." She cast a resentful glare at the group. "She'd anticipated my actions and had an enchantment already in place for when I licked the knife clean of my blood. When I kissed her, that blood was still on my tongue, and she was able to harness it. And here we are."

"To amass more power, yeah?" Ronan's was more a statement of fact than a question.

"She had me scry for you, Brenna. The moment you appeared in the park and your Siren took over it was too late. I wanted to protect you." Odessa shook her head, pleading on her face. "Can you ever forgive me for leading her to you?"

"For that, possibly. For what you did to Gran and intended to do to Eoin and Ronan? Never."

"Do you really think evil like that should be runnin' about free?" Ronan asked her with a tilt of his head toward his cousin. "Moira's fond of stabbing people in the back and attacking small children with the hopes of ending their lives to gain more and more magic. Sure, and she wants to be unstoppable in all ways. Should she be left unchecked, then?"

Meeting the woman's desperate gaze, Brenna shook her head. "No. She shouldn't be left unchecked, but is it really on us to murder a person? Do two wrongs make a right?"

Ronan cast a frustrated look in Damian's direction but focused on Moira again, as if afraid to remove his attention from her for longer than a second or two.

Determined to keep the blight from Damian's soul, Brenna tried another tactic. "Can't you simply remove her magic? Take her memories, relocate her far away... anything."

"It doesn't matter." The Aether shook his dark head. "She'll return and try another underhanded trick to steal it back. She has to die, Brenna."

Raised on the extreme tips of her toes with her back arched, Moira whimpered and her arms dropped limply at her sides.

"Damian, *please!*" Brenna was careful to keep the angst from her voice. She didn't know why this was important, but it was, and she strove for reason. "Would Sabrina want this?"

The flames died low for an instant but flared higher, swallowing Moira whole.

"Sabrina would want to live free of terror, Miss Sullivan." Damian's tone was arctic, and the bitterly cold wind slapped Brenna's face. "*Never* question my judgment again."

In a blink, he was gone, and she was left staring at the pile of ash that had once been Moira Doyle.

# CHAPTER 28

*K*nees weak from the confrontation, Brenna plunked down where she was. She gripped handfuls of earth, both grass and dirt, attempting to hang on as the world spun madly around her. The grisly, but probably justified, execution of Moira had pulled the rug out from under her. She had no sense of up or down.

But the grit under Brenna's nails worked to ground her and reminded her that life was a cycle. Birth, youth, maturity, and eventually death. For everyone. And in between those points were a few harsh lessons.

Moira was one.

There were also broken hearts.

For a brief time, there was love.

Very brief.

*Eoin.*

She really needed him to help her see the meaning of all this. Her Siren, curled up in a corner of her mind, sullenly trilled her agreement. He hadn't been far from her thoughts since Reggie's abduction.

"Brenna."

"Leave me alone, Ronan. All of you. Just leave me the hell alone for a little while."

"That's not a good idea, love," he said regretfully. "You can't be out here in the open, unprotected as you are."

"I don't even know where I am!"

"Sullivan land." Odessa approached and stared down at the ash at her feet. She kicked it. "The girl was a fool. Don't waste a second mourning her."

Shifting to kneel, Brenna glared up at her. "You and I are going to have a day of reckoning for what you did. It may not be today, but it will happen soon. Right now, I suggest you reverse any spells you've placed on me and go home. Hopefully, you recognize the error of your ways."

For once, Odessa didn't insult or try to order Brenna about. "I helped you keep your siren locked away."

"No! No, Aunt Odessa, you didn't. You practically kept *me* locked away. I didn't get a choice in the matter, did I?" Brenna glared her fury, still maintaining a modicum of vocal control.

"It was better that way."

"You're wrong. Friendships would have been nice. Maybe instruction on using my gifts." She shook her head. "You can't justify what you did. I'll never believe it wasn't to benefit you. Just go."

Odessa simply teleported away with a dignified nod.

Narissa touched Brenna's shoulder. "That was a mistake, honey. Leaving that mad cow to her own devices will end in another headache."

"One I don't want to deal with right now. I have to find Eoin."

Ronan squatted in front of her. "Look, and we're here to help you, Brenna."

"Your concern is appreciated, Ronan, but I need a minute. I…" She looked down at the ash and shook her head. "It's all new to me, this world. The senseless quest to always be on top. The taking of another life." She swallowed hard and willed herself not to cry for a hardened criminal she didn't know. It was pointless. "Please go."

With a nod and a wave of his hand for Narissa to precede him, they left.

She didn't know how long she sat and attempted to formulate a worthwhile plan to find Eoin. Ronan or Narissa would have a better idea how to search for him, but she needed a little longer to firm her resolve and shore up her courage.

"Damn you, Reggie," Brenna muttered as she viciously ripped out another patch of grass.

"Damn me? Now why would you do that, lovely?"

Heart in her throat, she twisted so quickly she flopped on her butt, scrambling back as she stared up at him in horror. He was, after all, a backstabbing sonofabitch and a liar to boot. And Brenna had stupidly sent away the only people who had her back.

"Why, my dear Brenna, you don't look thrilled to see me." Head cocked to one side, he smirked.

The desire to punch him in his smug fucking face overcame her, and she balled her hands into fists, barely managing to curb the impulse.

"You know I'm not. Where's Eoin? What have you done with him?" Her voice cracked, but she wasn't embarrassed by the raw emotion. She only regretted she couldn't hide it from Reggie, because he'd likely take great pleasure in her pain.

"Ouch. That hurts." He didn't bother to conceal his amusement. "I brought you a present, Siren. Don't you want to know what it is?"

Climbing to her feet, she lifted her chin and glared down the length of her nose, as she'd seen Alastair do. Hopefully, she could be at least half as intimidating as he was.

"No," she snapped. "Beware of Greeks bearing gifts, and all that."

Hands deep in his pockets, he shifted to study the cottage and the surrounding area. His sharp-eyed gaze missed nothing of the antiquated home or the work it needed. "This place is dreary, darling. Not at all where you and Eoin should be spending your days."

"We won't be spending our days together, thanks to you and your uncle." The venom eating her insides spilled over into her tone. "You took that away from us."

"Did I?"

"You know you did. What I don't understand is why. Eoin loved you like a brother, and you betrayed him."

"Maybe I wanted him to love me as more than a brother. Did you ever think about that?"

She refused to let her heart soften in sympathy. "You don't betray the ones you love, Reggie. Not if you truly care about them."

"And what should I have done? Languish while he spends his life with *you*?"

Instantaneous rage blurred her vision. His unkind words were unfair, and Brenna was tired of being made to feel worthless. Blinking rapidly, she backed up a step until her mind was once again clear. She couldn't be at a disadvantage and needed to be alert to his smallest move. "What is wrong with being happy for him? If you truly loved him, you'd want the best for him."

"And you think you're what's best for him, Brenna, dear? A Siren able to steal his power and render him a blubbering, broken man? Or possibly a dead one?" Anger settled on his sharp, pretty features, but it didn't detract from his handsomeness. It added to his appeal, painting him the tragic figure looking out for his friend.

"I don't know. But I'd have liked a chance to try." Her voice broke, and why shouldn't it? It was as shattered as the rest of her. "Why are you here? To finish what you started? To break Eoin completely?"

He shrugged coldly. "Perhaps."

"You won't. Even if you find a way to kill me—and good luck there, mister!—he won't be broken."

"Mmm, there you're wrong, Siren. Your death will completely destroy him."

"No. He's stronger than you and me combined, Reggie. I promise you that."

He tilted his head and studied her with new eyes. "You've come into your own, haven't you? Between Alastair Thorne, the O'Malleys, and Damian Dethridge, you've matured and grown a thicker skin. It's becoming."

She snorted. "I've always had to have a thick skin. I lived with your bosom buddy Odessa for the better part of my life."

"She's no friend of mine. Neither was Moira. Good riddance, there."

It occurred to Brenna that he'd somehow watched the action in play. She made a mental note to ask Narissa how such things were done.

Reggie strolled to an abandoned herb patch growing wild with weeds. He drew up his slacks and squatted, then fingered the tip of one plant stalk, pinching a sprig off and rolling it between his fingers. "Rosemary represents love and fidelity. Did you know that?"

"No. Where are you going with this, Encyclopedia Brown?"

He chuckled. "I think it's fitting, is all."

Rising, he returned to her side and held out the sprig, and Brenna instinctively accepted it. "Because we're discussing Eoin?"

"Yes. And because I believe you'll love him the way he deserves. Better than I ever could."

Unable to comprehend what he was telling her, she remained silent. The way he spoke made it seem like he had no intention of harming her, but his every action until that moment had been designed to hurt.

Reggie reached into his pocket and drew out Eoin's necklace. "Creating this was a foolish move, little Siren."

Her stomach plummeted into the ground at her feet. "How so?"

When she didn't take it, he lifted the amulet with his opposite hand and studied the crystalized blood at the disc's center as if it were the most fascinating thing he'd ever seen. She recognized the act for what it was. A pause to create drama. Reggie liked nothing if not delivering crushing news with a flare.

She waited him out.

"Do you know what a talented practitioner such as myself could do with one drop of your blood, darling?" When his eyes met hers, he lifted a brow in challenge. "With one drop, I can enthrall you. Have you do whatever I command." Placing his index finger over his mouth, he slowly tapped as if in deep thought. "Say, kill the entire O'Malley clan."

She shook her head. Horrified by the thought and knowing it was true. He really had the ability to control her with the weapon he possessed.

He dropped his arm and pinned her with a hard stare. "And you could, couldn't you? You're that powerful."

"I wouldn't. You couldn't make me do something so horrendous."

"Don't be naive, little Siren. With this, I could rule the world." Resembling a hypnotist on stage, he waved it back and forth.

Brenna waited for him to say something asinine like, "You're getting very sleepy." The darkest part of her soul laughed at her inappropriate humor while the part desiring to preserve the O'Malleys' lives struggled to find a way out of her current predicament.

"You're wrong, Reggie. I'd never hurt them. I'd find a way to off myself before I ever harmed one hair on Eoin's head or that of his family." Although her voice was jam-packed with conviction, inside she was dying a thousand deaths. If he could truly command her, she'd have no choice.

And for the first time as she thought about using her voice to kill him and stop their ridiculous cat-and-mouse game, she had a clear understanding why Damian had effected Moira's demise. Brenna would absolutely end Reggie's life to save Eoin.

His sudden sunny smile stunned her.

"That's what I expected." Reggie snapped his fingers, and the loud pop made Brenna jump. In his hand appeared a small clay pot with a lid. "I need a torch."

"I don't understand." Feeling as if she were on a movie set without a script, she looked to him for direction.

"We're going to melt this amulet down, darling. No one will be able to use your blood against you. Or at least not *this* blood. I can't say what they can do with Odessa's if she's ever caught unawares again."

Confusion drew her brows together as she stared at him in wonder. "You want to destroy the charm the Aether made for Eoin?"

"Yes."

*"No!"* Fists raised, she charged him, prepared to kick his ass and save the necklace. But the impact of her voice had already knocked him off his feet.

*"Brenna!"*

Eoin's commanding voice brought her up short, and she spun back toward the cottage to find him straightening from a slouched position in the doorway. He dropped his crossed arms, and the barest hint of a sound traveled to her. It was the sound of his myriad of bracelets clinking that snapped her out of her daze at seeing him.

"Eoin?" She shook her head but didn't approach him.

Possession of the necklace still belonged to Reggie. "What the hell is going on?"

"Reggie wanted to test your commitment. I told him it wasn't needed, but he insisted, all the same."

*"And you went along with it?"* Her screeching voice in no way sounded like the traditional dulcet tone of the Siren she'd been labeled. And Eoin clamped his hands over his ears and cried out.

"Of all the idiotic, foolish, dirty, rotten…" She sputtered to a stop, unable to come up with any more adjectives that didn't turn ugly. Facing Reggie, she bent down and ripped the chain from his fingers and, for good measure, punched him in the chest with all the meager strength she possessed.

With a shake of the necklace in his laughing face, she muttered, "I hate you both."

He ignored her as he peeled back the opening of his shirt to peer down at his chest. "That bloody well hurt! Who knew you had any muscle in those puny arms?"

"I'll give you puny, you asshat!"

"Brenna, leave off, love." Eoin, ever the peacemaker between her and his best friend, cautiously approached. With one finger, he rung out his inner ear. "Sure, and Reggie can't take another beating by your hand. He's a fragile flower, he is."

"You can bugger off, young scamp," Reggie said affectionately. He opened his mouth to say something, but whatever he'd intended died as the sky overhead turned an ominous black. Tossing the clay pot to Eoin, he snapped, "Destroy that thing. Immediately!"

# CHAPTER 29

*R*eggie lifted his arms and spun in a slow circle, prepared for Goddess knew what... or rather *who*.

With lightning-fast reflexes, Eoin ripped the amulet from her hand and looped the chain over his neck, then he gripped Brenna's wrist, prepared to drag her to the cottage.

"No! Eoin, I can help."

"I'll not have you a casualty of the O'Malley/O'Connor war, love. Sure, and I've said it before, haven't I? Don't think I won't carry you into that fecking cottage if I have to," he warned.

"In case you forgot, I'm extremely hard to kill."

Reggie's eyes remained locked on the horizon as he twisted to address her over his shoulder. "But not impossible for someone who has the right spell and ingredients. You should go, little Siren. If I'm not mistaken, Loman is about to make a spectacular entrance."

Reggie spared one second to smile at Eoin, and all the love he felt for him was packed into that lopsided grin. "Be happy, scamp, and save the girl like the hero I always dreamed you'd be."

With a campy wink, he turned to face the first opening rift.

As Brenna paused in her indecision, another hole appeared followed by two more. "He's outnumbered, Eoin. We have to help him!"

*"Fuck!"*

Appearing to make a decision, he tore the necklace from his neck and shoved it, along with the pot and a gold bracelet, into her hands. "Destroy the necklace, Brenna. If need be, the Aether can make another. But Reggie wasn't lying when he told you Loman was dangerous." His desperate gaze raked her face as if he feared he'd not see her again. "Listen, the bracelet will neutralize a person's magic. You can use it on Odessa when the time comes, yeah?" When she nodded her understanding, Eoin smiled sadly. "Go now, love. Close your eyes and visualize every detail of Alastair's garden. Imagine yourself on the outskirts just beyond the wards, with the smells, sounds, and breeze, and there you'll be."

"Kick their asses for me. For *us*."

As he jogged forward to join Reggie, he hollered, "That's the plan, love."

She waited for a few moments more, then closed her eyes and pictured the landscape beyond Alastair's garden. But her cells didn't warm in the form of any teleport she'd experienced. She tried again and again, growing panicked by the sounds of shouting and running feet.

Frustrated, she lifted her lids, but jerked back the instant she realized she stood face-to-face with the clapping man from the park. The fierce satisfaction in his cunning, reptilian eyes spoke volumes.

"Loman, I presume?" Trying to play it cool, Brenna inched back one step, then another, the plan to create distance. Everyone had warned her tales of this guy's treachery and cruelty. If Loman was targeting her directly, shit just got real. A small shift and a darting glance over her shoulder showed they were alone.

Brenna tucked her treasures behind her and tried her damnedest not to clink the tiny top of the clay pot as she slid the amulet inside. Pinching the lid's edge, she slipped the top into her jeans back pocket.

An image flashed in her mind, one of Gran showing her how to create fire when Brenna was a small child.

*Here goes nothing.*

With the tip of one finger, she brought a small flame to life, holding it against the edge of the charm's domed center to melt the glass and destroy the crystalized blood.

"Nah, uh, uh! Sure, and if I allow you to melt that little scrap of metal you're holdin', I'll likely never have what I need to destroy those fucking O'Malleys. You'll be handing me that amulet, girl. And do it soon, or I'm apt to get upset with ya."

The strain to undo what the Aether had created caused sweat to pool at her back and drip down her temples.

"Yeah, can't do that, I'm afraid." Where Brenna got the courage to stand up to Loman O'Connor, she couldn't begin to know, but the idea of being a robotic weapon used by this particular dude was terrifying to the extreme.

She heard the approach of another person from behind, and she had a momentary panic.

"You won't need to, Brenna."

*Ronan.*

The cavalry had arrived.

Though why he'd save her after she'd blown his eardrums and repeatedly rejected his help was a mystery to be solved.

Turning her back to Loman wasn't wise, so she inched sideways to look at Ronan. But upon closer inspection, it wasn't him at all, just someone glamoured to look like him. How exactly she knew, she couldn't say. The feeling was instinctual in nature. His aura was more muted, but still bright, with only the slightest hint of darkness. She almost asked the guy who he was, but the almost imperceptible shake of his head held her back.

Had Loman noticed?

"Ronan," Loman spat under his breath, and Brenna had her answer. The two were enemies, and the man posing as Ronan intended to fool him for reasons unknown. A little louder, Loman said, "This doesn't concern you, my boy."

Fake Ronan simply smiled, but the hate radiating from his eyes made Brenna's stomach flip-flop. Whoever he was, he despised the real Ronan's father.

The hiss Loman emitted reminded her of a terrified cat.

"Call off your army now, or I'll be locking ya in the tower until you die a shriveled-up, powerless old man."

The threat made Loman pale, and his wild look told of a very real phobia. Brenna didn't know the story behind the tower, but she reminded herself not to book it for an Airbnb stay.

"What do the O'Malleys have to sway you to their side?" Loman asked desperately. "We could have all the power again, my boy! You could help me defeat them, ya could."

"I already have all the power I need, to be sure." Fake Ronan's face spoke of his disgust. "How did you go about revivin' yourself after Castor won your match?"

With a scoff and a shake of his head, Loman said, "Hell didn't want me. Walkin' out the door was simple, to be sure. It was the finding and killing witches so I could be acquirin' their abilities that was a wee bit harder."

His comment seemed to mean something to the imposter Ronan because he swore resoundingly.

Brenna's heart rate increased, threatening failure, and she watched the two men volley comments like a spectator at Wimbledon.

Eyes narrowed, Loman lost all sense of fear and leaned

slightly forward. "You're not Ronan." A calculating smile curled his lips. "This changes everything, now, doesn't it?"

He raised his hands, and Brenna could only assume he meant to strike.

She stepped in front of the imposter as a fireball shot from Loman's palm. With her lids squeezed tightly shut, she waited for a searing pain that didn't come. With one eye, she peeked—and almost wet herself.

Everything and everyone around her was frozen in place. Weapons were suspended halfway to the mercenaries' shoulders. Reggie and Eoin were back to back, arms raised in anticipation of another attack, raw determination stamped in their immobile features. But more importantly, the fireball designed to fry her savior was paused midair less than a foot from her. The spiteful glee on Loman's normally attractive face made him positively freakish.

"What the hell?" Brenna whispered.

"Let me guess. You've never seen time suspended before," Fake Ronan said dryly from behind her. His accent was distinctly American in nature.

She squealed her surprise and spun to face him. Only this time, he didn't look like Ronan at all. At first glance, she thought Loman O'Connor had fooled her, but the energy was off for it to belong to a man so evil. And maybe she should've feared the stranger, but she didn't. "*You* did this?"

Amusement danced in his light-blue eyes as he approached her. "Did you think *you* did?"

"I'm discovering more abilities with each passing moment."

"Only a select few have my talent, sweetheart. It's doubtful you're one of them."

She tilted her head back as she looked up at him. "So who are you, really?"

"First, tell me how you knew I wasn't Ronan before Loman did. How well do you know him?"

"Just in passing, but your aura is darker. And not as wide-spread as his."

"Darker?" It appeared she surprised him with that comment.

Closing her eyes, she hummed a note and concentrated on the stranger's energy. When she looked at him, he appeared dazed. "Sorry. I forgot to warn you first."

"What the hell did you just do to me?"

"Nothing lasting. It's a way I have... I... to look at you...or rather, *into* you..." She shrugged off her lack of manners and control. It must've felt like an invasion of his privacy, not to mention the icky feel of another person poking and prodding all his hidden depths. How did she explain she was merely scanning his soul, looking for the cause of the darkness clinging to him? "I really am sorry."

Curiosity lit his face as he stared down at her. "What did you see?"

"Your wounds are self-inflicted. You beat yourself up over mistakes of the past."

"That's a freaky little gift, sweetheart." He shook out his arms, most likely to dispel the tingling sensation she'd created when she psychically explored his body.

"It's new, but I like it." She grinned when she registered he wasn't angry or put out by her soul scanning.

"Fair is fair, and I promised to tell you who I am." He only hesitated an instant before holding out his hand for her to shake. "I'm Ronan's uncle. Alexander Castor."

Castor. She'd heard the name in passing. She tucked the small pot and bracelet into her side, and careful to keep her thumb on the amulet, she offered her hand in return. "Not an O'Connor? Because you look eerily similar to Loman."

A grimace flashed across Castor's compelling face.

*Was everyone in that family hot enough to be an underwear model?*

She suspected they were.

"He's is what you would call my evil twin. And apparently alive and back to his underhanded ways, which was all news to me until a short while ago." He swore and ran a hand through his long white-blond hair. Blowing out a breath, he said, "I am an O'Connor by birth, but I was fortunate enough to escape the horrors of my family early on."

She glanced behind her at the dangling fireball. "Um, how long can you suspend time?"

"Not much longer without consequences. It's probably best you step to the side while I deal with my malicious brother."

Consequences sounded bad. Scooting out of range, she glanced over her shoulder at Eoin and shoved aside the building dread, prepared to take action. "Can we level the playing field first?"

"I think Ronan has that covered."

One by one, the weapons turned to metal scraps in the hands of the mercenaries as black tie wraps appeared from thin air and bound their wrists.

Before she completely processed the fact the tide had turned in Reggie's and Eoin's favor, time snapped back. The pressure in Brenna's ears was similar to the clogged sensation one got during a plane takeoff. With a slight wiggle of her jaw back and forth, she managed to clear her ears. She didn't expect the obnoxiously loud percussive sound in her head, though, and in reaction, she dropped the small ceramic pot containing the necklace.

As she reached for it, the amulet rose and drifted out of reach, then immediately flew toward Loman, whose expression was one of supreme satisfaction.

"No!" Brenna hollered as she ran, hoping to get to him before the necklace.

But she didn't need to, because it appeared to hit an invisible wall and dropped to the ground, cradled by the lush grass they were standing on.

"What the f—agghhh!" Loman's eyes bulged as he clutched his stomach and bent double.

"Ronan," murmured Alex. He retrieved the coveted prize from its resting place in the grass. "Cloaking spell."

It was the second time she'd seen cloaking in action, and now that she had, she intended to discover how it was done. It could be useful in future confrontations should she need it. Loman turned a concerning shade of fuchsia, and had Brenna not grasped how immoral the man was, she might've been concerned for him.

The ground rumbled, and the grass rolled back upon itself as a steel enclosure worked its way up from beneath the soil and encircled him. The pulsing silver bars caught the last of the sun's rays as they met overhead and fused together to completely contain him. Loman was a caged canary, and he was singing an ugly tune.

Ronan instantly appeared. His lack of emotion when he looked at his father was strange, but Brenna probably looked at Aunt Odessa in a similar fashion. There was no love lost between either couple.

"Let's hope that ends your fuckin' reign of terror."

"Likely it won't. We have to find out how he escaped the Otherworld before we attempt to dispatch him again." Castor strolled to the cage and tapped the bars. "They look good on you, Loman."

"Fuck off, you dryshite! Always the bleedin' hero, ya are!"

"I try."

Castor's delivery was so dry, Brenna fought the urge to laugh. "Will his temporary prison hold until reinforcements arrive?"

Ronan nodded. "Sure, and it should."

Eoin shouted Brenna's name, and she turned in time to see

him charging in her direction, worry for her etched clearly on his face. Behind him, Reggie followed at a more sedate pace.

"Don't!" She held up her hand to halt Eoin's progress. "I don't have the necklace."

He swore as he stopped short, roughly ten feet from her. "Did you destroy it, then?"

"Not yet. But I intend to."

A single tear trailed down her cheek as she thought about their future together—or rather their lack thereof.

Eoin jammed his fists into his jeans pockets and shook his head, his expression tortured. "Don't cry, love. We'll figure it out."

"There's nothing to figure, Eoin." She was a thousand-percent defeated. Moira and Loman had effectively destroyed her easier than they realized by giving her no choice but to permanently get rid of the amulet. If she didn't, someone would someday realize what that small blood droplet could do for them, and she'd be an empty-headed tool at the mercy of whoever possessed it. "We can't be together."

"Don't say that. Don't ever say it," he told her fiercely. "You and I were meant to be, Brenna Sullivan. We just have a few trials to face first, all the same."

A wave of dizziness hit her squarely between the eyes, and she dropped like a stone. Thankfully, Ronan was close enough to catch her.

*a*n eerie lavender and green infused light filled the clearing seconds before Narissa appeared with a surly Odessa by her side.

"Did I miss all the fun, sugar?"

"Not at all." Castor grinned. "Welcome to the party, sweetheart. We've been holding back all the fun while we waited for you to join us."

Brenna put a shaky hand on her forehead and rubbed. "I think I'm okay, Ronan. Thank you."

He released her but retained a hand on her elbow, and she appreciated the small courtesy.

"Give the reversal spell a moment to wear off, honey," Narissa advised. She shoved Odessa between the shoulder blades, none too gently. "Oh, and our auntie has a little something special for you." With an arched brow and a hard stare, she met Odessa's sullen glare. "Don't make me kick your butt from here to Savannah and back, you sow. Give it to her along with that apology you owe her. And mean it this time."

With trembling, obtrusively bright bejeweled fingers,

Odessa held out a check and a wide array of keys. "For you, Brenna."

She accepted both with a slight frown. "I don't get what's happening here."

"It's your portion of the proceeds from Sullivan Corp along with the keys for our European companies and estates." Odessa sent a resentful look in Narissa's direction. "I've been curtailed. Sentenced to reside in America."

"You're lucky you aren't sentenced to join my mother in the afterlife." Narissa sashayed forward in a wave of subtle perfume, and gazes of every man present, with the exception of Eoin and Ronan, dropped to her high, firm ass encased in a hip-hugging dress. She leaned in and gently patted Brenna's cheek. "That check is the remainder of Mama's estate. Odessa has found it in her black-as-tar soul to share with you, bless her heart."

"But..."

"Stupid girl! Take the feckin' money," Loman shouted. "I'll be acceptin' it from *you* soon enough. After I escape this bleedin' cage—"

Faster than any of them could form a coherent thought, Reggie produced a loaded crossbow and pulled the trigger. The thwack and thud of the impact as the arrow hit its target was sickening.

Loman dropped to his knees, clutching the shaft, shock stamped on his paling visage. "You were always the one to watch, Reginald." A ghost of a smile touched his mouth, and it was one of pride. "The person most like me. Ya should've been my son, to be sure."

"Thank the Goddess for small mercies," Reggie muttered as he flung the crossbow away. "Now die for good this time, you git." He waited only a heartbeat or two, then nudged Eoin. "Did you not hear the part about the reversal spell, young scamp? Go get the girl." With a sigh and a dramatic eye roll, he added, "I have to do all the heavy lifting around here."

Choosing to mentally reject Loman's brutal execution—too much death in so little time was mind numbing—Brenna concentrated on Reggie's comments. She cried out as what he'd said sank in, and she rushed to meet Eoin, where he swung her up and crushed her to him.

"This is my favorite part of a film," Reggie murmured in an aside to someone behind them. "The romantic climax."

"Sure, and I'm guessin' that comes later when the rest of you aren't watching us," Eoin retorted. Heat surged into Brenna's cheeks, and he chuckled as he kissed her lips. "There it is, love. Sure, and I adore the grand sight of your blushes."

She never wanted to stop touching him, but if she didn't, she was likely to go up in flames of embarrassment as well as desire.

"Now, little Siren, come give Uncle Reggie a resounding thank-you hug and walk off into the sunset with your hero." He opened his arms to her, and she dove into his embrace.

"I'm still salty about your trickery, Reggie." She kissed him on the cheek. "But thank you for taking Eoin away from Loman's reach and for all you've done for us."

His expression lost its haughtiness as he smiled down at her. "I knew you had a fire in you. *You*, however, needed to discover it for yourself. My machinations merely helped you along a little faster than you might have taken on your own. Love our boy enough for the both of us."

Brenna made a sound of protest. "Don't think you can escape us that easily. You're part of our lives forever."

"Sorry, darling. I don't burp babies or change nappies. I've standards to uphold." He sniffed, and his normal arrogance was back. With an unfeeling glance at Loman's lifeless body, he said, "One of you clean up the mess and take the rubbish out. I've a bubble bath in a high-rise suite calling my name."

"Not so fast, Reg." Ronan stepped toward him. "You have to answer for your part in blowing up the O'Malleys' pub."

For one with so much flash, Reggie left abruptly with minimal fuss.

Eoin laughed. "Sure, and he wouldn't know how to be repentant, our Reggie."

"Well, before we were so rudely interrupted, your Fairy Godmother—that's me in case anyone wasn't paying attention"—Narissa tapped her fingers to her chest with a cat-like grin—"was going to show you how to spend all that glorious money you inherited from my mama." She snatched the check from Brenna's fingers and waved it under her nose. "Come, honey. Vera has a classy little number I've had my eye on, but I've decided it would be perfect for you with your coloring."

"We have the same coloring," Brenna said dryly. "And who's Vera?"

"Wang," Narissa and Castor said in stereo as they shared a commiserating nod, as if the rest of them were provincial.

If they ever compared notes with Reggie, the three of them would find they had a lot in common.

Compressing her lips against a laugh, Brenna shook her head. "Shopping's going to have to wait. I'm going to use a page from Reggie's book and take a hot bath." She returned to Eoin's side and hugged his arm, resting her head against his shoulder as she smiled. "And a nap."

He turned slightly to hide his face from the others. "Sure, and if we're talking a bath and bed, it won't be sleepin' we're doing until much later."

Giving into the urge, she laughed and pressed a soft kiss to his smiling mouth. "Take me home, Eoin O'Malley."

"You weren't paying attention, Brenna Marie. You already *are*." Odessa waved a hand, and the forest of trees on the backside of the property shimmied and swayed, then repositioned themselves to stand guard on either side of a long, graveled lane. The driveway led to a four-story home.

Caught off guard, Brenna pressed a hand to her heart. There, in the distance, was the grand estate her grandmother had described in her childhood. "Gran's home!"

Eoin wrapped an arm around her upper body and drew her back to rest against him, and it was a good thing since her legs weren't doing a great job of supporting her on their own.

"Eoin, I can't believe it. It's like this is a dream."

"If it is, we're both livin' it, love."

"Our own home!" She turned, staring up at his bemused expression. Rolling back her enthusiasm, she asked, "Did I jump the gun?"

A soft smile curled his lips, and his emerald eyes developed a twinkle. "No."

"Do you think you might want to live here with me? I mean, I know it's probably too much, too soon, but…" She felt like ten kinds of fool for assuming he might want to reside with her on a permanent basis. Yes, he'd declared his love, and wicked intent was in his hot gaze every time he looked at her, but they'd never discussed forever. For that matter, they'd never talked about next week or any of the weeks thereafter.

"I'd be chuffed to live with you, Brenna, me love." He gripped her hand lightly in his and, in a leisurely manner, kissed her knuckles, very similar to when they'd shared a pint in the New York pub the night she escaped her life of drudgery. "Now let's be findin' that bed. I've a powerful need to hold you while we *nap*."

"Bath first," she reminded him.

"As if I'd be forgettin'."

Eoin was as excited as Brenna to explore their new home, but they were both knackered. The adrenaline rush was gone, leaving them battling sleep, and they climbed the remaining steps to the front door like wooden soldiers.

As he thumbed through the keys, trying to determine which would gain them access, the wooden door swung wide and they were greeted by a young, beefy butler.

"Name's Fintan," the man rasped out. No smile in greeting, no warm welcome. "And the key she's wearing would've opened the feckin' door."

He bore a striking resemblance to Brenna's family, with multi-colored hair and light sea-green eyes, a shade darker than Narissa's. Eoin searched his memory for any mention of a male Sullivan. Surely there had to have been one once upon a time to help continue the line, but he simply couldn't recall.

Then there was Brenna with her insta-love over Fintan.

She grinned happily from behind the man's back as he showed them to the master suite and offered to bring them a tray of food with a spot of tea to wash it all down.

"Isn't he great?" she whispered as Fintan headed to the door.

"No. He's a surly fecker." Eoin scowled. "And why is it ya become enamored with every new man you meet, love?"

She giggled and danced backward, dragging him farther into the room. "It's you I love, Eoin O'Malley. No one else. Promise."

"And don't ya be forgettin' it." Eoin playfully dodged to the left, then back right, scooping her into a fireman's hold. Brenna's laughing squeal made him grin. With a slight tap to her bottom, he carried her to the adjoining bathroom. But in the opening, he paused, not expecting to see a bath already drawn and candles dotting the window sills and vanity countertops.

"Sure, and this is queer," he muttered.

Brenna tried to peek under his arm, and when she released

a small squeak, Eoin could only assume she'd gotten a load of the romantic setting.

"How did Fintan know?"

Setting her on her feet, he surveyed their surroundings. "As much as I hate the idea of it, I think you should be calling Odessa to find out who this man is. Something's not right here, all the same."

Closing her eyes, Brenna turned her face up and inhaled deeply. After humming a barely discernible note, she gave him a soft, luminescent smile. "The ancestors say Fintan isn't a threat. He's their trusted caretaker." She caressed Eoin's cheek, and a second later, drew her sweater over her head and dropped it on the floor.

"Trusted, huh? Okay, and let's get to bathin'."

After he removed his shirt, she touched the disc resting on his breastbone. "I know they said the spell was reversed, but should we keep this just in case?"

"Tomorrow's another day, love. We'll worry about amulets and villains and potential future threats then, yeah? For now, we're going to enjoy a warm soak and a shag and maybe two days of sleep."

"That's a great action plan," she said primly, but her sparkling eyes were chock-full of happiness.

As she shimmied out of her jeans, the gold bracelet Reggie had used on him hit the floor with a clink. Eoin's heart thudded hard as an idea occurred to him.

"Don't take this the wrong way, love, but what do you think about sex with handcuffs?"

She halted halfway to pulling down her knickers and looked at him over her shoulder.

*Another painting to create.*

Eoin's attention was centered solely on her beautifully sculpted arse.

*Or perhaps a bronze.*

"No handcuffs and no nude paintings," she warned.

"We'll circle back around to this particular discussion later, to be sure," he told her with a wicked grin.

It did the trick, and a soft blush highlighted her cheekbones.

Painting. It was the only way to do justice to that particular shade.

"Have you always been into kink?" Her curiosity was priceless. The harder she tried to be casual, the more obvious it became that she was a novice in all things related to sexual game play.

Oddly, Eoin didn't mind. Once, he'd have been worried about boredom, but every hour spent with Brenna revealed a new facet to her personality, and it was anything but dull.

He sank into the tub across from her and drew her to straddle his lap. Her eyes rounded when she felt his fully erect cock rub against her nub. "I'm not answerin' that one, love. But I will say the handcuff idea was more to do with your Siren and less to do with you."

She scowled, and Eoin was surprised to see the flash of jealousy.

"I can see you're after misunderstanding me, Brenna." His lips twitched at her narrowed eyes. "The cuff suppresses magic, and my guess is your Siren, too. My thinkin' was if you wear it when we shag, you've less chance of losing control of her."

Her brow cleared, and she nodded as she immediately comprehended what he was telling her. "Suddenly, I'm very into handcuffs," she confessed with a grin.

"Let's try the one on for size, and if it works, grand. If not, we'll talk to the Aether about craftin' what we need." But in his mind, Eoin was already designing the perfect armbands for her. Silver, to catch the light when her skin glowed with its iridescent light.

"I can see your artistry at work. Does this mean I really am your *moose*?"

Eoin laughed as he shoved away the metalwork project for another time. Here and now, his main focus was Brenna and providing all the love and pleasure she could handle.

"My heart is full when I look at you, Brenna."

His confession brought wonder to her eyes.

"Even on my most optimistic of days, I didn't think I could ever have this. Have you." She shook her head with a soft smile. "How did I get so lucky?"

"We both did," he managed past the thick lump forming in his throat. A more poignant moment, he'd never experienced. Everything he never knew he wanted was now within his grasp, and he never intended to let her go.

# EPILOGUE

## ONE MONTH LATER...

*a* door slammed somewhere in the distance, and the forceful sound disrupted Eoin's thought process as he molded the clay in front of him. He'd been trying to get the Siren's wings right for hours. With a sigh, he abandoned his worktable, but not before covering the clay with a magically infused cling film to help preserve it and prevent it from drying out.

An indignant shriek echoed through the halls as he exited his studio, and he had a moment's pause.

"'Tis your sister and her friend from America. The Aether's sister-in-law."

He jumped when Fintan stepped from the shadows, standard scowl in place.

"Jaysus, man. You're like a fecking ghoul, ya are! Lurkin' in the shadows."

The caretaker's hard features morphed into a grin. "Have to keep ya on your toes, now, don't I?"

"Consider it a job well done," Eoin muttered. He nodded toward the main section of the house. "What's Dubheasa carryin' on about?"

"What else? Ronan Fucking O'Connor."

"Should I head back into the studio, then?"

"I would." Fintan shot a look toward the hallway as if demons lurked just around the corner. "As a matter of fact, I might be takin' up art meself."

"You're afraid of my sister?" Eoin was incredulous that the towering fella next to him was scared of a woman. Dubheasa was a force of nature all her own, but she had a softer side, all the same.

"Not *her*." Fintan turned his back and headed the way he came. "Save yourself the headache, O'Malley. Lock yourself in the studio, and don't come out for the next week and a half."

"Sure, and now you've got me curious."

"It's your head, man." With an abrupt wave, Fintan was gone, leaving Eoin with a burning curiosity.

"Feck."

He trudged down the long corridor from the south wing toward the main stairwell, questioning his sanity in seeking out Dubheasa while she was in a temper. But he felt her unspoken disquiet, and it was what compelled him to continue until he found her. Eoin entered the salon, crossed to kiss Brenna, then flopped on the sofa, one arm behind his head. "What did I miss?"

"Ronan Fucking O'Connor!" Dubheasa threw her hands up. "We need to kill the man!"

Thunder boomed overhead, and the ground rumbled in response.

A single check showed Brenna behind his sister, frantically shaking her head. *Don't get her started again. It's the Guardian-mate thing.*

*"She's in a snit because he refuses to give up on courtin' her?"*

Brenna gave a single nod, and as she selected a pastry from the tray, one of her newly designed silver bracelets clinked against the plate. And as she bit into a *pain au chocolat*, her eyes rolled back in ecstasy, not dissimilar to her expression from last night.

Turned out, her charmed jewelry worked brilliantly to keep her Siren contained while they made love.

She caught his stare and frowned slightly.

Eoin grinned, when she misinterpreted his look.

*"I still don't know how Fintan anticipates all our needs. But that man is a miracle worker."*

"He's a Seer, love. It's his gift."

"How—"

"Eoin! Are ya even payin' attention to me here?" Dubheasa demanded, interrupting his telepathic conversation with Brenna.

"Aye. You're *still* right fierce in your determination to shun Ronan O'Connor and avoid becoming a Sentinel of Magic." He gestured to the window with his thumb. "Was the thunder your doing? That's new."

Taryn Stephens, Dubheasa's best friend and coven mate, snorted and choked on her tea. When she had her coughing under control, she shoved her thick titian- and mocha-colored hair behind her ears.

It occurred to Eoin that she was just the type of woman to appeal to Fintan, and he understood exactly why the man was hiding; he was running from his feelings. Fintan and Dubheasa were two peas in the same pod. Both feared what would happen if they fell for their prospective mates.

But Eoin could've told them to stop running and give in to fate's design. Because the last month with Brenna had been the best of his life.

*Heaven on earth.*

*"That's exactly how I would've described it. I love you, Eoin."*

From across the room, he met her sparkling, soul-stealing eyes.

*"I'm sorry it took me four years to wake the fuck up, love."*

*"Better late than never."*

She smiled her Madonna-like smile, so different from the wicked Siren she'd unleased in the bedroom, and Eoin fell for her all over again. Just like he would every day from here to the end of his life, days numbered or not.

"You're a right tool for not showin' the proper degree of concern, Eoin," Dubheasa said as she plopped down on the opposing sofa and eyed the expansive tray of food.

"Aye, well, I've been thinkin' he's not as bad as I first imagined." Eoin grinned. "Sure, and maybe the plonker is your perfect match."

Dubheasa threw a croissant at his head.

"Ronan Fucking O'Connor," Fintan intoned from the doorway, then he glared at Taryn and disappeared as mysteriously as he'd appeared.

In his place, Ronan strode through the door, and all his attention was hyper focused on Dubheasa. "Is that to be my new name, then? I'd have thought you'd come up with something a little more original than that, to be sure."

"How about—" She was saved from commenting by Taryn's hand clamped over her mouth.

The devil danced in his blue eyes as he watched Dubheasa wrestle Taryn away with a growl. Without a by-your-leave, he sat next to Dubheasa and filled a plate from the tray. "You can come up with all the nicknames you want after we're mated, love." He took a healthy bite of his pastry as if he had no care in the world.

With a strangled cry, she jumped up, only to be pulled back down again by Ronan, closer to his side than when he first sat down. "And you can plot my demise later, too. But right now, we've another problem." He paused, likely for effect. "My father's escaped the Otherworld... *again*. And the Goddess Anu is initiating a lockdown. I'm to stay here for the foreseeable future... with all of you."

Dubheasa gaped at him, too appalled to speak.

Ronan tapped her chin closed and grinned like he'd won the fecking lottery.

*"Fuck!"* As one, they all turned toward the door where Fintan had been lurking, but his fierce gaze was locked on Taryn. "When will this bleedin' lockdown be startin'?"

"Right now." Ronan sounded far too gleeful for Eoin's peace of mind.

---

Thank you for reading Eoin and Brenna's story. If you want more of the O'Malley family, be sure to look for ***Wine & Warlocks***, book 5 in *The Unlucky Charms* series, around mid-March 2023! Ronan and Dubheasa's dance is sure to entertain. ;)

As a special gift to you, I've created bonus content for Eoin & Brenna. Simply text GIFT to **1-877-795-1526** to get a link. For those outside the US, please check out links in the FOR FANS section of my website.

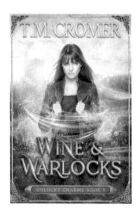

If you never want to miss a release or sale, be sure to sign up for my text alerts. Currently for North American residents only, but the UK and Ireland will be coming soon.

Text **JOIN** to **1-877-795-1526** to subscribe.

Also, if you haven't already subscribed to my newsletter, tmcromer.com/newsletter, or joined my Facebook reader group, tmcromer.me/vip-readers, I encourage you to do so. It's the best way for you to stay current on upcoming stories.

After I'm done with the O'Malleys, I'll be introducing the Aether and friends, and you won't want to miss it.

---

### *Books in The Thorne Witches Series:*
*SUMMER MAGIC*
*AUTUMN MAGIC*
*WINTER MAGIC*
*SPRING MAGIC*
*REKINDLED MAGIC*
*LONG LOST MAGIC*
*FOREVER MAGIC*
*ESSENTIAL MAGIC*
*MOONLIT MAGIC*
*ENCHANTED MAGIC*
*CELESTIAL MAGIC*

### *Books in The Unlucky Charms Series:*
*PINTS & POTIONS*
*WHISKEY & WITCHES*
*BEER & BROOMSTICKS*
*COCKTAILS & CAULDRONS*

*WINE & WARLOCKS (Mar 2023)*

**Books in The Sentinels of Magic Series:**
*THE AETHER (Nov 2023)*

**Books in The Holt Family Series:**
*FINDING YOU*
*THIS TIME YOU*
*INCLUDING YOU*
*AFTER YOU (Jul 2023)*

Ingram Content Group UK Ltd.
Milton Keynes UK
UKHW021314210623
423813UK00022B/760

9 781956 941159